THE CART PUSHER

by
Phil M. Williams

Printed in the United States of America.
First Printing, 2022.
Phil W Books.
www.PhilWBooks.com

ISBN: 978-1-943894-90-1
Print Edition

A Note from Phil

Dear Reader,

If you're interested in receiving two of my popular thriller novels for free and/or reading many of my other titles for free or discounted, go to the following link:

www.PhilWBooks.com.

You're probably thinking, *What's the catch?* There is no catch.

Sincerely,
Phil M. Williams

CHAPTER 1

HODL

"What time's your class?" Tucker asked, his eyes glued to his laptop, and his fat fingers tapping away.

Scot slipped a fleece over his head. "In about fifteen minutes." It was the first day of class for the spring semester.

Tucker looked up from his laptop, still in his pajamas. "I won't take any class before ten. Shit, I'm a paying customer. The school needs to accommodate *my* needs."

Technically, Tucker's father was a paying customer.

Scot slipped on his sneakers. The top edge was worn from shoving his feet into the perpetually tied shoes. "I don't have much choice. It's Manufacturing Processes. I need it for my major." Scot was majoring in Industrial Engineering.

"Did you still wanna buy some Bitcoin? I'm on Coinbase now."

Scot stepped across the well-appointed dorm room, complete with a flat-screen television, entertainment center, three game consoles, and a minifridge. Almost everything was Tucker's, except the old dartboard.

Scot stood next to his sitting roommate, with a view of his laptop, and pointed at the screen. "Is that the price of Bitcoin?"

Tucker nodded. "That's the bid. The ask is 264.09." The ask price was a few dollars higher than the bid price.

Scot pursed his lips. "I don't know, man. I'm still worried about the Mt. Gox bullshit."

Mt. Gox was the largest Bitcoin exchange from 2010 until 2014, when it collapsed, filed for bankruptcy, and claimed they had lost their customers' cryptocurrency. Like magic, the digital wealth had disappeared. It was fitting that Mt. Gox stood for Magic, the Gathering Online Exchange.

"That was a long time ago," Tucker said. "Coinbase is much more secure."

Scot tilted his head. "That was last year."

Tucker shrugged. "A long time ago for a new technology."

"Do you think it's a good investment at this price?"

"I don't know. I don't think anyone knows. When I bought at thirteen dollars, I thought it was a lot. I wish I would've bought a lot more back then."

"I wish I would've bought when it was a penny."

"That's the thing. People who bought at a penny probably thought it was expensive when it finally reached parity with the dollar. People who bought at a dollar probably thought I was crazy for buying at thirteen dollars. Bitcoin's a fucking bullet train. You have to get on and hold on for dear life."

Scot nodded. "HODL." He pronounced it *hoe-dle*.

Tucker nodded back. "That's right. HODL."

"I can afford ten. I'll look at it when I get back from class." Scot had savings from his summer job as a cart pusher at Big-Mart, as well as his work-study job in the cafeteria.

The ask on the screen ticked up to $267.09.

"You sure you wanna wait?" Tucker gestured to the Bitcoin live quote. "You just lost thirty bucks."

"I have to go. I can't be late."

"I can buy 'em for you. You can send the money to my PayPal account when you get back, and I'll transfer the coins to your wallet, when you get it set up."

Scot paused, unsure.

"There are only twenty-one million Bitcoin. They're not making anymore."

"All right. Let's do it."

Tucker grinned.

Scot knew Tucker wasn't being completely altruistic. He wanted a buddy to share in the ups and downs of the Bitcoin experience. Of course, losing or earning money would have a much bigger impact on Scot's life.

Tucker bought ten Bitcoin for $267.09 each.

Scot hurried off to class.

CHAPTER 2

False Start

Scot fast-walked to class, his eyes watering and his head tilted down against the wind. Snow piles covered the dormant flower beds along the sidewalk. He entered the gothic three-story building. *ENGINEERING* was etched in the stone over the entrance.

Scot found his class on the second floor. He removed his coat, settled into a front-row seat, and opened his laptop. *ENGR 420: Manufacturing Processes, Professor Evan Sanders* was scrawled in large black letters across the whiteboard.

Scot's classmates filled the seats around him. While he waited for class to begin, Scot sent $2,670.90 to Tucker via PayPal.

The middle-aged professor appeared at the head of the class. Without uttering a word, he set his laptop bag on his corner desk, then went to the whiteboard, holding a single sheet of paper. He glanced at the paper, then he wrote two names on the bottom right corner of the board—*Dexter Williams and Scot Caldwell.*

Scot's stomach tumbled, as a wave of anxiety passed over him.

The professor set the marker on the pen tray, tossed the paper in the trash, and turned to the class. "Welcome to Manufacturing Processes. I'm Professor Sanders. You may call me … *Professor Sanders.*" His joke elicited a few muted chuckles. "Too early for jokes?" Professor Sanders waited for laughter that never came. He cleared his throat, as if to signal the fun and jokes were over. He gestured to the board and the two names at the bottom corner. "If your name is written here, please go to student accounts immediate-ly."

Scot shut his computer and shoved it into his laptop bag, feeling the stares from his classmates. He put on his coat and shouldered his laptop bag. He hurried from the classroom, tripping on someone's coat in the aisle, and nearly falling face-first on the linoleum. Scot righted himself amid more laughs than the professor had garnered with his stale comedy routine.

Scot left the classroom, his face beet red. He fast-walked to student accounts, an office in the Admissions Building. He was met by a twenty-something receptionist.

"Can I help you?" she asked.

"My professor just told me to come down here," Scot replied. "I'm assuming there's a problem with my account."

The receptionist took his name and pointed to the students sitting in plastic chairs along the wall. "Have a seat. Someone will be with you shortly."

Shortly turned out to be forty-nine minutes later.

Scot sat across from a birdlike woman in her sixties, her glasses perched on the end of her nose. She tapped her mouse and squinted at the screen. "I'm surprised you were able to register for classes. Technically, your account is a year past due."

Scot furrowed his brow. "That can't be."

"We haven't received a payment in a year, not since last January."

"How much do I owe?"

"That depends on whether or not you wish to withdraw or to continue."

Scot drew back. "Withdraw? I only have three semesters left."

"If you want to continue, you owe $36,400. That's for last semester and this one. It must be paid in full."

Scot slumped his shoulders. "I need to call my mom."

The woman looked at Scot over the top of her glasses. "You don't have much time. If you withdraw in the next two weeks, you'll have a withdrawal fee of $1,000, but you won't have to pay for the semester, which would lower your total due to $19,200."

CHAPTER 3

Casualty of Divorce

As he walked back to his dorm, Scot called his girlfriend, Charlotte. His call went to voice mail. Scot disconnected the call, knowing her voice mail was perpetually full. He stopped walking and thumb-typed a text.

> **Scot:** Call me when you get this. I have a BIG problem

Then he called his mother, walking again with his phone to his ear.

"Hi, honey," Laura answered.

"I just got kicked out of class," Scot replied.

Her voice went up an octave. "*Why?*"

"Because my account's past due, two semesters past due."

"That can't be right. Your father was supposed to take care of it."

Technically, Eric Manning was Scot's stepfather, but Eric had been around since Scot was four, so Scot considered him to be his father. However, since Laura and Eric had divorced last year, Scot had seen very little of Eric.

"There hasn't been a payment since last January," Scot said.

"I'll call him and get to the bottom of this," Laura replied. "This is your education. He has no right to do this."

"When you talk to him, tell him that I owe $36,400, and, if I don't have the money in the next two weeks, I have to leave school."

"Well, we can't have that. We'll figure it out, honey. Don't you worry. I'll call you back, as soon as I talk to your father."

"Thanks, Mom. I love you."

"I love you too, honey."

Scot disconnected the call and walked back to his dorm. He tossed his laptop bag and coat on his bed. He found Tucker sitting on the edge of the leather couch, playing Halo on the big screen.

"Can you sell my Bitcoin?" Scot asked.

Tucker paused his game and looked up at Scot. "What are you talking about?"

"I just got kicked out of class. My account's past due. I owe like thirty-six grand."

Tucker sank back into the couch. "Shit. Sorry, bro."

"Can you sell my Bitcoin?"

"You sure you wanna do that? You might lose a few bucks." Tucker winced. "Price went down a little after you left, and with the bid/ask spread …"

"Forget it. Just leave it. It's not enough money to make a difference anyway."

"What are you gonna do?"

Scot removed his cell phone from his pocket. "I need to find out why my bill wasn't paid."

Tucker went back to his game.

Scot called his mother and paced in front of his bed, a polite distance away from Tucker. "Did you talk to him?"

"He's not answering his phone, but I'm still trying," Laura replied.

Scot let out a heavy breath.

"I'm so sorry about all this. I wish I could send you a check. Disability only pays a thousand a month."

"It's okay, Mom."

"Your father really screwed me in the divorce. Alimony's next to nothing. It's a struggle just to buy groceries and keep the lights on. That's fine if he wants to screw me over, but I won't let him do it to you."

"We don't know anything yet. I should try calling him."

"Good idea, honey. I'll keep trying too."

"Thanks, Mom." Scot disconnected the call, then called his stepfather.

Eric's voice-mail recording said, "You've reached Eric Manning, Manager, Quality Pest Control. Leave your name and number, and I'll get back to you."

Scot left a message after the tone. "Dad. It's me. I have a serious problem with my account here at school. Call me back as soon as you get this." Scot disconnected the call and put on his coat.

"Where are you going?" Tucker called out from the couch.

"To see my dad."

CHAPTER 4

The Stepfather

Scot drove his seven-year-old Hyundai Elantra away from Philadelphia and the University of Pennsylvania, toward his hometown of Lebanon, which was ninety minutes to the north. The sky was gray, the trees along the roadside devoid of leaves.

As he drove on US 422, his cell phone chimed. Scot glanced at the screen and answered. "Hey."

"I got your text. What's going on?" Charlotte asked.

Scot explained the situation to his girlfriend.

"Hopefully, your dad just made a mistake."

"I hope so. It worries me though. Everything's been fucked since the divorce."

"Try to think positively."

"Thanks. I love you.

"Love you too."

Lights flashed behind him. A lifted pickup truck was on his bumper.

Scot moved out of the left lane. "I should get off. I need to concentrate on the road. I'll call you after I talk to my dad."

"Drive safe. Good luck," Charlotte replied.

"Thanks."

Around lunchtime, Scot parked in front of a warehouse. A handful of pickup trucks with spray tanks in the back were parked in the lot. A sign over the garage read Quality Pest Control. Eric's old Ford Ranger was in the lot. Scot walked into the office.

The plump receptionist smiled. "*Scot.* What a pleasant surprise."

Scot forced a smile. "Hi, Dottie."

"Your dad's in his office. Swamped with renewals. It's that time of year. How's school going?"

"Good."

"You're going to Penn, aren't you?"

"That's right."

The desktop phone rang, but Dottie ignored it. "That's a great school. Your dad must be so proud."

Scot forced another smile and pointed toward Eric's office, beyond the reception desk. "I should …"

"Of course. It was so nice to see you."

"You too."

Dottie finally answered the phone.

Scot walked past the reception desk. The office area had white walls, marked with dirty fingerprints, and gray carpet, stained and worn by boots. Scot knocked on Eric's office door.

"Come in," Eric called out.

Scot opened the door. "Hey, Dad."

Eric's desk was cluttered with contracts. He turned from his computer and forced a tight-lipped smile, purposely hiding his yellow teeth. He was a thin man, with a ruddy complexion, beady blue eyes, and a salt-and-pepper mustache. "Scot. What are you doing here?"

"I called you an hour ago."

"Come in. Have a seat." Eric waved Scot into his office. Scot sat in the plastic chair across from his father. "Sorry. I'm slammed with renewals. I haven't had time to go through my messages yet."

"Mom said you were supposed to pay for my tuition, but they told me that nobody's made a payment in a year."

Eric's forehead erupted with deep grooves. "That's not true. She knows I don't have the money for that."

Scot held up one hand. "Wait a second. She knows you don't have the money?"

"Yeah."

"Why didn't anyone tell me?" Scot asked, his voice higher.

"Your mom told me that she'd handle it. I assumed she talked to Ray."

Ray Caldwell was Scot's biological father, a man who had left when Scot was two.

"What does Ray have to do with this?" Scot asked.

"He's supposed to pay for your college," Eric replied. "Marie's too. It's in their divorce settlement. Of course, he never did. I think he might've sent a few checks for Marie, but it wasn't enough, and we couldn't afford it at the time."

Ray and Laura had divorced nineteen years ago, but the settlement wasn't news to Scot as his mother had often complained about Ray not living up to his end of the contract. "I thought Marie dropped out to marry Frank?"

"Well, I suppose she did, but if money wasn't an issue, maybe she would've waited to get married and finished her degree. She's way too smart to be at Frank's beck and call."

Scot ran his hand over his face, his head suddenly pounding. "If he wouldn't pay for Marie's college, why would he pay for mine?"

Eric swallowed, his large Adam's apple bobbing up and down. "I don't know."

"I need your help."

Eric looked at his desktop. "I'm sorry, Scot. With the divorce, the lawyers, now paying for two houses, I, uh, … I don't have the money. I'm scraping by as it is." Eric raised his gaze. "I'm sorry. I wish I could help."

Scot glared at his father. "How's Janine?" Eric's girlfriend was sixteen years his junior.

"Uh, … she's fine."

"Heard you bought her a new car."

"Well, … uh, … I mean, she has to get to work."

Scot frowned. "Right." He stood from his seat. "I'll see ya, Dad." Scot left the office.

Eric called after him, but Scot didn't turn around.

CHAPTER 5

Frank, the Banker

Scot parked at a Sheetz gas station a few miles away from Quality Pest Control. He called his older sister, Marie. It went straight to voice mail. He sent a text.

Scot: I need to talk to you. It's important.

He entered Sheetz, used the restroom, grabbed lunch, and returned to his car. He checked his texts. Still no response from Marie. He sent another text.

Scot: I'm coming over. I'll be there in 90 min.

Marie lived in Villanova, just outside of Philly and on the way back to Penn. While he ate, he called Charlotte, updating her on his conversation with Eric.

"Do you think he's telling the truth?" Charlotte asked.

Scot swallowed a bite of his sub. "I don't know. Maybe. I need to talk to Marie." He took another bite.

"I can't listen to you eat in my ear. It's gross." Her tone was harsh.

"*Sorry,*" Scot replied, his mouth full.

"I have to go. My break's almost over."

Charlotte was a cashier at the Big-Mart in Lebanon, which was where they had met last summer.

Scot swallowed. "All right. I'll call you later, … if you want."

"Bye."

Scot said, "I love you," but she had already disconnected the call.

He set his phone in the cupholder and rubbed his temples. He finished his lunch, then drove toward Philly.

Ninety-five minutes later, Scot drove through an exclusive neighborhood of mansions on two-acre lots. The trees were barren, yet not a leaf covered the dormant lawns. Scot parked in the driveway of a stone-and-stucco-faced McMansion, with multiple peaks, multiple chimneys, and a four-car garage.

He exited his car and peeked in the garage windows on the way to the front door. Their cars were there. Frank's Porsche and BMW and Marie's Lexus. Frank was his older sister's husband. *If she's home, why didn't she text me back?* He rang the doorbell. After several seconds, he rang it again.

Marie answered the door, an apron covering her peasant dress, a look of confusion on her face. "Scot. What are you doing here?"

"I sent you a text."

"Sorry. I've been away from my phone. Frank doesn't like me to be tethered to it."

"I really need to talk to you."

"Of course." Marie stepped aside. "Come in."

Scot followed Marie inside. The open-plan interior was impeccably decorated with modern decor. Lots of black and white, leather and right angles. An impractical death trap for a child, but Frank had had his kids. Marie was twenty-four, half Frank's age, and the prototypical trophy wife.

As they walked toward the kitchen and the smell of broiling steak, Frank called out from his office. "Who the hell was that?"

Marie said to Scot, "I'll be right back." She fast-walked to Frank's office.

Scot stood in the family room in front of the dormant big screen.

Marie spoke in a hushed whisper, her words too quiet to decipher.

Frank asked, "What the hell does he want?"

Marie shushed him. "He just wants to talk to me."

They argued back and forth in harsh whispers.

Frank ended the argument, stating clearly, "Bring my lunch in here."

Marie returned to Scot, forcing a smile, her face flushed. "Let's go in the kitchen. You can talk to me while I finish lunch."

In the kitchen, salad ingredients were spread across the center island. Marie checked the steaks, then went to the center island.

Scot leaned on the granite counter, facing his sister.

"So, what's up?" Marie asked, grabbing her serrated knife and a tomato.

Scot explained the situation at school. Then he recapped his conversations with Laura and Eric.

"Mom says that Eric was supposed to pay for my college, but Eric said that he doesn't have the money, with the divorce and all, and that she knew that," Scot said, referring to his stepfather as Eric because Marie had never viewed Eric as her father. She was too old to build the same connection that Scot had had with Eric.

Marie shook her head and tilted the cutting board toward the salad bowl, the diced tomatoes sliding onto the spinach.

"What?" Scot asked.

Marie shrugged. "I know how you feel about Mom."

"Just say it."

"She's a liar. I'm not surprised."

Scot drew back. "It could be a misunderstanding."

"Maybe. Either way, if they're having money troubles, they should've told you." Marie shook a container of balsamic vinaigrette unnecessarily hard. "You shouldn't have to find out like you did. They're so irresponsible."

"There's more to it. Eric said he thought Ray would pay, since it's in the divorce agreement."

Marie rolled her blue eyes, as she applied the dressing.

"Is that not true?" Scot asked.

She set down the dressing. "It's true. I just, … I really shouldn't say. I don't want to start anything."

"What? Tell me."

"It's not important."

Scot frowned. "You can't bring it up, then not tell me."

Marie hesitated for a moment. "When I was at Temple, the same thing happened to me. Mom *claimed* that Ray was supposed to pay."

"When I talked to Eric, he mentioned Ray not paying for your college."

Marie pursed her lips. "Eric's getting that from Mom."

Scot tilted his head, confused. "I don't understand. Is that not true?"

"At the time, Ray said he sent the check to Mom, but Mom claimed she never got it."

"Did he actually send the check?"

"I don't know. Either he did, and Mom spent it, or he's lying. Either way, I got kicked out of school. I could've tried to get more loans, but I had just met Frank. It was easier to …" She sighed. "I don't know."

"Shit. I didn't know that. Who do you think was lying?"

"Mom bought her BMW right after that."

"I doubt she paid cash for that."

Marie shrugged again. "I guess."

"Should I go to Ray and ask him? I haven't seen him since I was little."

"It might be worth a try."

"I can't imagine he'll just hand me a check. I've had no contact with him."

"What other choice do you have?"

Scot sucked air through his teeth. "Um, … I was thinking, … maybe you and Frank could loan me the money. I would pay it back as soon as I graduated—"

"Loan?" Frank walked into the kitchen, wearing a shirt and tie, his shirttail out, and sweatpants. "Did I hear someone say something about a loan?"

Frank was an investment banker for Goldman Sachs. In an effort to save on office space, they were experimenting with telecommuting, so Frank worked from home several days per week.

"Well, um …" Scot started.

Frank faced Scot, towering over him, his arms crossed over his chest. Frank was tall, with large hands and feet, and a full head of gray hair, well-built for a man half-a-century old.

Marie shook her head at Scot discreetly.

Scot continued. "I need $36,000 for school. I was hoping you guys could loan it to me. I could pay you back as soon as—"

"I'll stop you right there," Frank said. "What do you see when you look around my house?"

Scot scanned the kitchen, confused. "Uh, … I don't know."

"Come on. Be honest. You think I'm rich, don't you?"

"*Frank*," Marie said.

Frank showed his palm to Marie, silencing her.

"I guess. I don't really think about it," Scot said.

Frank gestured to his surroundings. "You see all this wealth, and you think, *What's thirty-six grand to someone like me?* I probably wipe my ass with hundreds. Right?"

Marie dipped her head.

"I wouldn't put it like that," Scot said.

"What you don't see are the eighty-hour weeks I worked for two decades. You don't see the hard work. The daily grind."

"He knows you work hard," Marie said.

Frank pointed at Marie. "That's not the point." He turned his attention back to Scot. "The point is, if someone gave me thirty-six grand when I was your age, I wouldn't have had the desire to work my ass off. This country is full of opportunities. Go find yours."

Scot nodded.

Frank went to the oven, opened it a crack, and sniffed the steak. "Don't overcook the steaks."

Marie grabbed her oven mitt and took out the steaks. She used a steak knife to check the pink inside.

Frank peered over her shoulder. "A little overdone but not too bad." He started back toward his office, then stopped and pivoted to Marie. "Make me an old fashioned too. Use the Macallan."

Macallan was an expensive brand of single-malt Scotch whiskey.

Once he was out of earshot, Scot whispered, "Your husband's a douche."

Marie glared at Scot and whispered back, "Don't do that. Don't come here and make judgements."

"I'm sorry." Scot blew out a breath. "What am I supposed to do?"

"I could call Ray for you. Set something up."

"Do you have much contact with him anymore?"

"I'm on their Christmas card list, but we haven't spoken in a few years. I do still have his number, provided it hasn't changed."

"What am I supposed to say? *I know we haven't talked in thirteen years, but will you give me $36,000?*"

Marie deadpanned, "I wouldn't lead with that."

CHAPTER 6

Dear Old Dad

Two days later, Scot and Charlotte sat at Ray Caldwell's dinner table in Altoona, Pennsylvania. Charlotte had taken off work, accompanying Scot for moral support. Ray twirled spaghetti with his fork. His wife, Brenda, picked at her salad. Their fifteen-year-old son leered at Charlotte's low-cut sweater.

"So. What made you want to reach out after all these years?" Brenda asked, her dark eyes boring through Scot. She was a dead ringer for Sandra Bullock.

Scot's mother, Laura, had always hated Brenda. Laura referred to her alternately as the "little slut" or the "child," depending on the context. According to Laura, Ray had met Brenda at a traffic stop, while Ray and Laura were still married. Brenda had flirted, hoping to get out of a speeding ticket. She was eighteen at the time, and Ray was thirty-three. One year later, Ray had left, divorced Laura, and married Brenda shortly thereafter.

Scot set down his fork. "Like I said over the phone, I wanted to see how you guys are doing." Scot cleared his throat. "I also wanted to talk to you about my college."

Brenda narrowed her eyes.

Ray continued to eat, sitting at the head of the table, unfettered by the topic.

"As you probably know, my parents got divorced last year," Scot said.

"Laura and—was it Aaron?" Brenda asked.

"Eric."

Brenda nodded. "Right. Eric. Was that her third husband?"

Junior, the teenager, stifled a grin.

Scot clenched his jaw. "She's only been married twice."

"Well, you never know with your mother."

Scot hesitated, taking the insult like a jab to the mouth. "Since the divorce, money's been tight. Lawyers. My mom's on disability. Her hip's in bad shape. She can barely walk. Anyway, I was hoping you guys could offer some assistance, so I could finish my degree. I would pay you back."

Ray set down his fork with a *clang*. "How much do you need?" Scot's biological father was a fit man with a white buzz cut, birdlike nose, and thin lips. His polo was buttoned to the top, the collar tight around his neck.

Scot cleared his throat. "Thirty-six thousand."

Brenda let out a high-pitch groan.

Junior smirked at Scot.

"He's a good student, Mr. Caldwell," Charlotte said.

Scot was actually an average student, struggling to maintain a passing GPA in his math-and-science-heavy major.

Ray nodded to Scot. "That's a lot of money."

"Like I said, I'll pay you back. I just need to finish," Scot replied.

"I can appreciate your situation, but you have to understand the facts. Retired cops aren't rich." Ray pointed at Junior across the table. "Plus, this one will be in college in less than three years. I can't jeopardize his future."

"For me," Scot said.

Ray cocked his head. "Excuse me?"

"For me. You can't jeopardize his future *for me*."

"Would you expect me to?"

"No, but the divorce settlement you signed does."

Brenda groaned again. "There it is."

Scot swallowed, his throat dry. "You said I have to understand the facts. That's a fact, isn't it?"

"Your father doesn't hear from you in fifteen years, and you expect us to throw money at you?" Brenda asked, her voice shrill.

Ray showed his palm to his wife. "It's okay, Brenda."

Brenda's eyes welled with tears. "It's not okay. After what *that* woman put us through." Brenda addressed Scot. "Your father tried to have a relationship with you, but your mother made that impossible. And now you think he should pay for your college?"

Scot stared at the tabletop.

"*Enough*," Ray said.

"Chill, Mom," Junior said.

Brenda sniffled and wiped her eyes with her napkin.

"You're right, Scot," Ray said. "It's in the divorce settlement, but, at that time, college was a lot cheaper than it is now, and your mother made it impossible for me to have a relationship with you. Part of the settlement was that you and your sister would spend every summer and every other Christmas with me. How often did that happen?" Ray waited for an answer that never came. "The bottom line is that your mother didn't hold up her end of the deal. Therefore, the deal is null and void. You can take me to court, but it won't get you what you want."

"That's bullshit," Charlotte said. "Just because you didn't get to see him doesn't mean the whole divorce contract thing is wrong."

Brenda huffed at Charlotte, one side of her mouth raised in contempt.

Scot raised his gaze to his father. "You paid for some of Marie's college."

Ray pushed aside his empty plate. "I paid for *all* of it, until your mother stole my check, and Marie had to drop out, but Marie sent me letters. Called me. She had a relationship with me. I would like to have a relationship with *you*, but this isn't the best way to start one."

"That's not Scot's fault. He was just a kid," Charlotte said, her voice going up an octave.

Scot covered Charlotte's hand with his. "We should go." Then Scot stood from the table and said to Ray, "This was a mistake. You're obviously not going to help me."

Charlotte stood too, glowering at Ray. "You should be ashamed of yourself."

"Just like Laura," Brenda said. "Playing the victim."

"Fuck you," Charlotte said to Brenda.

Brenda shot out of her seat. "You little bitch."

"Whoa," Junior said, also standing.

Ray stood too. He pointed toward the door. "Get out of my house."

"No problem, *Dad*," Scot replied.

Scot and Charlotte left, leaving the front door open in their wake.

CHAPTER 7

Back Home

Scot dropped Charlotte off at her mom's double-wide trailer, then drove home. His mother and his younger sister lived in an end-unit townhome, with a single car garage. Scot parked behind his mother's four-year-old BMW. He stared at the moldy siding on the north-facing townhome.

He smacked his steering wheel several times, then screamed at the top of his lungs, "Fuck!" He held the *uh* in *fuck* like an opera singer. He leaned his forehead on his steering wheel, thinking about the last forty-eight hours. *I'm totally fucked.* He thought about what Marie had said about Laura stealing her college money to buy that car. *Mom wouldn't do that, would she?*

Scot exited his car and walked inside, his shoulders slumped.

Laura lounged on the couch, watching television, an open bag of chips on the coffee table. The frumpy fake blonde sat up and muted the television, when she saw her son. "Was that you yelling?"

Scot diverted his gaze. "It was someone down the street."

"How did it go?"

Scot sat on the edge of the recliner, kitty-cornered from his mother. "Not well. He won't help me."

"That bastard," Laura replied.

Scot detailed his visit with Ray and Brenda. Laura was equal parts outraged, indignant, and furious.

"I guess I'll go to Penn tomorrow, get my stuff, and withdraw,"

Scot said, his voice monotone.

A car door shut outside.

"I'm sorry, honey," Laura replied. "You'll get through this. It'll just be a blip. You'll see. You can take off this semester, save some money, then get a better financial aid package next year because my income went way down when I went on disability."

Scot hung his head. Not wanting to kill his mother's optimism, he kept his thoughts to himself. *Even if I get a great financial aid package, I still need $19,000 just to pay off my past-due bill.*

Heather breezed into the living room, coming from outside. Her hoodie was partially unzipped, revealing deep cleavage. Scot's younger sister was Eric's only biological child. Technically, she was Scot's half sister, although he didn't think of her that way.

Heather stopped and addressed Scot. "What are you doing home?"

"Your brother's taking off a semester," Laura said, interjecting.

"Why?"

"Financial difficulties," Scot said.

"Sucks." Heather went upstairs.

Scot wondered if Heather would go to college. She was eighteen and had graduated high school last June. There had been talk of community college, but as far as he knew it was just talk.

As if reading Scot's mind, once Heather was out of earshot, Laura noted, "Luckily, your sister doesn't want to go to college." Laura huffed. "I can barely keep the lights on around here while your deadbeat father runs around with his little slut."

Scot knew Laura was talking about Eric's girlfriend, Janine, but it was the same way she'd described Ray's wife, Brenda. Scot wondered if Laura picked the same type of man, the type who would leave their family for a younger woman, or was the stereotype of the older man going for the younger woman just that pervasive?

"You know your father bought that little slut a brand-new car," Laura continued.

"I know. You told me," Scot replied.

Laura sniffed. "It's frivolous."

"What does Heather want to do?" Scot asked, changing the subject, desperate not to be sucked into his mother's vortex of slutty second wives, deadbeat ex-husbands, and broken dreams.

"She wants to be an Instagram something or other."

"Influencer?"

"Yes. That's it. Instagram influencer. I don't know how you make any money doing that, but that's what she wants to be."

Influencers typically fell into one of two categories—many times both. Famous and hot. Heather wasn't famous, but Scot wasn't blind to the effect she had on men. The first time he'd noticed it was when she was thirteen, and they went to the shore for a family vacation. She walked around the boardwalk in her bikini and cutoff shorts, the men rubbernecking as they passed. Scot had been embarrassed for her, but Heather had been empowered by her newfound curves. Eric had been oblivious. *What about Laura?* He couldn't remember. *Was she proud? Jealous? I can't remember.*

"Honey?" Laura asked.

Scot woke from his thoughts and stood from the recliner's edge. "I should go to bed."

"Everything will look better in the morning."

Scot forced a smile. "Good night, Mom."

"Good night, honey."

Scot trudged up to his bedroom, kicked off his shoes, undressed, and climbed under his covers. Thoughts of his future, or lack thereof, made his head hurt. He thought about what his mother had said. *Everything will look better in the morning.* He rolled to his stomach, hugging his pillow. *I don't think it'll look better for a long time.*

CHAPTER 8

Six Months Later

Scot stood in the back of the break room, his coworkers standing around him, everyone wearing their khakis, gray T-shirts, and red vests.

Ron gestured to Charlotte, blushing next to him. "I'd like to recognize our very special associate of the week, Charlotte Carey."

The wall behind Ron had BIG-MART painted in large block letters, with the slogan underneath in smaller block letters that read *BIG SAVINGS. BIG SELECTION. BIG SMILES.*

Ron was the general manager of Big-Mart and Scot's boss. He was in his mid-thirties, with thinning brown hair combed forward to hide his receding hairline. Scot thought Ron resembled a pedophile, not that he'd ever met one to make the comparison.

"Charlotte is the perfect example of what we want in an associate," Ron said in his nasally voice. "She's always well-groomed, pleasant to the customers, and reliable."

Technically, she was only reliable because Scot drove her to work, allowing her to do her makeup in the car.

Ron continued. "Her beautiful smile brightens the day for everyone at Big-Mart. I'm so proud to present this certificate and a twenty-dollar Big-Mart gift card." Ron handed Charlotte a certificate printed on blue paper, along with an envelope. "Let's give Charlotte a Big-Mart round of applause." Ron clapped, as if he'd just presented an Oscar.

A spattering of applause came from the Big-Mart associates, Scot being counted as one of the clappers. More than a few associates didn't clap, their hands occupied with their phones or their sugar-filled breakfast items.

Ron leered at Charlotte during the applause.

Kyle leaned toward Scot and said, "Ron's checkin' out your girl."

Scot frowned. "She wouldn't give him the time of day."

Kyle worked in the warehouse. He was a nineteen-year-old stoner, with a blond beard and a mop of wavy hair to match. He could pass for a hipster or a homeless person.

When the applause died, Ron said, "All right, let's get pumped for the day." Ron paced in front of the audience, nodding, and making eye contact with the associates. "Let's get our squirm on."

Groans came from the audience.

"Come on, everybody. Wake up. Let's get squirmy." Ron gyrated back and forth, his legs bending left and right, his fists pumping over his head. "Come on, everybody. Get your squirm on!"

A handful of associates wiggled back and forth, without enthusiasm.

After a painful twenty seconds, Ron stopped dancing and started clapping rhythmically. "All right. Now that we're awake, you know what time it is. It's time for the Big-Mart cheer. Let's get it." He paused for a beat. "Who's number one?"

Some of the associates said, "The customer."

Ron put his hand to his ear and leaned toward the crowd, doing his best Hulk Hogan impression. "I can't hear you. Who's number one?"

A few more associates answered, "The customer."

Scot stood silent as usual.

"I still can't hear you," Ron said, putting his hand to his ear again. "Who's number one?"

"The customer!" the associates shouted.

At the same time, Kyle shouted, "Deez nuts!"

A few associates laughed.

Ron scanned the crowd for the offender, scowling, but gave up his search after a few seconds. Ron then held up his arms, like a conductor, and said, "*Goooo*," holding the *O* until the entire room held the long *oh*.

Then Ron dropped his arms, as if starting a drag race, and everyone shouted, "Big-Mart!"

Except Kyle, who shouted, "Deez nuts!"

CHAPTER 9

The Cart Pusher

Scot stood in the shade of the shopping cart shelter, watching a man load his groceries into the back of his Range Rover SUV. The man had parked near the back of the lot, thirty yards from the shelter, away from other cars. After working the lot as a cart pusher for nearly two years, if you count the previous four summers as well as the past six months, Scot had become adept at predicting which customers would return their carts to the shelter and which customers would leave their carts elsewhere.

Scot classified customers into one of five categories.

The Do-Gooders were people who returned their cart, regardless of the circumstance. Many times these people returned their cart to the store, not just to the nearest cart shelter. The Do-Gooders were often full of smiles, like returning their cart was great fun.

The Entitled never returned their carts. They believed it was Scot's job to collect their carts, which it was, but only because people like them were entitled. Scot thought the guy with the Range Rover was likely Entitled.

The Lazy only returned their carts if the shelter was near their car.

The Guilty only returned their carts if Scot watched them.

The Riders were a derivation of the Do-Gooders, often riding on the back of the cart or running with their child in the cart back to the shelter. The Riders smiled and giggled, likely having actual fun, whereas the smiles of the Do-Gooders may or may not have been genuine.

Scot watched the man with the groceries shut his hatch, then climb into his Range Rover. Predictably, he drove away, leaving his cart stranded. Scot thought of the irony. The Range Rover douchebag had parked in the back of the lot to keep his precious car safe from other cars and runaway carts, yet he left a runaway cart. *Entitled.*

"Hi, Scot," Anna said, stopping at the cart shelter, her keys in her hand.

"Hey," Scot replied, lifting his chin.

Anna was a cashier, like Charlotte, but, unlike Charlotte, Anna was a plain Jane, rarely wearing makeup, her brown hair always in an unintentionally messy ponytail.

"I forgot my lunch at home, so I'm going to Chick-fil-A," Anna said. "You want anything?"

Scot shook his head. "No. I'm good." Scot thought about the fact that Charlotte would be pissed if she found out Anna had picked up lunch for him, not to mention he had a bagged lunch in the associates' fridge.

"Okay." Anna smiled and waved. "See you later." She walked toward her old Honda Civic.

Once she was gone, Scot headed to the errant cart left by the Range Rover guy. As he did, he thought about what Kyle had said about Ron checking out Charlotte. Scot pictured Ron on top of Charlotte, pumping away. The image made him queasy. He tried to think of something else, wiping the image from his mind, but the concept remained.

Maybe not with Ron but she could be cheating. She doesn't text me right back. It takes her hours sometimes, and I know she's on her phone all the time. That's the other thing. She goes into the other room to text sometimes. She wasn't doing that four or five months ago.

Scot grabbed the errant cart unnecessarily hard and pushed it back toward the shelter, still thinking. *We're barely doing it anymore. When we do, it seems like a chore for her.* Scot thought about the fact that Charlotte could do much better than a garden-variety white boy, who was unremarkable in every way. Scot was an average height and build, with a too-small chin and a too-big forehead. He couldn't even grow a decent beard to cover his weak chin. He was twenty-one but could still pass for a baby-faced teenager.

Scot pushed the lone cart into the back of the line of carts already in the shelter, slamming it into place. *Fuck my life.* Then he moved the train of connected carts out of the shelter. He pushed the carts back toward Big-Mart, leaning into the heavy train, his sneakers gripping the macadam. The slight incline added additional difficulty.

As he neared the building, a Mustang turned in front of him rapidly, nearly hitting the train of carts. The man in the black Mustang leaned on the horn, causing Scot to flinch. Then the man gunned the V-8, driving from the parking lot much too fast.

Scot put his hand over his chest, his heart pounding.

Henry ambled over to him, coming from a bench just outside Big-Mart, a book in his hand. "You okay?"

Scot's face reddened, fear giving way to embarrassment. "I'm fine."

Henry was a Big-Mart greeter. He often sat out front, reading during his break. The eighty-year-old was a tiny man with more wrinkles than a box of raisins.

"You sure?" Henry asked.

Scot glanced at the shopping cart train. "This job sucks sometimes."

"Demosthenes once said, 'Small opportunities are often the beginning of great enterprises.'"

CHAPTER 10

The Job Offer

"What did Ron want?" Scot asked, walking with Charlotte in the Big-Mart parking lot.

Just moments ago, at the end of the workday, Ron had asked to see Charlotte in his office.

"He offered me a job," Charlotte replied, with a small smile.

Scot furrowed his brow. "You already have a job."

"A better one."

Scot unlocked his Hyundai Elantra and climbed into the driver's seat. Charlotte slipped into the passenger seat next to him.

"What do you mean, a better one?" Scot asked.

"Assistant manager," Charlotte replied, still smiling.

Scot started his car. "Wow. You planning to take it?" Scot tried to act happy for her, but the assistant manager worked directly with Ron.

Charlotte shrugged. "I'm thinking about it. It pays $40,000—plus bonuses and health care. I could get my own place."

Scot nodded, driving away from Big-Mart and toward Charlotte's home.

They drove in silence for a minute, the late-afternoon sun high in the sky.

"You don't seem happy for me," Charlotte said.

Scot glanced over at his girlfriend. "No. I am. It's just, ... I didn't think you wanted a career at Big-Mart."

"I don't. You know I wanna be a stay-at-home mom. I was hoping that you'd graduate and get an engineering job, so we could get married and have kids."

Scot let out a breath. "I'm working on it."

"Do you think you'll get back to school this fall?"

"I doubt it. I won't have enough money. The spring semester's possible."

Charlotte nodded and retrieved her cell phone from her purse. Scot focused on the road, also content to end the conversation. Charlotte spent the rest of the ride scrolling on her Instagram feed.

When they arrived at Charlotte's mother's double-wide trailer, Charlotte grabbed her purse and said, "See you tomorrow."

Scot unbuckled his seat belt. "You don't want me to come in?"

They had been spending most evenings watching Netflix in Charlotte's room, although Charlotte alternated between watching Netflix and scrolling on her phone, even though she chose all the shows they watched.

"I'm tired." Charlotte leaned over to give Scot a kiss.

Scot tried to meet her lips, but Charlotte kissed his cheek, her lips barely making contact. Then she left his car, without looking back. Scot gripped the steering wheel, watching her enter the trailer through his windshield. *Something's not right. It feels like she's pulling away.* His chest tightened at the thought of losing her.

CHAPTER 11

Points

The next day Scot pushed a train of shopping carts toward Big-Mart.

A customer shoved their empty cart toward Scot, letting go, the momentum causing the cart to collide with Scot's train. The customer smiled. "Here you go."

Before Scot could tell her to take the cart to the shelter, she'd turned and marched to her car. Scot grabbed the cart and added it to his train. Then he positioned himself behind the train, leaned into the carts, and pushed, the train of carts moving toward Big-Mart again. Scot pushed the carts through the automatic doors and into the nearly empty shopping cart area.

Scot leaned on a cart, catching his breath, as he turned to look into the store.

Henry stood just beyond the entrance, greeting customers with a smile and a "Welcome to Big-Mart."

Many people ignored the old man. Some people nodded. A few thanked him.

Henry waved at Scot, with the same cheesy grin he'd had for the customers.

Scot waved back, no smile. Scot turned back to the carts, straightening them, and organizing the inside cart area. When he was finished, he grabbed his phone from his pocket and checked the price of Bitcoin. It was $285.83. He'd purchased ten Bitcoin for $267.09. Scot calculated that he'd made a 6 or 7 percent profit in six months.

That's 12 to 14 percent per year. A lot better than my bank account. He thought about buying more Bitcoin. Scot had saved nearly $5,000 over the past six months, all of it sitting in his PNC Bank account, gaining zero interest.

"You know you can't be on your phone," Ron said.

Startled, Scot shoved his phone into his pocket. He turned to his boss. "Sorry, Ron. I was just checking something real quick."

Ron frowned. "Rules are rules. I have to give you a point."

It was the first point Scot had ever gotten at Big-Mart. Like all Big-Mart associates, if Scot received five points in a six-month time span, he'd be terminated.

CHAPTER 12

A Real Man

In the break room, Scot scanned his associate ID card, effectively clocking out and ending his workday.

Anna walked to the time clock, also scanning her ID card. Then she smiled and said, "Hi, Scot. How was your day?"

Scot shrugged. "Just another day with big savings, big selections, and big smiles."

Anna giggled, snorting a little. "You're so funny."

"Yeah."

"Did you hear about Henry?"

"What happened to Henry?"

"He had to leave early because his legs were hurting. He asked for a chair, but Ron wouldn't give him one, and he gave him a point for leaving early." Anna put her hands on her hips. "Can you believe that?"

Scot nodded, thinking about the point he had received earlier that day for looking at his phone. "Unfortunately, yeah."

"You know what Ron said?"

"Let me guess. *Rules are rules*?"

Her eyes bulged. "That's *exactly* what he said."

"Ron's a dick."

Anna nodded. "He is. I still can't believe he did that to Henry."

Scot shrugged again, nonplussed.

"Are you leaving? I could walk out with you."

"I'm waiting for Charlotte."

Anna dipped her head. "Of course. Right. Well, I should go. Bye." She waved and forced a smile.

"See ya," Scot replied, without emotion.

Kyle sauntered up to the time clock and swiped his card, smelling like marijuana. His eyes were bloodshot and dilated. "What up, Scotty."

Scot lifted his chin to the young stoner. "Kyle."

"Waitin' for your girl?"

"Yeah."

Kyle smirked. "Might be a while. I saw her flirtin' with Ron."

"When?"

Kyle shoved his ID card into his pocket. "A few minutes ago. Flippin' her hair. All giggly and shit. Ron was leanin' in real close too, checkin' out her tits."

Scot thought about the V-neck T-shirt Charlotte had worn. The shirt was a little too tight, and the neckline was a little too deep. "Bullshit." Scot didn't sound confident that it was, in fact, bullshit.

Kyle shrugged. "Girls are always monkey branchin'. It's in their nature."

Scot scowled at Kyle. "What the hell's *monkey branching*?"

"It's when a girl's in a relationship, but they're lookin' for someone better. They'll hang on to you like a branch." Kyle mimicked holding on to a branch at eye level with his left hand. "But, when they find someone better, they grab the new branch, the higher branch." Kyle mimicked grabbing a higher branch with his right hand. "Then they'll let you go, like you were nothin'." Kyle let go of the imaginary branch in his left hand, grinned, and dropped both hands. "Monkey branchin'. That's why I don't fuck with relationships. I like to hit it and quit it. Pump and dump." Kyle rapped Scot on the back. "You know what I'm talkin' about."

Scot stepped away from Kyle, still scowling.

Kyle chuckled. "Or not."

★★★

On the way to Charlotte's mother's trailer, Scot glanced at his girlfriend sitting in the front passenger seat of his Hyundai, and asked, "What took you so long to clock out?"

Charlotte looked up from her phone. "I don't know. Guess I lost track of time."

Scot gripped his steering wheel. "Talking to Ron?"

"Yeah. So?"

Scot clenched his jaw. "Kyle said you were flirting with Ron."

Charlotte twisted her face in disgust. "You were talking to Kyle about me? What the fuck does he know?"

"He was just telling me what he saw."

"And you believe him?"

"No. That's why I'm asking you." Scot's voice was whiny.

"Kyle's white trash. I can't believe you'd even let him talk about me like that."

Scot glanced from the road to Charlotte. "It's not like that."

"Whatever."

"What am I supposed to think?" Scot glanced at Charlotte again. "I feel like you're pulling away from me. We haven't had sex in like three weeks."

Charlotte huffed. "*Sex.* That's all you care about, isn't it?"

"No. I mean, it is important, but it's not just the sex."

"You expect me to have sex with you while my mom's home? Or your mom? Maybe if you had your own place …"

"But that was never an issue before. We found time alone."

Charlotte shook her head. "You don't get it. I need a man, not a little boy. Men have houses and nice cars and good jobs. Men get married and take care of their wives."

"I'm working on it."

"Show me." Charlotte picked up her phone, alternately tapping and scrolling, signaling the end of the discussion.

When they arrived at Charlotte's home, she exited Scot's car without a word and certainly without a kiss.

CHAPTER 13

The Gram

Scot drove home, replaying his argument with Charlotte, and feeling guilty for letting Kyle get under his skin. He parked in a visitor's spot, across the street from his mother's townhome, and sent a text to Charlotte.

> **Scot:** I'm sorry. I was an idiot. I really do want what you want. Please forgive me.

Scot waited several minutes, hoping for an immediate response that never came. He exited his car, slammed the door behind him, and walked across the street to his mother's house. As he walked up the driveway, the growl of a flat-six engine approached.

A red Porsche 911 parked behind Laura's BMW. Heather exited the front passenger seat, wearing a short dress and high heels. Scot gawked at her, as she strutted around the car, leaned into the driver's side window, and kissed the driver. Then she said something inaudible to the man, pivoted, and sauntered toward Scot. The driver backed out of the driveway and drove away, his engine revving unnecessarily loud.

"Who was that? Your boyfriend?" Scot asked.

"Just some guy I met at Panera," Heather replied. "Let me take some pictures with his car for the Gram."

"Be careful."

"He's harmless."

Scot and Heather walked into the house together. Laura sat on the couch, watching a cop show on television. Heather went upstairs to her room. Scot made himself a sandwich and sat with his mother while he ate dinner. Then he went upstairs to his room too.

Scot had a single bed in the corner, which was simply a single mattress. He had a desk made from particle board, along with a dresser and an end table made from the same cheap wood. A dartboard hung from a hook on his closet door. He changed from his work clothes to shorts and a T-shirt, then sat at his desk.

He checked his texts, hoping for a response from Charlotte, but still nothing. A Facebook notification buzzed on his phone. He had a friend request from Anna. He wondered if Charlotte would notice that they were Facebook friends. *Would she be jealous? It might be good for Charlotte to see that other girls are interested in me. She probably won't even notice though. Says Facebook's for old people.* Scot accepted the friend request.

Then he tapped the PNC app on his phone, initiating a wire transfer, transferring most of his money to his Coinbase account, so he could purchase more Bitcoin. He estimated that he'd be able to purchase fifteen more Bitcoin, provided the price didn't rise too much over the next day or so, as he waited for the wire transfer to complete.

Another Facebook notification came to his phone. It was a DM from Anna.

> **Anna Fisher:** Thank you for accepting my friend request! By the way, I called Henry. He said his legs are feeling better, so hopefully he'll be back tomorrow. Thanks again. Have a good night.

Scot didn't respond to the DM. Instead, he tapped his way to Instagram, checking Charlotte's page, and viewing her latest images. The most recent one was from that morning, showing Charlotte in the tight V-neck shirt she'd worn to work. The image had received over one hundred likes. Scot scanned the comments, his body tense as a drum.

> **Big_Boy_533** Nice rack!!!
> **HectorMacho789** Damn girl. DM me

TerranceUnnn Love them tig ole bitties
Ron_Singleton31 Beautiful

Scot tapped Ron_Singleton31, confirming what he already knew. It was Ron from work. Scot went back to Charlotte's page, checking other pictures, and finding that Ron had liked and commented on each and every one. *Fucking douchebag.*

CHAPTER 14

Late

Scot watched the digital clock in his Hyundai change to 7:52 a.m. *Shit. We'll be late.* He checked the front door of Charlotte's mother's trailer, willing Charlotte to appear, but she didn't. He sent another text.

Scot: Hurry up!!! We're running late!!!

The last text he'd received from Charlotte said she'd be out in a minute. That was eight minutes ago. After the fight they'd had, if Charlotte hadn't responded, Scot might've thought she'd caught a ride with Ron.

Scot beeped the horn. Just a polite tap. He stared at the door, still mentally willing Charlotte to appear. If she came now, they still had a chance, depending on the traffic lights. Scot beeped the horn again, this time leaning on the horn a little longer. The front door opened, and a wave of relief passed over Scot, quickly replaced by dread as Charlotte's mother, Helen, stepped out, wearing her robe and slippers.

Helen worked at a dental office as an administrative assistant. She was around forty but appeared much older, with a puffy face and a puffy body. She had been a teenager when she'd had Charlotte. According to Helen, her parents were devout Christians, who'd been appalled that she'd had sex outside of wedlock. Consequently, she'd been kicked out. Charlotte's father had abandoned Helen too, supposedly moving to Alaska to work on the oil pipeline. Helen often reminded Charlotte that he never sent the checks she'd been promised. Charlotte thought that was a lie. She thought Helen didn't actually know who Charlotte's father was.

Helen marched to Scot's Hyundai and knocked on the driver's side window.

Scot powered down the window. "Good morning, Mrs. Carey."

Helen sneered, her nostrils flaring, and her face blotchy without makeup. "Don't be comin' here honkin' the horn at my daughter. If you need to talk to her, knock on the door like a gentleman. You treat her with the respect she deserves."

Scot stared at the steering wheel. "I'm sorry, Mrs. Carey."

Helen pivoted and marched back inside.

Charlotte finally appeared, strutting to the car with her makeup bag in hand, and her purse over her shoulder. Her hair was done, but her eyes appeared small and her lips appeared thin without makeup.

When she sat in the passenger seat, Scot immediately reversed and said, "We're going to be late."

Charlotte unzipped her makeup bag. "It's fine."

Scot rolled past a stop sign and gunned the engine. "It's not fine. I got a point yesterday. Now I'll have two."

Charlotte checked herself in the mirror, dotting foundation on her cheeks, nose, and forehead.

Scot glared at her. "Don't you care?"

"Ron won't do anything."

"To you maybe." Scot gripped the steering wheel, his knuckles white. "He's probably in love with you. You know he's all over your Instagram page."

"So what?"

"So what? *So what?* If some girl was all over me like that, you'd be pissed."

Charlotte unscrewed the cap on her eyeliner. "I wouldn't care."

Scot gunned the engine, crossing the double-yellow line to pass a slow-moving Buick. "I guess you wouldn't."

Charlotte held her eyeliner at the ready. "I can't do my eyes when you're driving like a crazy person."

"It's not my fault we're late."

"Do you want me to stab myself in the eye?"

Scot didn't respond, but he did slow down, and Charlotte finished her makeup in silence.

They arrived at Big-Mart at 8:03 a.m., three minutes late. Scot ran into the store, thinking there might be a five-minute grace period. He had heard that once from another associate, although it was not confirmed. Charlotte strolled after him, unconcerned.

Scot clocked in at 8:04 and exited the break room, just as Ron exited his office, definitely catching a glimpse of Scot leaving the employee-only area. Scot fast-walked toward the exit and the Big-Mart parking lot.

Henry waved and smiled. "Good morning, Scot."

Scot nodded but didn't break stride.

"Hold on, Scot," Ron called out.

Scot stopped in his tracks, just short of the exit, his heart pounding. He pivoted to see Ron about thirty feet behind him, near Henry.

Ron motioned with his index finger. "Come over here."

Scot trudged to Ron.

"In my office."

Scot followed Ron into his office, passing Charlotte along the way. She appeared unconcerned for Scot or even her own tardiness.

Ron's office was decorated with inspirational posters. One poster showed a golf course green with the word *SUCCESS* printed in big letters. Underneath it said, *Some people dream of success, ... while others wake up and work hard at it.* Another showed a rock climber with the message, *Know what you want and reach for it.*

Ron gestured to the plastic chair in front of his desk. "Have a seat."

Scot slumped into the seat.

Ron sat across from him, bouncing a little in his leather swivel chair. "You were late this morning."

"I know. I'm sorry. Traffic …" Scot trailed off, knowing that was a lame lie, as traffic was rarely an issue in Lebanon.

"Well, I suggest you leave earlier." Ron opened a folder on his desk. He wrote on a piece of paper for a minute, while Scot fidgeted in his seat. Finally, Ron slid the paper over to Scot with a pen. "This acknowledges that you were late this morning, and I gave you a point. Sign at the bottom if you agree that this is true."

Scot signed the paper and slid it back to Ron.

Ron leaned forward, his elbows on the desk and his fingers steepled. "This is two points in two days, Scot. Remember. If you receive five points within a six-month period, you'll be terminated."

Scot nodded. "I know."

Ron gestured to the door. "Get to work."

Scot left the office and trudged for the parking lot. Along the way, he caught a glimpse of Charlotte smiling and scanning at her checkout stand. *I bet Ron doesn't give her a fucking point.*

Near the entrance, which was also an exit, Henry said, "You okay, Scot?"

"I'm fine," Scot replied, his head bowed, and his shoulders slumped.

"You sure?"

Scot glanced around, making sure no customers were in earshot. "It's bullshit. It wasn't my fault. Ron ..." Scot shook his head. "You know how he is."

"Epictetus once said, 'It is our attitude toward events, not events themselves, which we can control. Nothing is, by its own nature, calamitous. Even death is terrible, only if we fear it.'"

CHAPTER 15

Celebration

Scot swiped his ID card at exactly 4:00 p.m., then stood near the time clock, waiting for Charlotte. He had been angry with her for making him late that morning, but, by the end of his shift, he had let it go.

Anna swiped her card immediately after him. "Hi, Scot."

"Hey, Anna," Scot replied.

Henry entered the break room, his posture hunched. He trudged to the time clock and swiped his card. He smiled at Scot and Anna, nodding to each of them. "Good afternoon, Anna, Scot. How was your day?"

"Pretty good," Anna replied. "How was yours?"

Another associate clocked out.

Henry smiled at the associate, then answered Anna. "Not too bad. My legs are holding up. Thank you for asking, my dear." Henry addressed Scot. "How about you, Scot? How was your day?"

Scot smirked. "Big smiles all day."

Anna giggled.

Henry chuckled. "I detect a hint of sarcasm, but I like it." He winked at Anna. "I should be going. I need to get off my feet."

"Bye, Henry," Anna said in his wake. Then she turned to Scot. "Don't you just love Henry?"

"Yeah. He seems nice," Scot replied, watching the door for Charlotte.

"He *is* nice."

Scot didn't reply.

"Well, … see you tomorrow," Anna said.

"Yeah."

Anna left the break room.

Three more associates entered the break room, their ID cards in hand. Kyle was last in line. He clocked out and lifted his chin to Scot. "What up, Scotty. Waitin' for your girl again?"

Scot nodded.

"She's with the boss man. I heard he's makin' her assistant manager. She'll be his right-hand woman. Lots of late nights together." Kyle pumped his eyebrows.

Scot put up his hand like a stop sign. "Don't be a dick. She hasn't even decided yet." Scot wasn't actually sure if she *had* decided. Communication had been an issue lately.

Kyle grinned. "So fuckin' sensitive. Learn to take a joke."

Charlotte bounced into the break room, all smiles.

As she clocked out, Kyle said, "Heard you're the new assistant manager. Congrats."

Charlotte put one hand on her hip. "How did you know that? It just happened."

Kyle smirked. "I know everything that happens around here."

Charlotte twisted her face in disgust. "You're so creepy."

★★★

On the way home, Charlotte said, "It's a *lot* more money. Plus the benefits. You can't beat it. I can finally get out of my mom's house, buy a car."

"That's great," Scot said, without enthusiasm.

"I think you should take me to The Harvest tonight to celebrate."

The Harvest was a farm-to-table fine-dining restaurant in Harrisburg.

"You're the one making all the money. You should take me."

Charlotte huffed. "What's your problem? Why can't you be happy for me?"

Scot stopped at the stoplight and turned to Charlotte. "I am, but I can't afford The Harvest. We'll spend like two hundred dollars."

"You have way more than that in savings."

"It's for college."

A honk came from behind them.

Scot checked the green light, pressed on the accelerator, and drove through the intersection.

"Two hundred dollars won't make a difference," Charlotte said.

"That's almost three days of work for me, after taxes." Scot replied, his voice going up an octave.

Charlotte crossed her arms over her ample chest.

They didn't talk for several minutes.

Scot parked in front of Charlotte's mom's double-wide.

She glared and said, "You're jealous."

Scot turned to Charlotte, his face contorted in confusion. "What are you talking about? Why would I be jealous?"

"Because I'm successful, and you're not."

"You think being an assistant manager at Big-Mart is success?"

"Fuck. You." Charlotte exited the Hyundai, slamming the passenger door behind her.

CHAPTER 16

The New Manager

The next morning Scot sent Charlotte a text.

Scot: Do you still want me to pick you up?

A response came a few minutes later.

Charlotte: YES. I don't have a fucking car

Thirty minutes later, Scot parked in front of Charlotte's mother's double-wide trailer. He didn't dare honk the horn. Charlotte exited the house, her face a mask of barely contained fury.

When she entered the Hyundai, she said, "I'm not talking to you."

So they didn't talk. Scot drove them to work in silence, while Charlotte did her makeup.

At the start of the workday, Ron called a meeting in the break room. Scot stood in the back with Kyle.

Ron said, "I'm thrilled to announce that Charlotte Carey is our new assistant manager." He began to clap.

A handful of associates joined in the applause, Scot not among them.

Charlotte stepped out of the crowd and stood next to Ron, beaming and blushing. Ron handed her a new name tag and a red polo shirt, like the one Ron and the department managers wore. Then Ron hugged Charlotte.

Scot clenched his fists.

Kyle leaned in to Scot and said, "Ron's coppin' a feel."

CHAPTER 17

Management Has its Privileges

Scot clocked out at 4:00 p.m. on the dot and sat at a nearby table. A few associates came and went, also clocking out. He checked his Coinbase account on his phone. The wire transfer had gone through. The price of Bitcoin was $279.47, down about six bucks since he had checked it a few days ago. He estimated that he'd lost sixty dollars in Bitcoin in that time, only slightly less than what he had made working that day. Scot initiated a buy order for fifteen Bitcoins. The buy order was accepted at $280.05 for each Bitcoin.

"I'm gonna have to give you a point. You know you can't be on your phone," Kyle said, mimicking Ron's nasally voice.

Scot scowled at Kyle and set his phone facedown on the table.

Kyle grinned and showed his palms in surrender. He sat at the table across from Scot. "Relax, Scotty. I'm just fuckin' with you."

Charlotte entered the break room and marched to Scot, her expression like stone. The polo Ron had given her was a size too small, emphasizing her curvaceous figure. "I'm going out."

Scot stood from the table. "Where?

Kyle leaned back in his chair, watching the couple with a slight smile.

"Ron's taking me and the department managers out to Texas Roadhouse to celebrate my new job," Charlotte said.

"That's great. Can I go?" Scot asked.

Charlotte shook her head. "It's just for management."

"Oh." Scot looked down for a beat. "You ready to go home?"

"Ron's gonna give me a ride."

"I bet he is," Kyle said, under his breath.

Scot frowned at Charlotte. "I don't feel comfortable with that."

"You tell her, Scotty."

Charlotte glowered at Kyle. "Shut up, Kyle."

"Is that your management style? Just tell us lowly associates to shut up?"

Charlotte ignored Kyle, taking Scot by the arm and walking him to a corner of the break room, out of Kyle's earshot. She said in a hushed whisper, "I'd rather go to The Harvest with you, but you couldn't do that."

Scot held out his hands. "I'm trying to save money."

"What do you expect me to do? Stay home with you on a Friday night and play video games?"

Anna and Henry entered the break room, headed for the time clock.

"I have to go," Charlotte said. "I don't have time to argue with you."

"Will you text me when you get home?" Scot asked, his voice pleading.

She rolled her eyes. "Depends how I feel." Then she pivoted and left the break room.

Scot felt his pockets, suddenly aware that his phone wasn't on him. He glanced across the break room. It was on the table near the time clock, next to Kyle. Scot walked back to the table and snatched his phone.

Kyle leaned back in his chair, his hands behind his head. "That was cold."

Anna and Henry stood nearby.

"What was cold?" Anna asked.

"Charlotte's going out with the managers, leaving my man Scotty high and dry on a Friday night," Kyle said.

Anna winced. "Sorry about that."

"It's not like that," Scot said.

"It's not? She said she was going to Texas Roadhouse, but it was just for managers. Lowly associates aren't allowed."

"That's rude," Anna said.

"I'm grilling burgers tonight," Henry said. "You all are welcome to come by."

Kyle stood from the table and patted Henry on the back. "Thanks for the invite, Hank, but I got a hot date. Check you guys later." Kyle left the break room.

"I'd love to come," Anna said. "What time?"

"How about seven?" Henry asked.

"That's fine with me." Anna turned to Scot. "Are you coming?"

Scot hesitated.

"I grill a pretty good burger, if I do say so myself," Henry said.

Scot addressed Henry. "I appreciate the invite, but I, uh ..." Scot struggled to come up with a believable lie.

"Plato once said, 'We can easily forgive a child who is afraid of the dark. The real tragedy of life is when men are afraid of the light.'"

Scot tilted his head. "I'm not sure what that means."

"It means, you should come over," Anna said, her hands on her hips.

Scot thought about Charlotte going out with Ron and the managers. "Yeah, okay."

CHAPTER 18

Henry's House

Scot parked along the curb in front of a redbrick rambler. It was nearly seven, but the summer sun was still high in the sky. The grass was long and weedy. The hedges were overgrown, partially covering the bay window. Scot double-checked the address, making sure he was at the right place.

He debated driving away. He could say that he got sick or that he had a family emergency. *That's good. A family emergency.* Scot put his Hyundai into Drive, just as Anna parked her Honda Civic behind him. She gave him a polite beep. Scot checked his rearview mirror, and Anna waved from her car.

Scot blew out a breath and put his car back into Park. He met Anna in the street. Her brown hair was down, and she had changed into capri pants and a light-blue blouse. They went to the front door together. Anna brought a pie for dessert. Closer to the house, Scot noticed that paint peeled off the window frames, and the concrete walkway was cracked.

Henry opened the door, before they could knock. "Come in. Come in."

Anna handed Henry the pie. "I brought you some apple pie."

Henry beamed. "Thank you, dear. I love apple pie."

Scot held out his empty hands. "Sorry. I, uh, forgot to bring something."

Henry touched Scot's forearm. "I'm happy *you're* here. We have everything we need."

Scot followed Henry and Anna into the kitchen. Along the way, they walked through the dimly lit living room, with seventies-era furniture, faux wood walls, and a dingy mustard-colored carpet.

The tiny kitchen held a round table with three wooden chairs. It was already set with glasses, plates, and salad bowls. The old refrigerator rattled in the background.

Henry said, "I have to apologize for the appearance of my house. I have so many projects to do, but these old bones are just too darn tired to get to them. I've been meaning to replace my carpet with hardwood for quite some time. I'm embarrassed to say that the hardwood's been in my garage for seven years."

"I think your house looks great," Anna said, scanning the kitchen. She turned to Henry. "I'm not very handy, but, if you ever need help, I can do manual labor."

Scot thought Henry was fishing for free labor. *I'm not falling for that.*

Henry touched Anna's forearm. "That's sweet of you, dear, but it's not necessary." Henry offered and poured iced teas for his guests. Then he said, "I need to put the burgers on. I've had them marinating since last night. I'll be right back."

"Do you need help with anything?" Anna asked.

"No. You two have a seat. Relax." Henry grabbed the burgers from the fridge and went outside to the deck and the grill.

Scot glanced out the kitchen window at Henry working the grill. The deck was gray and weathered from the elements. Part of the railing was missing. Scot sipped his iced tea, then pivoted to Anna. She was at the refrigerator, perusing the pictures held by magnets. Scot joined her at the fridge. A half-dozen pictures portrayed Henry with a sickly woman, slightly taller than him.

The pictures appeared relatively recent, as Henry didn't appear much older today. One showed the couple standing on a beach, the ocean in the background. Another showed them at a fancy restaurant.

Another showed them by a lake. One showed the woman, shriveled and pale in a hospital bed, with Henry's arm around her, both of them smiling.

Anna said, "This must've been Henry's wife."

"Did she die?" Scot whispered.

"Breast cancer two years ago but don't mention it. I asked him about his wife a few months ago because he still wears his wedding band, and he told me about her dying." Anna bit her lower lip. "He seemed so sad about it, so I never brought her up again. I felt awful for opening my big mouth."

"That sucks."

Anna nodded.

"Do you know what he used to do for a living before Big-Mart?" Scot asked.

"I think he was a philosophy professor at HACC."

HACC stood for Harrisburg Area Community College.

The back door opened and shut.

"Burgers are on the grill," Henry said, as he stepped into the kitchen.

Scot and Anna turned from the fridge, their teas in hand.

"Are you sure there's not something I can help you with?" Anna asked.

Henry waved her off. "Salad's already done. Baked beans just need to be heated. And the burgers will be done soon." He gestured to the kitchen table. "Why don't we sit?"

Scot and Anna sat at the table.

Henry groaned as he sat.

"Are you okay?" Anna asked.

"Fine. My old legs get tired, but I'm fine." Henry smiled at Anna and Scot. "So, what do you young people like to do for fun?"

"I'm pretty much a homebody," Anna said. "I like to play with my cat, Patches. I also like to play this game, Terraria. I'm kind of obsessed with it at the moment."

Scot stared at Anna in the bright fluorescent light of the kitchen, watching her pink lips as she spoke.

"What's a Terraria?" Henry asked.

"I'm not sure what the name means," Anna said. "It's a game that lets you explore, build, craft, mine. I actually like the farming part the best."

"I grew up on a farm. My dad raised chickens. I learned one thing about farming."

"What was that?"

"That it's hard work." Henry chuckled.

Anna laughed. "Real farming does look like hard work. I'll stick to computer-simulated farming."

"What about you, Scot?"

Scot shrugged. "I play Halo sometimes. I go out with Charlotte. We watch movies. Hang out and stuff."

Henry covered his heart with his hand. "Ah, young love. It's a feeling like no other."

Scot flushed and changed the subject. "I'm actually saving up to go back to school. I'm going to Penn. I'm three semesters away from finishing my Industrial Engineering degree."

"You have a bright future, Scot. Your mother must be proud."

Scot shrugged again. "I guess."

"Don't downplay your accomplishments. They're impressive and should be valued accordingly."

Scot nodded.

Henry gestured to Anna. "My dear Anna is studying to be a veterinarian."

"Not exactly," Anna said, cringing. "I'm saving up, like Scot, but I have a long way to go."

"You'll get there," Henry said. "You keep plugging away, and you'll get there. Small pluses make big pluses."

★★★

After dinner and dessert, Scot and Anna thanked their host and left together.

As they walked to their cars, Anna asked, "What are you doing now?"

Scot fiddled with his keys. "I guess going home and going to bed. I'm working this weekend."

Anna glanced at her watch. "It's only 9:30. Um, … you want to come over and play Terraria with me? The graphics are kind of lame, but it's really fun."

"I should go home and get some sleep."

Anna wrung her hands. "Right. Sure. I should go to bed too. Maybe another time."

"Yeah. Maybe." Scot watched her walk to her car.

Before she entered her car, she smiled at Scot and gave him a little wave.

Scot waved back, blushing, suddenly feeling self-conscious.

CHAPTER 19

A Mother's Love

The next morning Scot silenced his alarm on his phone. He tapped on his texts, checking to see if Charlotte had responded. Still nothing from her. Four unrequited texts since last night. Scot went to the bathroom, peed, and brushed his teeth, then changed into his work clothes. Khakis, gray T-shirt, and his red vest, with his name tag that read *Scot, Associate*.

He trudged downstairs, intent on having a decent breakfast, since he didn't have to pick up Charlotte, as she was off that Saturday.

His mother was in the kitchen, wearing her robe, hovering over the brewing coffeepot.

"Morning, Mom," Scot said, entering the kitchen.

Laura smiled at her son. "Good morning, honey. You want some breakfast?"

"Sure. That'd be great."

"How about scrambled eggs and toast with strawberry jam?"

Laura cooked the eggs, while Scot prepared the toast and set the table.

"Should I set a place for Heather?" Scot asked.

Laura turned from the stovetop. "Don't bother. She was out late. It'll be nice, just the two of us." Laura limped to the table, holding the pan of scrambled eggs. Using the spatula, she heaped eggs onto Scot's plate.

Scot sat at the table. "Thanks, Mom."

"Of course, honey." Laura limped back to the counter, setting the pan on the stovetop. She grabbed three individually wrapped pastries from the cupboard to go with her coffee. Then she joined her son at the kitchen table.

"You're not having any eggs?" Scot asked.

She opened a cheese Danish. "It's too much food for me in the morning. I need to lose some weight."

Scot ate his eggs and toast, while Laura devoured all three pastries.

Scot checked his texts. Still no response from Charlotte. He wondered how late she was out. *Did she go home with Ron? Did she have sex with him?*

"Is something wrong, honey?" Laura asked.

Scot set down his phone and exhaled. "Charlotte and I are fighting."

Laura leaned forward. "What happened?"

"I don't know. We've been drifting apart for a while now. I think she wants me to be more successful."

"Of course she does. Women love successful men."

Scot frowned. "Too bad I'm a loser."

Laura reached out and slapped his hand, not hard. "Don't say that. You are *not* a loser. You go to Penn for Christ's sake."

Scot slumped his shoulders. "I *went* to Penn. Now I work at Big-Mart."

"This is temporary, honey. What's important is that you have a brilliant mind and a kind heart. That's what matters."

Scot smiled. "Thanks, Mom."

"Charlotte will come around. You'll see. Maybe she needs more commitment. Women like commitment."

CHAPTER 20

People of Big-Mart

Scot restocked shampoo and conditioner in the Health and Beauty Department. His eyes were bloodshot, and his feet ached. He glanced at the clock on the wall. It was 11:29 p.m. He had volunteered to work a double shift, after several associates called off for the night shift. From his perspective, it sucked, but he was well into overtime, so every extra hour was time and a half.

An obese woman waddled into the aisle, wearing purple stretchy pants and a purple tank top. Scot moved the box of shampoo to the side and stood tight to the shelves to give her room to pass. He smiled at the woman. She ignored him. Kyle appeared behind her, with his cell phone in hand, and a smirk on his face. He snapped a few photos of her ample backside, before she left the aisle.

Scot frowned at Kyle. "What are you doing?"

"Takin' pictures for my website," Kyle replied.

"What website?"

"People of Big-Mart. I take pictures of all the freaks who come in here, then I post them on my site with a funny caption. I was thinkin' of makin' a Barney reference to that purple whale you just saw. Maybe 'Barney in retirement,' or 'Barney really let himself go.'"

Scot glanced around, making sure they were alone. "You can't do that."

"Sure I can. It's my First Amendment right. Big-Mart's in public. There's no expectation of privacy when you're in public."

"That doesn't mean Ron won't fire you, if he finds out."

Kyle shrugged. "Big fuckin' deal. Shit, if my site keeps growin', I won't need a job. I just landed a sponsor that pays eight hundred bucks a month. Pays for my new car."

"Good for you." Scot went back to the shampoo box, grabbing several bottles, stocking the shelves.

"Why are you still workin'?" Kyle asked.

"I took the extra shift. I need the money," Scot replied.

"That's not what I mean. The managers left an hour ago."

"I'm on the clock for another thirty minutes."

Kyle rolled his eyes. "Fuck, Scotty. Don't you ever wanna break the rules?"

"I need this job." Scot grabbed two more shampoo bottles.

"You're entitled to a break."

Scot set the bottles on the shelf. "I already had my break."

"I wonder if Ron's with your girl, while you're workin' a double shift?"

Scot clenched his jaw. Kyle had hit a sore spot. Scot still hadn't heard from Charlotte. He was up to nine unrequited texts, making him feel like a stalker. "Fuck it. I'll take a break."

Kyle rapped Scot on the back. "My man. Let's go to the warehouse and get high."

"I don't get high," Scot protested.

But Kyle was already walking toward the back of the store and the warehouse. Scot followed, fast-walking to catch up.

The warehouse featured five shut garage doors, which opened to the loading docks. Rows of metal racks were filled with pallets of shrink-wrapped consumer items. A forklift sat dormant between the racks.

They went into the warehouse bathroom.

Kyle flipped on the fan. "This is the best place to get fucked-up. No cameras. No customers." He pointed to the overhead fan. "And that fan is strong." Kyle turned on his vape pen. "It needs to heat up."

"I don't do drugs," Scot said. "I don't care if you do, but …"

Kyle frowned. "Come on, dude. Quit bein' a pussy. It's just weed."

Scot flushed, embarrassed by his pussified persona. "How often do you get high?"

"Every day. No way I could work here sober."

Once the vape pen was warm, Kyle took the first hit, inhaling through the end of the pen, then exhaling the vapor. Scot expected a pungent odor from the marijuana, but it was nearly nonexistent. Kyle handed the pen to Scot.

"How do I do it? Do I push a button?" Scot asked.

"It's an autodraw. Just inhale," Kyle said.

Scot inhaled, the vapor tasting slightly minty. Then he exhaled. He felt nothing.

They passed the vape pen back and forth for a few minutes.

Scot began to feel a sense of relaxed euphoria. He giggled for no reason. "I feel … happy."

Kyle laughed. "You're fucked-up."

Scot giggled again.

Kyle turned off the pen, smacked Scot across the back, and opened the bathroom door. "Let's go."

"Where are we going?" Scot asked, following Kyle back into the store.

"To have some fun," Kyle replied, over his shoulder.

"What about the cameras?"

"They only check 'em if there's an incident."

Big-Mart was open, but very few customers occupied the aisles and even fewer associates. Scot followed Kyle to the ammunition counter in the Sporting Goods Department. Scot's jaw dropped when Kyle produced a key to open the counter. "Where did you get that?"

"Stole it from Kent," Kyle replied, opening the counter access door.

Kent was the Sporting Goods Department manager.

Scot worried that Kyle planned to shoot up the place. Instead, he grabbed two Ping-Pong paddles and a ball hidden behind the ammo.

They played Ping-Pong on the table that was for sale for $499.99. Kyle was pretty good, spiking the little plastic ball each time Scot's return was weak. They laughed and talked trash too loudly. A few customers looked at them side-eyed, as they walked past.

After Kyle handily beat Scot in Ping-Pong, they wandered over to the toy section. They tossed a nerf football back and forth. Kyle booted a kickball into the Home Goods Department. Another into the Hardware Department.

Then they mounted two bikes and raced around the store, cackling like jackals, both of them much too big for the kid-size bicycles. Kyle's bike was pink, with a basket in front. He had mounted his phone to the basket, recording the journey. On the last turn, Kyle crashed into a cardboard display, filled with marshmallows. Scot, who was right behind him, crashed into Kyle, and fell on the marshmallows, popping several bags.

They lay on the linoleum, under the bright fluorescent lighting, giggling their asses off. Kyle ate a marshmallow off the floor. Scot did too.

"I'm really hungry," Scot said, his mouth full.

"Me too," Kyle replied, his mouth also full of marshmallows.

Scot righted the display and restocked the marshmallows, despite Kyle's admonishment.

"Just leave it," Kyle said, holding a split bag of marshmallows.

"Are you *trying* to get fired?" Scot asked, still restocking the display.

They rode their bikes back to the toy section, Kyle hauling all the open bags of marshmallows in his basket. They took their marshmallows to the Furniture Department, crashing on beanbags, then stuffing their faces with white gooey goodness.

"That was pretty fuckin' fun, *huh*?" Kyle asked.

Scot smiled. "Yeah, it was."

They ate marshmallows in silence for a moment. Scot thought

about Charlotte, wondering what she was doing.

Kyle broke the silence. "If you could fuck any girl who works here, who would you pick?"

Without hesitation, Scot replied, "Charlotte."

Kyle threw up his hands in disgust, his marshmallows in his lap. "Come on, dude. You can't be serious. She's got you all twisted."

Scot looked down. "I love her."

"Dude, stop. You're killin' my buzz. I bet she's fuckin' around on you with Ron right now."

Scot glared at Kyle. "She wouldn't do that to me. She's at home. I just talked to her. I heard her mom in the background." That was all a lie.

"I'm tellin' you, man. You can't trust these hoes. So fuckin' *scandalous*. That's why I smash, but, as soon as they want a relationship, I'm out."

"Who do *you* want to have sex with?" Scot only asked to change the subject.

Kyle nodded, a small smile on his lips, as if savoring a thought. "That nerdy chick, Anna. I know she looks plain, but I would love to hit that. There's somethin' about her, you know?"

Scot gritted his teeth, an unexpected wave of jealousy crashing over him.

Kyle checked his phone. "Shit. Shift's over." Kyle groaned and stood from the beanbag. He stretched his arms over his head, then tossed a half-eaten bag of marshmallows to Scot, several marshmallows spilling from the bag to the floor. "Later, player." Kyle pivoted and left Scot sitting on the beanbag, with three half-eaten packages of marshmallows resting on his midsection.

Scot stared at the mess he'd made, regret setting in. *If Ron finds out about this, I'm done.* Scot took the open bags of marshmallows with him to clock out. Then he took them to the self-checkout, scanned them, and paid for them. He dumped them in the trash on the way out, his appetite gone.

CHAPTER 21

Repercussions

Charlotte had finally texted back on Sunday night, making sure Scot was coming to pick her up on Monday morning for work. No mention of what she did over the weekend or acknowledgment of Scot's unrequited texts. Scot chose to take the high road, letting it go in the hope that they were on the mend.

During the icy trip to work, Scot glanced from the road to Charlotte, who was doing her makeup, and said, "I really want this to work, Charlotte."

She continued to apply eyeliner, unresponsive.

"I'm serious. I really want this to work. Whatever you need from me, I'll try to do it."

Charlotte applied lip gloss and puckered her lips in the mirror.

Scot stopped at a traffic light and turned in his seat to Charlotte. "Is it commitment? Because I'm totally committed to you. I don't want anyone else. I want you."

Charlotte shut the sun visor and mirror, then turned to Scot, a scowl on her face. "I don't think you're going anywhere. I mean, I make more money than you, and I've never even been to college."

Scot hung his head and pinched the bridge of his nose. When he looked up, the light had turned green. He drove through the intersection. They continued in silence the rest of the way to Big-Mart.

Scot parked his car and said, "Is this about Ron? Is there something going on?"

Charlotte didn't bother looking at Scot when she said, "No." She grabbed her purse and makeup bag, and exited Scot's Hyundai, not waiting to walk in together.

After the morning meeting and group cheer, Ron summoned Scot to his office.

Scot wrung his hands, his underarms sweating, sitting across from Ron at his desk. Scot's employee file sat on the desktop.

"Do you know why you're here?" Ron asked.

"I'm on the schedule to work today," Scot replied, feigning ignorance.

Ron shook his head. "Do you know why I wanted to talk to you this morning?"

Scot shrugged. "You wanted to thank me for filling in on Saturday?"

Ron shook his head again. "Guess again."

Scot swallowed hard. "I don't know."

"I think you do know." Ron tapped on his laptop, then turned the screen to face Scot.

A security video was on the screen, showing Kyle pedaling a girl's bike, then crashing into the marshmallow display, causing Scot to crash as well.

Scot swallowed again, his throat dry.

"What do you think I should do about this?" Ron asked, his face like stone.

"Well, uh, … give me a strong warning not to do it again—"

"I should fire you is what I should do."

"Please, Ron. I'm sorry. I really need this job. I won't do anything like that ever again."

Ron glowered at Scot. "I know you won't because, if you do, I'll fire your ass so fast it'll make your head spin. You understand me?"

Scot clasped his hands together like he was praying. "I understand. Thank you, Ron."

"You're lucky you paid for those marshmallows. Otherwise, I would've fired you and Kyle on the spot for theft. I'm giving you two points for being a moron. That's four in less than a week." Ron held up one finger. "One more and you're gone. I suggest, from now on, you make sure you're on time, and you stay off your phone, and, for the love of God, stay away from that idiot Kyle."

CHAPTER 22

Simpin' Ain't Easy

After Scot's near firing, he'd spent the workday focused on his job, careful not to break any rules. Late in the afternoon, with the sun high overhead, Scot pushed a cart toward the shelter. He slammed the cart into the train of shopping carts. A sparkling silver Subaru STI with temporary plates parked next to the shelter. Bass thumped from the vehicle, along with the low growl of the boxer engine. The driver cut the engine and rap music.

Kyle stepped out of the driver's side door, smoking his vape pen. "What up, Scotty?"

"Did you talk to Ron?" Scot asked, standing under the shelter next to the train of shopping carts.

Kyle blew minty marijuana vapor in Scot's face. "About what?"

"About Saturday night. He had video of us riding those bikes around the store."

Kyle walked into the shelter. "He didn't say shit to me."

Scot frowned. "Why not? He gave me two points."

"You remember that chick Jasmine?"

"Yeah."

Kyle sat on the railing. "Last year, I caught Ron makin' out with her in the warehouse. Got some video too. If he fucks with me, he knows I'll go to corporate, get him fired." Kyle grinned and took another hit from his vape pen. "I'm untouchable."

"You think you can help me get rid of my points? If I get one more

I'm gone." Scot glanced back at Big-Mart, making sure Ron wasn't watching him talk to Kyle. "I've been stressed all day, making sure I don't make any mistakes."

"No can do, my man."

"Why not?"

"Why do you want another man to fix your problems?"

Scot held out his hands, annoyance in his voice. "You're the reason I got the fucking points in the first place."

Kyle slid off the railing and took another hit from his vape pen, vapor spewing from his mouth as he spoke. "This job sucks anyway. Gettin' fired would be doin' you a favor."

"I need this job. I'm saving to get back to school."

"There are other jobs."

Scot ran his hand over his face. "Whatever, man."

"This place ain't good for you. Ron's bangin' your girl and holdin' your job over your head at the same time."

Scot glared at Kyle. "That's bullshit. Where's your evidence?"

Kyle shrugged and turned off his vape pen. "I don't need any evidence. I can tell by the way she treats you and flirts with Ron."

"I thought we were cool after Saturday, but you really are an asshole."

"I might be an asshole, but I'm right about her. Don't be a simp, dude." Kyle pivoted and walked toward Big-Mart.

CHAPTER 23

Last-Ditch Effort

Despite the silent treatment, Scot still drove Charlotte home from work. He had thought about telling her to find her own way home but had chickened out, worried that Charlotte might break up with him and that Ron would gladly take her home. Despite their recent tumult, Scot still hoped for reconciliation and a return to the relative bliss they'd shared in the beginning of their relationship.

Charlotte tapped on her phone, as Scot turned his car into her neighborhood of mobile homes.

Scot tried to break the icy silence. "I was thinking we could go out and celebrate your job tonight."

Charlotte scowled at Scot. "On a Monday night?"

"Yeah. There'll be less people. We could go to The Harvest, like you wanted." Scot had planned to sell half of one Bitcoin to pay for the meal.

"I'm tired. I'm gonna go to bed," she replied, not making eye contact.

Scot parked in the driveway, behind Charlotte's mother's Pontiac Grand Am. "I could come in. We could watch TV for a while. Maybe mess around after your mom goes to sleep?"

Charlotte twisted her face in disgust. "I don't think so." She opened the passenger door.

"I guess I'll see you tomorrow," Scot said to her back, just as she shut the car door.

Scot watched her bubble butt, as she walked to the front door. She didn't look back when she entered the trailer. Scot gripped the steering wheel, thinking about what Kyle had said about Charlotte having sex with Ron.

Scot reversed out of the driveway, driving back the way he came in. Instead of turning to exit the little neighborhood, he drove into a cul-de-sac and turned around, parking behind a Honda Accord. Charlotte's neighborhood had one entrance and one exit. From his vantage point, he could see anyone entering or leaving. *She's blowing me off. Maybe she is seeing Ron.* Scot let out a heavy breath. *I'm about to find out.*

Scot waited for an hour, watching the residents come and go. Finally, he spotted Charlotte's mother's Pontiac Grand Am. Helen was driving, with Charlotte in the front passenger seat. Scot followed them, allowing at least one car between them. They ended up at the Lebanon Chevrolet dealership. Scot didn't stick around, fearing he'd be spotted and outed for stalking. He figured Charlotte was car shopping, given her new salary, and didn't tell him because she's still angry with him. *At least she's not cheating.*

CHAPTER 24

Common Courtesy Isn't Common

The next morning Scot parked in Charlotte's mother's driveway, and sent a text.

Scot: Here

After a few minutes of no response, Scot called Charlotte. His call went straight to voice mail. He waited a few more minutes, then went to the front door and knocked.

Charlotte's mother, Helen, answered the door in pajama pants and a T-shirt. "What do you want?"

Scot drew back, surprised by the question, since he'd been driving Charlotte to work for seven months straight. "I'm just here to pick up Charlotte. Do you know if she's ready?"

Helen furrowed her brow. "She left already."

Scot winced, as if he'd been slapped. "Did someone pick her up?"

"Why would someone pick her up? Didn't she tell you about her new car?"

Scot forced a smile. "Right. I don't know what I was thinking. Sorry." Scot fast-walked back to his car, then drove toward Big-Mart.

Along the way, he thought about following Charlotte to the Chevy dealership the night before. Scot hadn't stayed to see Charlotte buy a car, figuring that she was just browsing, and feeling satisfied that she wasn't cheating on him with Ron. It had never occurred to him that she'd buy a car and not have the common courtesy to let him know that he didn't have to pick her up for work.

As Scot drove into the Big-Mart parking lot, he spotted Charlotte, Ron, and another male manager fawning over a candy-apple-red Camaro. Scot parked nearby and approached them, the immaculate sports car sparkling in the sun. Scot ignored Ron and the other manager, making a beeline for Charlotte. "I went to your house to pick you up."

Charlotte gestured to the Camaro. "I drove myself to work."

"You bought this last night?"

Ron opened the driver's side door and slipped into the black leather seat. "This is *nice*."

Charlotte stepped to the open door, ignoring Scot. "Don't change my seat. I have it set perfectly."

Ron showed his palms. "I'm not changing anything."

The other manager slipped into the passenger seat. "This *is* nice."

Scot stood behind Charlotte, talking to her back. "Why didn't you tell me that you were getting a car?"

"I don't have to tell you anything," she replied, over her shoulder.

"I didn't say you did. I just ..."

Ron tapped his watch, turning to Scot. "It's almost eight. You're gonna be late."

Scot checked his phone. It was two minutes till. He sprinted to Big-Mart, his hands balled into tight fists, and the managers laughing in his wake.

CHAPTER 25

Is it Over?

Around lunchtime, Scot grabbed an errant shopping cart, dumped on the grassy median along the eastern edge of the parking lot. If he left the cart, other customers would copy the bad behavior. Heat reverberated off the macadam. Sweat slipped down his spine and collected in the seat of his khaki pants. As Scot pushed the cart toward a shelter, he thought, *Is it over? Did she just break up with me? She didn't say it was over. Maybe she's just really mad at me. Or disappointed that I turned out to be such a loser.*

Scot pushed the cart into the shelter. He hid in the shade of the shelter, taking an unauthorized break from the heat. He looked toward the back of the lot, at Charlotte's sparkling new sports car. *Why wouldn't she tell me that she was buying a new car? Then she's showing it off to Ron. It's so fucked-up.*

Scot spotted a mother pushing a full shopping cart, with a toddler sitting in the seat, and several six-packs of sodas wedged onto the sides. Scot left the shelter, intent on offering to help load her car. On the way, he spotted Charlotte leaving Big-Mart. He turned, making a beeline for Charlotte.

She scowled at the sight of him, not breaking stride.

Scot walked alongside her. "What's happening to us? I don't understand."

Charlotte lifted one shoulder, not looking at Scot.

"Are you breaking up with me?"

"If that's what you want." She spoke in a detached monotone.

"How can you be so cold?" Scot asked, his voice going up an octave.

"If I'm so cold, why do you care?"

Scot held out his hands like a beggar. "Because I love you."

Charlotte shook her head, her face like stone. "You're a *boy*. You don't know what real love is. If you really loved me, you'd find a way to marry me. You'd buy me a house. We'd have children. You can't give me any of that."

"I'm only twenty-one. What do you expect?"

Charlotte stopped next to her Camaro and fished her key fob from her purse. She glowered at Scot. "You're a *boy*. I need a man. What do you have to offer? You can't even take me to a nice restaurant."

Scot crowded her. "I said I'd take you to The Harvest. You didn't want to go."

She held out her hand like a stop sign, one side of her mouth raised in disgust. "Back up. You're all sweaty."

Scot stepped back, tears welling in his eyes. His voice cracked, as he asked, "Are you breaking up with me?"

She pressed the button on her key fob, unlocking her car. "This has been over for a long time. You're just too stupid to notice."

"Why are you just telling me now?"

Charlotte climbed into her car and slammed the door. She started the engine and drove away, revving the V-8.

Scot watched her taillights, and then it hit him like a ton of bricks. *She strung me along because I was her ride.*

CHAPTER 26

Obsession

Scot sent another text. It was his fiftieth unrequited text that day.

> **Scot:** Please talk to me. I love you. Please give me a chance. I love you I love you I love you I love you I love you I love you. CALL ME PLEASE

Scot sat on his bed, his back against the wall, staring at his phone, willing Charlotte to call or text. As Scot stared at the string of texts he'd sent Charlotte, he noticed a discrepancy. His previous texts all had a little tag at the bottom that read *Delivered*. But his most recent text didn't have the Delivered tag. *She blocked me.* Scot threw his phone across the room, hitting his closet, then falling to the floor.

He rushed to his phone, worried that he'd destroyed it. Scot scooped it up and checked it. Thankfully, the protective case had saved it.

Scot went to his sister's door and knocked.

Heather answered the door in a string bikini, her breasts mashed together for maximum cleavage. Pop music spilled from her bedroom. "What do you want?"

"What are you doing in your bikini?" Scot asked.

"Pictures for the Gram. What do you want?"

"Can I borrow your phone?"

Heather frowned. "No way." She shut her door in Scot's face.

Scot went downstairs, finding his mother on the couch, watching a cop show. "Can I borrow your phone?"

Laura turned from her show. "Is your phone broken?"

"I'm just checking something."

Laura gestured to her phone on the coffee table. "Go ahead, honey."

Scot took his mother's phone back to his bedroom. He paced in his room, thinking about what to say, knowing that he'd likely only have a few seconds to talk. Then he dialed Charlotte's phone number.

Charlotte answered on the third ring with a tentative "Hello?"

Scot spoke rapidly. "I love you. Don't hang up—"

The call ended.

Scot called again. His call went directly to voice mail. He sent a text.

> **717-555-8765:** Please talk to me. Just five minutes. I love you

Scot tapped Send, watching to see if the text was tagged as Delivered. It wasn't. Scot tossed Laura's phone on his desktop. He lay on his bed, his face buried into his pillow. He sobbed for a long time.

Scot went to the bathroom. In the mirror, his face was blotchy, his eyes red and puffy. He washed and dried his face, taking a moment to compose himself. Then he went downstairs and set his mother's phone back on the coffee table.

"Are you okay?" Laura asked, sitting up straight, staring at her son.

"I'm fine. I'll be back." Scot made a quick exit, before he dissolved into tears again.

He drove to Charlotte's trailer park, driving past her house. Her Camaro and her mother's Pontiac were in the driveway. Scot drove back to the trailer park entrance, parking discreetly behind the same Honda Accord he'd parked behind the night before.

An hour later, the sun was orange and nearing the horizon. Scot heard the low drone of an engine he'd heard recently. A silver Subaru STI drove into the neighborhood. *Kyle?*

"What the hell's going on?" Scot asked himself. "She calls me a boy? If I'm a boy, Kyle's a fucking infant."

Shortly thereafter, the Subaru left the trailer park. Scot got a glimpse of Kyle in the driver's seat with Charlotte next to him. Scot followed them to Chipotle, always keeping a safe distance between them, not because he was afraid of being caught but because he didn't want his presence to alter their behavior. He needed to know the truth.

Scot parked on the opposite side of the lot from Kyle's Subaru. From his vantage point, Scot had a good view of the restaurant. Through the restaurant windows, he watched Kyle wait in line, while Charlotte saved a table. He watched them eating, talking, and laughing. *When was the last time she laughed with me?*

They finished eating, cleared their table, threw away their trash, and stacked their trays. Kyle actually held the door for Charlotte, as they exited the restaurant.

Scot exited his car and fast-walked across the parking lot, his fists clenched. Kyle and Charlotte stood next to the Subaru, about to enter the vehicle.

They both turned to Scot, as he approached Charlotte.

"What are you doing?" Scot asked Charlotte.

Charlotte shook her head. "You're pathetic. Go home."

"You broke up with me for *him*?" Scot asked, gesturing to Kyle. "I'm a boy, but *he's* mature?"

Charlotte crossed her arms over her chest. "It's over, Scot. If you keep harassing me, I'll call the police."

Scot held out his hands. "You won't talk to me."

Kyle appeared, moving between Charlotte and Scot. Kyle was a big guy, standing six inches taller than Scot. Kyle put his hand on Scot's chest, pushing him back, not hard. "Come on, Scot. Don't be a little bitch."

"Fuck you, Kyle." Scot slapped Kyle's hand off his chest.

Kyle sneered and grabbed Scot by his upper arm. He marched Scot back toward his car, away from Charlotte.

"Let me go," Scot said, wiggling in Kyle's grasp.

Kyle gripped Scot tighter. "You gonna go home?"

"Yeah. I'm going."

Kyle let go but still escorted Scot.

"You stole my girlfriend," Scot said, sounding like a child.

"She was never yours, dude. It was just your turn. Now it's mine."

CHAPTER 27

Desperation

The next morning Scot waited in the Big-Mart parking lot, obscured by an SUV. He had parked his car far from his current location, knowing that Charlotte would be unlikely to park near his Hyundai.

Charlotte's Camaro appeared in the distance. She parked her car near the back of the lot, as she had done the day before. Scot hid behind the SUV, near the lane that led directly to the Big-Mart entrance, and the likely path for Charlotte to walk.

A few minutes later, Charlotte did exactly that.

Scot stepped out into the lane.

Charlotte stopped in her tracks and inhaled a sharp breath, her hand over her chest. "You *asshole*."

Scot showed his palms. "I didn't mean to scare you."

She fast-walked toward Big-Mart.

Scot walked alongside her. "How long have you been seeing Kyle?"

Charlotte glowered at Scot. "It was one date, not that it's any of your business."

They passed Henry, who also walked toward the Big-Mart entrance. He said, "Good morning, Scot, Charlotte."

Neither of them acknowledged Henry.

"Did you have sex with him?" Scot asked, talking loud enough for Henry and a nearby customer to hear.

Charlotte stopped, turned to Scot, and pointed her finger in his face. "Leave me alone, or I'll make sure Ron fires you." She pivoted and continued to Big-Mart.

Scot walked behind her, his head bowed, tears welling in his eyes. He went directly to the bathroom. A customer was inside, washing his hands. Scot shut himself into the last stall on the row. Scot sat on the toilet cover and leaned over, his head in his hands, crying as quietly as possible.

A knock came at his stall.

Scot sniffled and said, "Someone's in here."

"It's Henry," he said. "I was checking to see if you're okay. It's almost eight."

Henry was referencing the fact that Scot would be late soon if he didn't clock in.

"I don't care. They can fire me. Fuck this job."

"Is that what you want?"

Scot sniffled again. "I don't know. I don't know anything anymore."

"I couldn't help but hear a little of your conversation with Charlotte."

"That's just *great*."

"I'm sorry, Scot. I wasn't trying to pry."

Scot didn't reply.

"D.H. Lawrence once said, 'A woman has to live her life, or live to repent not having lived it.'"

"Are you saying she's not living her life with me?"

"No. I think *she's* saying that."

Scot swallowed the lump in his throat.

"It's three minutes till," Henry said. "Why don't you hand me your ID card, and I'll clock you in while you collect yourself."

Scot removed his lanyard and ID card from around his neck. He stared at his chubby baby face in the picture, thinking that all he had to do was hold the ID card for three minutes, and then he'd never have to come back to Big-Mart again.

Henry said, "Scot?"

Scot still stared at his ID card.

"Quitting should be your decision, not theirs."

Scot tossed his ID card under the stall at Henry's orthopedic shoes.

CHAPTER 28

Intentions

At lunchtime, Scot pushed shopping carts together to make a large train, with the intention of moving them back inside Big-Mart.

Kyle exited Big-Mart, headed for his car and likely lunch.

Scot mean-mugged Kyle as he walked past, but Kyle ignored him. Scot followed Kyle to his car, leaving his train of carts unattended. "I thought you didn't want a girlfriend," Scot said to Kyle's back.

Kyle pivoted to Scot, now standing by his car. "I don't."

Scot moved within striking distance of Kyle, his fists clenched. "Then why are you seeing Charlotte?"

Kyle frowned. "I'm not tryin' to be her boyfriend. I'm tryin' to fuck her."

Scot swung wildly, his weak punch glancing off Kyle's chin.

Kyle shoved Scot, pushing him to the macadam, then stood over him. "I'm gonna let that go because she's got you all fucked-up."

Scot rose to his feet, his face flushed. "You lied. You said she was having sex with Ron."

Kyle shook his head. "She is." Then he entered his car, started his engine, and drove away.

CHAPTER 29

Glutton for Punishment

After work, Scot followed Charlotte's Camaro. She drove directly home, alone. Scot waited near the trailer park entrance again, parked behind the old Honda Accord. An hour later, Charlotte left the trailer park in her Camaro.

Scot followed Charlotte across town. She turned into a little town-home community, parking in a visitor's spot at the end of the cul-de-sac. Scot parked across the street behind a box truck. He exited his car, peering out from behind the truck, squinting into the afternoon sun. From his elevated vantage point, he watched Charlotte go to the front door of a middle unit townhome, entering without knocking. She wore a short sundress with chunky heels, showing off her assets.

Scot felt sick to his stomach. He knew from the car in the drive-way, the Chrysler Sebring convertible, that it was Ron's house. Scot crept across the street, walking around the back of the row of town-homes. A terrier barked from the backyard of the end unit. Scot hid behind a burning bush hedge in the common area.

The back door of the end unit townhome opened, and a woman said, "Come in, Pippa."

The dog yipped again and scurried inside.

Scot breathed a sigh of relief.

He found Ron's backyard. It was enclosed by a wooden privacy fence. Scot opened the gate and slipped inside. The grass was freshly cut, and a second-floor deck ran along the back of the house. He crept to the back windows, under the second-floor deck, and peeped inside. A large-screen TV hung from the far wall, facing a black leather couch and the windows. Scot sat on the patio, his head below the windows. Periodically, he peeked inside but saw nothing.

Then Ron stepped onto his deck, twelve-feet above Scot. Ron worked the grill, and shortly thereafter Scot smelled the grilling steaks. Scot pictured Ron and Charlotte having dinner. Laughing and talking. *What am I doing? I need to go home.* But Scot couldn't bring himself to leave. He had to see for himself.

Just after dark, Ron and Charlotte descended the steps to the walkout basement. Scot peeped through a back window, as they sat on the couch, close together, the backs of their heads facing Scot. Ron flipped on the television and surfed through the channels. They settled on the latest Spiderman movie. Scot imagined Ron's hands roaming up Charlotte's thigh.

Ron waited until halfway through the movie to make his move, putting his arm around Charlotte, kissing her open-mouthed. Scot felt nauseated. They made out for several minutes. Then Ron guided her head down toward his crotch, Charlotte now hidden from view by the couch. Scot's stomach tumbled, bile creeping up his throat. His heart raced.

Ron leaned his head back in ecstasy, his arms across the back of the couch.

Scot could count on one hand the number of times Charlotte had done that to him during the thirteen months they'd dated.

Scot staggered away from the house and vomited in the common-area grass.

CHAPTER 30

Why?

Scot staggered back to his car, blinded by tears. He rested his head on his steering wheel and cried like a baby.

When the tears finally dried, Scot asked himself, "Why? Why? Why?" He banged his forehead on the steering wheel with each *why*. "What does *fucking* Ron have that I don't have?" Scot peered through his windshield at Ron's townhome. "Big deal. He has a shitty house. He's like thirty-five."

Scot rubbed his temples, then rested his head on the steering wheel again. *I don't understand. What the hell's wrong with her?* In his mind, Scot replayed the deterioration of his relationship with Charlotte, trying to figure out why, and not sure exactly when things started to fall apart.

The roar of a V-8 engine woke Scot from his thoughts. Charlotte's red Camaro drove past. Scot started his Hyundai and pressed the accelerator, the front wheel kicking up gravel from the roadside. He followed Charlotte to her mother's double-wide trailer, parking right behind her Camaro.

Charlotte and Scot exited their vehicles at the same time. Charlotte glanced at Scot, then ran up the driveway toward the house, tottering on her wedged heels.

Scot ran too, making it to the trailer before her, blocking the door. "I love you, Charlotte. Why are you doing this to me?" Scot asked, his voice quivering.

Charlotte glared. "Get the *fuck* away from my door. How many times do I have to tell you that it's over?"

Helen opened the front door. "Get inside, Charlotte."

Scot turned, both women now in view.

Charlotte slipped past Scot, into the trailer.

Helen stepped onto the stoop, causing Scot to step back. She pointed a shaky finger in Scot's face. "I'm gonna tell you this once. Stay away from my daughter. If I see you here again, I'll call the police. You understand me?"

Scot dipped his head. "Yes, ma'am."

"Now get the hell off my property."

CHAPTER 31

The Announcement

At the morning meeting, Ron said, "I have a very special announcement to make."

Scot stood in the back of the break room, brooding, and mean-mugging Ron from afar. *Fucking douchebag.*

"Come on up here." Ron gestured to Charlotte.

Charlotte stepped out of the crowd and stood next to Ron, blushing.

"Charlotte and I are officially dating," Ron said, grinning.

The suck-ups cheered. A few associates gawked at Scot, likely expecting a reaction from Charlotte's ex-boyfriend.

Ron leaned over and pecked Charlotte on the lips, causing her blush to turn bright red.

The cheers intensified with the PDA.

"Fucking nauseating," Scot mumbled to himself, the cheers drowning out his words.

Kyle sidled up to Scot and said, "I told you these hoes are scandalous."

"Fuck you," Scot replied, before moving away from Kyle.

Ron showed his palms. "Thank you. We appreciate it."

Scot bristled at Ron's use of the word *we*.

Ron continued. "I'm making this announcement because we don't want there to be any rumors. Also, here at Big-Mart, we're a family. It's important to share happy news with your family. For the record, we've already informed corporate, so we're doing this by the book."

"Happy news, *huh*?" Scot mumbled to himself.

Two Latina associates, probably in their mid-twenties, glanced at Scot and giggled.

When Scot scowled at them, they turned away, no longer giggling but still smiling, now speaking in hushed Spanish.

"All right, let's get pumped for the day." Ron clapped, pacing back and forth in front of the crowd, making eye contact with the associates. "Come on, everybody. Let's get pumped."

Half-hearted clapping came from the audience.

Still clapping and pacing, Ron said, "You know what time it is. It's time for the Squirmy Dance!" Ron gyrated back and forth, his legs bending left and right. "Come on, everybody. Get your squirm on!"

A handful of associates wiggled back and forth.

Scot exited the break room, headed for the parking lot, while his coworkers got pumped.

"Scot," Henry called out.

Scot stopped and pivoted near the Big-Mart entrance, which doubled as an exit.

Henry and Anna walked toward him. They must've followed Scot out of the morning meeting.

"You okay?" Henry asked.

Scot looked away for a beat. "I'm fine."

"Are you sure?" Anna asked.

"I said I was fine." Scot walked outside.

CHAPTER 32

Lover's Hate

At lunch, Scot sat in the back corner of the break room, scrolling on his phone, stalking Charlotte's Instagram page. Every picture she'd had of them together had been scrubbed from her page, like Scot had never existed. Just like that. They were together for over a year. Then, just like that, they're over, and she's already moved on. Scot stared at a picture of Ron and Charlotte, posing in front of her Camaro.

Scot mumbled to himself, "Nice glasses, dickhead."

Henry and Anna approached Scot's table with their lunches in hand.

"Can we join you?" Anna asked.

Scot shrugged and placed his phone on the table facedown. "It's a free country."

Henry and Anna sat at the round table for four.

"How are you doing?" Henry asked.

"How do you think I'm doing?" Scot replied, with a frown.

"Well, I don't know. That's why I asked."

Scot rolled his eyes. "I thought you knew everything. Don't you have some old philosophy quote that'll fix all my problems?"

"Don't be rude," Anna said.

Henry gave Anna a small smile. "It's fine, dear."

Henry and Anna unpacked their lunches. Anna opened her Terraria-themed lunch box and removed a sub wrapped in wax paper. Henry had a ham and cheese on white bread.

"Did you bring a lunch?" Anna asked.

"Not hungry," Scot replied. That was a lie. He'd forgotten his lunch and his wallet at home.

"You have to eat something." Anna set half of her sub on a napkin, then pushed the other half of her sub to Scot, with the wax paper doubling as a plate. "You can have half of my turkey sub. I can't eat it all anyway."

Scot grabbed the wax paper, pulling the sub toward him, his stomach growling. "Thanks."

Anna smiled. "You're welcome."

The three of them ate for a few minutes in silence.

Henry broke the silence. "Euripides wrote, 'Stronger than lover's love is lover's hate. Incurable, in each, the wounds they make.'"

Scot stared at Henry for a moment, speechless.

Ron entered the break room and marched over to their table. He beckoned Scot with his index finger. "I need to talk to you in my office."

Scot took a bite of his sub and replied with a full mouth, "I'm eating."

"*Now*. I'm not asking." Ron left the break room, presumably heading back to his office.

Scot set down his sub, swallowed, and stood from the table.

"You want me to go with you?" Henry asked, also standing.

Scot shook his head. "That's not necessary, but thanks."

Scot left the break room and walked down the hall to Ron's office.

"Shut the door," Ron said, when Scot entered the doorway.

Scot shut the door and sat in the plastic chair across from Ron at his desk. Scot didn't say a word, refusing to talk first.

After an uncomfortable silence, Ron said, "After that stunt you pulled at Charlotte's last night, I think it would be best for everyone if you resigned."

Scot stared at Ron, stone-faced.

"I'll give you a good reference. Target would hire you today."

Scot thought about the fact that Big-Mart was the only place he'd ever see Charlotte. "I'm not quitting."

Ron frowned. "I could fire you."

"For what? Fucking my girlfriend?"

Ron held up his hand like a stop sign. "That's enough."

Scot stood from his seat. "You're not getting rid of me, Ron."

Ron stood from his seat. "One more point and you're gone."

"You're interrupting my lunch break." Scot left the office, leaving the door open in his wake.

CHAPTER 33

Opportunity Knocks

At the next morning meeting, Ron said, "We have too many people who are calling off for the weekend. I know it's summer, and everyone wants to go to the shore, but Saturday and Sunday are our busiest days of the week. When you call off, you're not hurting me, you're hurting your coworkers who are left to pick up your slack." Ron clasped his hands together, as if he were praying. "So please don't call off on the weekend, unless absolutely necessary." Ron scanned the room, making eye contact with various guilty associates, cementing his point.

Many of the associates looked down or away. Scot stood near the front, his arms crossed over his chest, glowering at Ron.

Ron continued. "We're still very short-staffed for this weekend. Would anyone like to add a shift on Saturday or Sunday?"

Scot raised his hand and said, "I'll work twelve hours Saturday and Sunday." It was a spur-of-the-moment decision. Ron wanted Scot to quit. Well, Scot decided he'd do exactly the opposite.

More than a few associates gawked at Scot, like he was insane.

"You've already worked a lot of hours this week," Ron reminded Scot. "Someone else might need the hours." Ron scanned the crowd again. "Anyone else? Anyone?"

Nobody raised their hand.

"Give Scot the hours," Kyle called out from the back. "Nobody wants to be here on the weekend."

Ron blew out a heavy breath. "All right, Scot."

CHAPTER 34

Small Pluses

At lunch, Scot sat in the break room, eating a bologna and cheese sandwich on stale bread. His mother hadn't been to the store in weeks, and the cupboards were nearly bare. To take his mind off Charlotte, he tapped on his phone, checking the price of Bitcoin—*$288.13*. Up eight dollars since he'd last checked. Scot did some mental math, figuring that his twenty-five Bitcoin had gained two hundred dollars in value in eight days. If they kept up this pace for an entire year, his Bitcoin would appreciate over $9,000. Scot smiled to himself. *Beats the hell out of a savings account. Maybe I really can get back to school for the spring semester. I'll show her that I'm not a boy.*

Kyle swaggered into the break room, an energy drink in hand. He tapped on Scot's table with his knuckle. "What up, Scotty."

Scot looked up from his phone and shrugged. "What do you care?"

"It's like that?"

Scot went back to his phone, pretending to be engrossed in the Bitcoin price chart.

"Dude. You need to stop simpin'."

Scot looked up again, his face beet red. "I'm not a simp."

Kyle smirked. "You let Charlotte play you like a simp."

"It's none of your business."

"If you wanna flip the script, don't act so desperate. Act like you don't give a fuck."

"I'm not talking to you about this. Leave me alone."

Kyle flashed his palms. "Whatever, dude." He left the break room.

Scot stared at his phone, but he wasn't processing what was on the screen. He was thinking about what Kyle had just said, knowing his advice held some hard truths.

"These seats taken?" Henry asked.

Scot woke from his trance to see Henry and Anna.

"Mind if we join you?" Henry asked.

Scot shook his head.

Henry and Anna sat at the round table.

"More hours, *huh*?" Henry asked, unpacking his lunch.

"Yeah. I need the money," Scot replied.

"I admire an industrious man. You'll do well in life."

"Good for you, Scot," Anna said, also unpacking her lunch. "You inspired me to take a shift on Saturday too."

Henry nodded to Anna. "That's great, dear. I'm in the company of greatness."

Scot suppressed a grin, soaking up the compliments like rain in a desert. He addressed Henry. "Don't we get a philosophy quote for the occasion?"

Henry smiled, his face erupting with deep grooves. "Let me think for a bit. You've put me on the spot." Henry tapped his temple. "My memory's not what it once was."

"It's okay. I wasn't serious."

Henry held up one finger. "Hold on. I think I have one." He paused for an instant. "Plato once said, 'Apply yourself both now and in the next life. Without effort, you cannot be prosperous. Though the land be good, you cannot have an abundant crop without cultivation.'"

CHAPTER 35

Working on the Weekend

On Saturday morning, Scot pulled into the Big-Mart parking lot. He was surprised to see Charlotte's Camaro already there. She usually skated in late. It's not like Ron would fire her. Scot parked one row away from Charlotte's car, not wanting her to accuse him of stalking again. He'd finally gotten it through his thick head. He was desperate to get her back, but letting her see that he was desperate to get her back was repulsing her, not to mention it might get him arrested. He hated to admit it, but Kyle's blunt advice woke Scot to reality.

Scot exited his car and walked toward Big-Mart. Heat already reverberated off the macadam. He'd brought an extra shirt and deodorant for the occasion. Quick steps came from behind.

Scot turned to see Charlotte jogging toward him, her breasts bouncing under her polo. He stopped, his stomach fluttering, waiting for her to catch him.

She slowed to a walk as she approached. "I need to talk to you. It's important."

"About what?" Scot asked, leaning toward her.

Customers walked past them, toward the store.

"I'd rather not say in the middle of the parking lot," Charlotte said. "Let's talk in my car."

Euphoria washed over Scot. *She wants to get back together.* He held back a cheesy grin. "Sure."

They walked back toward her car, away from Big-Mart.

Anna fast-walked toward them, glancing at her watch. She gaped at Scot walking the wrong way. "Where are you going? We have five minutes."

Scot stopped in his tracks and stared at Charlotte.

Her lip twitched.

It hit him like a freight train. "You're trying to make me late."

She opened her mouth, but nothing came out.

His nostrils flared. "What the hell, Charlotte? I need this job."

"That's a lie." Charlotte placed her hands on her hips, her lips curled into a sneer. "You could work at Target or Costco, but you're so *obsessed*—"

"I'm *not*."

"Yes, you are."

"Come on, Scot," Anna said, tugging on Scot's elbow. "We'll be late."

Scot pivoted to Anna, noticing her touch. "You're right. Thanks."

Charlotte mean-mugged Anna.

They walked toward Big-Mart, leaving Charlotte behind.

"She's trying to get you in trouble," Anna said, as soon as they were safely out of Charlotte's earshot.

"She's trying to get me fired," Scot replied, his head bowed.

"That's messed up."

Scot nodded. "Yeah."

They walked into Big-Mart. An elderly woman greeted them. Henry was off.

Anna waved at the greeter.

Scot ignored her, still thinking about Charlotte. *She must still have feelings for me. That's why she wants me to leave. It's hard for her to see me.*

They clocked in two minutes before eight.

As they waited in the break room for their shift to start, Anna asked, "How late are you working tonight?"

"Until eight," Scot replied.

"That's a long day," Anna said.

Scot nodded again.

"You think you might have enough energy to go minigolfing with me after work? I hear there's an alligator at the end that opens and closes its mouth."

Scot tilted his head, confused. "Are you asking me out?"

Anna blushed. "As friends of course. I know, with everything, now's probably not a great time …"

Scot thought about Kyle's advice. What better way to show Charlotte that he doesn't care than to go out on a date with someone else? "Yeah, sure."

CHAPTER 36

First Date

By eight o'clock, Scot was beat and sweaty and had planned to cancel on Anna. He clocked out just as Anna appeared in the break room. She had been off since four. They had planned to meet at Big-Mart at eight, when Scot's shift was over. She wore flats and a sundress that fell just below her knees. She'd let her hair down, her blue eyes popping with a little makeup.

Scot gaped at her.

"You ready?" she asked.

"You look, … uh, … you look great."

She reddened from the compliment. "Thanks."

He inspected his rumpled and sweat-stained clothes. "I'm really dirty. I don't know if I can …"

"You look fine to me, but we can run by your house, and you can shower and change, if you want. They don't close until eleven tonight."

They took Scot's Hyundai, leaving Anna's car at Big-Mart, with plans to grab it later.

On the way to Scot's mother's townhome, Anna asked, "So, you live with your family?"

Scot glanced from the road to Anna, finding it difficult to keep his eyes on the road. "My mom and my younger sister."

"That's nice."

"What about you?" Scot asked.

She hesitated. "I'm on my own. I have a roommate, but I don't live with my family."

Scot nodded. "Good for you. I can't wait to get my own place."

Anna didn't reply.

Scot turned into his neighborhood, parking in a visitor's spot across from his mother's townhome. They walked up to the house, stopping at the front door, Scot's hand on the doorknob. He said, "My mother can be a little, uh, overly comfortable with people. She means well, but …"

Anna smiled. "I'm sure it'll be fine."

They entered the townhome. As usual, Laura sat on the couch, watching a cop show. An empty bag of Cool Ranch Doritos sat on the coffee table.

Laura straightened up at the sight of Anna, then stood, wiping crumbs from her oversize T-shirt. "Scot. Who's your friend?"

Scot gestured to Anna. "This is Anna. We work together. We're going to play minigolf, but I need a quick shower."

"It's so nice to meet you, Anna." Laura reached over the coffee table. "I'm Laura, Scot's mother."

They shook hands.

Anna smiled again. "It's nice to meet you too."

Laura looked Anna up and down. "Aren't you just the cutest little thing? I used to look like you, when I was your age. Can you believe that? Now I'm this big old hag." Laura chuckled.

"Don't say that, Mom," Scot said.

"Well, she has eyes."

"I think you look great," Anna said.

Laura pointed at Anna. "This one's a keeper."

After a few more niceties, Scot and Anna went upstairs to his room. Scot's bed was unmade. He snatched a few pairs of boxer briefs and dirty T-shirts from the floor, shoving them into the overburdened hamper. Scot flushed, embarrassed by his room. "Sorry. I need to clean up and do a wash."

"Don't worry about it," Anna replied, scanning his room.

Scot grabbed some clothes from his dresser.

Anna walked over to his closet, staring at the dartboard. "I like your dartboard."

"It's old. My dad gave it to me."

Anna pivoted to Scot. "Mind if I play, while you're in the shower?"

"Go right ahead."

Scot took a shower, put on clean clothes, and brushed his hair and teeth. Then he returned to his room.

Anna whipped a dart at the dartboard, nearly hitting the bull's-eye.

"Wow. Nice one," Scot said.

Anna grinned. "Thanks. I'm a bit of a gamer. Not just video games but any game you can think of. Board games, sports, whatever." She stared at him, unblinking. "You look nice and clean, by the way."

"Thanks." Scot noticed her noticing him. His stomach fluttered at her obvious interest. "You ready?"

They left Scot's house, saying goodbye to Laura on their way out.

On the way to minigolf, Anna asked, "Where's your dad? You mentioned that he got you the dartboard."

Scot stopped at a stop sign. "He lives in Lebanon, with his girl-friend. My parents divorced last year."

Anna winced. "Sorry. Divorce is … really hard."

Scot drove through the intersection. "Technically, my birth par-ents divorced like sixteen years ago. Then my mother remarried. I consider my stepfather more of a father than my biological father, although it's been different between us since he left."

"Different how?"

Scot shrugged. "I don't know. He has this young girlfriend. She's not young like us but a lot younger than my dad. Everything's about her now."

Anna nodded. "They always go younger."

Scot turned right onto US 422. "What about your parents?"

Anna sighed. "Same as you. Divorced. My dad left when I was really young. We don't have any contact. It was a revolving door of men most of my childhood."

"That sucks."

"My mom finally married when I was sixteen. My stepdad has three kids of his own, and he has custody, so their house is really crowded. I had this closet of a room, sharing a bathroom with two boys. I was like Harry Potter, living under the stairs, but without magical powers." She chuckled to herself, but it didn't sound jovial. "It was clear my stepdad didn't want me there, and my mother didn't want the conflict. I think they were happy when I left."

"You left home when you were sixteen?"

"Seventeen. I stuck it out for a year."

"*Shit*. That's rough."

Anna pointed at the windshield. "It's coming up on the left."

"I see it." Scot turned into the parking lot of Adventure Sports. "Do you ever see your mom?"

"Only on major holidays, and even then …"

Scot parked his Hyundai and turned in his seat toward Anna. "I'm really sorry."

Anna turned in her seat too. "Do you mind if we talk about something else?"

"That's fine with me. What do you want to talk about?"

She lifted one shoulder and grinned. "We could talk about how you're about to get your butt kicked in minigolf."

"Oh, really? We'll see about that."

They grabbed a hot dog and hit the links. Anna was competitive but in a funny way. She made Scot laugh by making weird noises during his backswing, costing him a few strokes. Another time, with Scot's ball inches from the cup, he shanked it after Anna whispered, "Don't miss, big boy," in a sultry voice.

By the time they hit the last hole, the course was deserted, and Anna was winning by fifteen strokes.

Scot's cell phone buzzed in his pocket. His first thought was that it was a DM from Charlotte, apologizing for trying to get him fired. He leaned his putter against a bench and picked up his phone. It was a Facebook notification from Anna.

Anna set her putter next to Scot's, strutted over to him and said in Ron's nasally voice, "You can't be on your phone. I'm gonna have to give you a point."

Scot laughed. "This is from you." Scot read the Facebook DM silently.

> **Anna Fisher:** I'm having a great time with you. Thank you for coming out with me!

Scot blushed. "When did you send this?"

"A few minutes ago, when you were lining up your putt," Anna replied.

"I'm having a great time too."

Anna stepped closer, nearly touching him.

Then she slid her hands up his back, sending a jolt of electricity through Scot's body. Reflexively, Scot pulled her close, his hands on her waist, breathing in her vanilla body wash. She tilted up her head, staring into his eyes. He stared back for a beat, leaned in, and pressed his lips to hers.

She reciprocated, her lips pressing harder than his own.

CHAPTER 37

Snooze

Scot's phone chimed, doubling as his alarm. His eyes fluttered, his mind hazy. He groped for his phone on his bedside table. He swiped his finger across the screen, intending to tap the snooze but actually turning off his alarm.

★★★

Sunlight filtered between his blinds, warming his face. Consciousness seeped into his brain. He had an inkling that something was wrong, but his mind was too fuzzy. *What time is it?* Scot shot upright in bed, realizing the potential problem. He grabbed his phone and checked the time—*7:51.*

"Shit!" Scot jumped out of bed and ran to the bathroom down the hall. He gargled some mouthwash while he peed. Then he ran back to his room, wearing only his boxer briefs. He dressed in his khakis, gray T-shirt, and vest in less than sixty seconds. He grabbed his wallet and keys from his desktop and exited his room. Halfway down the hall, he pivoted and ran back to his room. He retrieved his phone and lanyard with his associate ID card from his bedside table, then ran from his room.

His mother was still asleep on the couch as he ran from the town-home, toward his car in the visitor's parking spot. He started his Hyundai and chirped the front tire as he left his parking space.

Scot drove on the two-lane road, passing farmland, forest, and cheaply built vinyl-sided homes, his foot heavy on the accelerator. He turned onto US 422, tailgating a minivan driving exactly the speed limit. His cell phone chimed. He glanced at the number, swiped right, and put his phone to his ear.

"Please tell me that you're in the parking lot," Anna said, not waiting for his greeting.

"I'm on 422, five or six minutes away," Scot said. "I'm stuck behind a minivan."

Her voice was frantic. "It's two minutes till. You'll never make it."

Scot eased off the accelerator, no longer tailgating the minivan. He sighed and said, "It's fine."

"It's not fine." Anna whispered, "What's your associate ID number? I'll clock you in."

If a Big-Mart associate forgot their ID card, which wasn't uncommon, a keypad on the time clock allowed for manually entering associate ID numbers.

"You could get into trouble," Scot said.

"It's my fault. I kept you up until two," Anna replied.

Scot smiled at the thought of their late-night date. "It's not your fault, and it was totally worth it."

"It's one minute now," she said in a hushed whisper. "Please, Scot, just give me your number."

He lifted his associate ID, glancing at the familiar number. "Four-seven-seven-three-two-six." Scot paused for an instant. "Anna? Did you get that?"

She didn't answer, but the call was still connected.

A moment later she whispered, "I clocked you in. Try to sneak into the meeting."

"Thank you, Anna. I had a really great time last night."

"Me too. I have to go. The meeting's about to start."

"See you soon."

"Bye."

Scot disconnected the call. For the rest of the drive, he thought about Anna and their date, the talking, the laughing, the kissing. A sense of euphoria washed over him.

He parked at Big-Mart and jogged inside. Scot slipped into the break room, just as Charlotte said, "Who's number one?"

"The customer!" the associates shouted.

Ron was off on the weekend, so the Big-Mart cheer fell to the new assistant manager.

Scot melted into the crowd, but Charlotte followed him with her eyes. He moved to the back, searching for Anna. She found him first, sidling up to him, and squeezing his hand. He wanted to kiss her but knew it wasn't appropriate at work.

He smiled and whispered in her ear, "Thank you."

She whispered back, "Of course."

The Big-Mart cheer continued around them, as Charlotte said, "*Goooo*," holding the long *O* for several seconds.

Anna stepped back and checked out his rumpled clothes and disheveled hair. She giggled, then leaned in and whispered, "Walk of shame?"

Charlotte dropped her hands, like she was starting a race.

The associates completed the cheer with a hearty "Big-Mart!"

Scot laughed and whispered back to Anna, "I literally just rolled out of bed."

"You're still cute," Anna replied.

Scot blushed.

The associates filtered out of the break room.

"I think Charlotte saw me come in," Scot whispered.

"Tell her that you were in the bathroom," Anna replied.

Charlotte stood by the exit, fake-smiling at the associates. Scot and Anna were the last associates to approach the break room exit. They didn't make eye contact with Charlotte, as they reached the exit.

"Scot. Anna. I need to talk to you both," Charlotte said, her voice as cold as ice.

Scot swallowed and turned to Charlotte. "About what?"

"In my office."

"Do you even have an office?"

Charlotte stiffened. "I'm using Ron's."

Kyle sauntered into the break room, bleary-eyed, with an energy drink.

"You're late, Kyle," Charlotte said.

Kyle didn't acknowledge Charlotte, as he went to the time clock.

Charlotte's face reddened. She called out to Kyle's back. "I'm telling Ron."

Kyle scanned his card, then returned to the break room exit. He said to Charlotte, "Go ahead."

"I *will*."

Kyle chuckled. "Good luck with that." He opened his energy drink.

"Get to work," Charlotte said, her face twisted into a scowl.

Kyle took a long swig of his drink, then let out an exaggerated "*Ahhh.*"

"You are so fired."

Kyle turned his attention to Scot and Anna, unconcerned about Charlotte's threat. "What does she want with you two?"

"That's none of your business." Charlotte opened the break room door and said to Scot and Anna, "Let's go."

Scot and Anna followed Charlotte down the hall. They glanced at each other, each making a pained face. They sat across from Charlotte in plastic chairs at Ron's desk.

"You were late," Charlotte said to Scot. "You have five points now. You're done."

"I was in the bathroom," Scot replied.

Charlotte raised one side of her mouth in a crooked grin. "That's a lie. I can prove it too with the cameras."

Scot swallowed hard. "Come on, Charlotte. Give me a break."

Charlotte narrowed her eyes at Anna, glancing at Anna's ID card hanging from the lanyard around her neck. "I saw you typing on the time clock keypad right before the meeting. Why would you do that if you have your card?"

Anna chewed on her bottom lip. "I didn't …" She didn't sound confident.

"Go ahead and fire me," Scot said, interrupting. "I don't give a shit, but Anna didn't have anything to do with it."

"After Ron sees Anna clocking you in on video, he'll fire both of you," Charlotte said.

"Anna has nothing to do with this," Scot said.

"Then she doesn't have anything to worry about. Ron's gonna look at the video, and he'll do what he has to do." Charlotte leaned forward, her elbows on the desk. "You know that clocking in for someone else isn't just a point, but you can get fired for that. I learned that in my training."

"Please, Charlotte. Just fire me. Why do you have to do this to Anna?"

Charlotte shrugged and glared at Anna. "I'm not doing anything to her. She did it to herself."

Tears welled in Anna's eyes. She stood and rushed from the room, leaving the door open in her wake. Scot ran after her.

Kyle stopped Anna in the hall, just outside the break room. "What happened?"

Scot caught up to Anna and said to Kyle, "It's none of your business."

Anna sniffled and wiped her eyes with her index finger. "Charlotte's firing us."

Kyle pulled a face. "She can't fire anyone. She's an *assistant* manager."

"She can tell Ron to fire us."

"I'll take care of this." Kyle marched past Scot and Anna, headed for Ron's office.

"What are you doing?" Scot called out to his back.

"I got this," Kyle replied, over his shoulder.

Kyle entered Ron's office, the door open.

Charlotte yelled at Kyle, telling him to get to work. Then they argued back and forth at a lower decibel, their words inaudible.

Scot and Anna crept down the hall, hoping to eavesdrop. They stopped a few doors down.

"Ron's not gonna fire either of them," Kyle said.

"Yes, he will. And he'll fire you too," Charlotte replied.

"When you talk to Ron, give him a message from me. Tell him, if he fires Anna or Scot, I'll go to corporate."

"Go to corporate for what?"

"None of your business. Just let him know."

Kyle left Ron's office. As he walked past Scot and Anna, he winked at them and said barely above a whisper, "You're good."

Scot followed Kyle down the hall, with Anna right behind him.

"Kyle," Scot said, once they were a safe distance from Ron's office.

Kyle stopped and turned to Scot and Anna. "What?"

"Why did you help us? When I asked you before …"

Kyle shrugged. "Bitch needed to be humbled."

At lunchtime, Scot sat in the break room, checking the price of Bitcoin on his phone. It was $293.62, up five dollars since he had checked it two days ago.

Anna approached his table, holding her lunch box and two purple vitamin waters. "I got us some drinks."

Scot looked up from his phone. "Thank you for sharing your lunch." In the rush to work that morning, Scot had forgotten his lunch.

Anna sat next to him at the table. "You're very welcome."

Scot half stood, removed his wallet from his back pocket, and sat down again. He opened his wallet and said, "I can give you some cash."

Anna waved him off. "The waters were cheap."

Scot put his wallet back in his pocket. "Thank you. I'll buy lunch next time."

"I saw Kyle leaving for lunch. I waved at him and smiled, but he just nodded all cool, like he didn't save our butts this morning."

"That sounds right. It was probably nothing to him. I think Kyle does whatever Kyle wants to do."

"Luckily, he wanted to help us." Anna opened her lunch box and removed two homemade chicken salad sandwiches, handing one to Scot, along with a vitamin water.

"That's for sure."

As they ate their lunch, Scot glanced at the Bitcoin price again, thinking about making another purchase.

"What's that?" Anna asked.

Scot swallowed a bit of his sandwich. "It's the price of Bitcoin."

"What's a Bitcoin?" Anna asked.

Scot explained the cryptocurrency and how, instead of saving in dollars, he was saving for school in Bitcoin.

"If you don't mind me asking, how much do you need to get back to school?" Anna asked.

"Depends on my financial aid package, but I think I'll need around 46K to finish."

At a minimum, to return to Penn, Scot would have to pay the $19,200 that was past due, plus one semester, which used to be $18,200, but, with a better financial aid package, he estimated that it would be around $9,000 per semester. It would likely cost him 28K to get back to school, but Scot didn't want to run into the same problem. Therefore, he wanted to have the money to finish his final three semesters prior to returning. Three semesters at $9,000, plus his past due bill, came to roughly 46K.

"How much do you have?" Anna frowned. "Sorry. That was a rude question. You don't have to answer."

"It's okay. I have a little over seven thousand." Scot took a sip of his vitamin water. "If I work every day, including weekends, I might be able to get back in two or three years, but it still feels like a long way off."

"I know the feeling."

"What about you? Is vet school expensive?"

"I have to transfer to a four-year school to finish my bio degree first. I finished my associates degree from HACC last May. That'll be at least $25,000, plus another 150,000 for vet school."

His eyes bulged. "That's 175K."

Anna nodded. "Technically, I only need 173,000. I've saved a whole two thousand bucks."

Scot winced. "I thought my situation was tough."

"It's not that bad. I think financial aid will cover a lot of it, but it won't cover everything, plus my living expenses. I think I need around $50,000, but, with tuition going up every year and my savings rate, I'll be older than Henry by the time I make it to vet school."

"I'm sorry, Anna."

She lifted one shoulder. "Don't worry about it. You didn't create the world."

Scot stared at his sandwich. "Are we hopeless?"

"Maybe. At least we'll be hopeless together."

They smiled at each other. Then they grabbed their sandwiches and took big bites.

CHAPTER 38

Enemy or Ally?

"I'm disappointed with you, Anna," Ron said, shaking his head at her.

On Monday morning, Scot and Anna sat across from Ron at his desk.

Anna dipped her head.

Ron gestured to Scot. "From him, I'm not surprised, but from you ..."

"None of this is her fault," Scot said.

"That's not what the evidence says."

"We *should* talk about evidence. Like the evidence Kyle has about you and Jasmine."

Ron clenched his jaw, his face reddening. "For the record, Kyle's wrong about me. I didn't do anything wrong."

Scot tilted his head. "Then why are you letting him blackmail you?"

"He has a picture, but it's not what you think. I was comforting an associate, who had lost her mother. That was all, not that I owe you two an explanation."

Bullshit.

"It's a mistake to associate with that degenerate Kyle," Ron said.

"We're not associating with Kyle," Scot replied. "We didn't ask him to do anything."

"I could've been an ally. Instead, you both made a powerful enemy."

"How could you be an ally? You would've fired us."

"You don't know that."

"That's not what Charlotte said."

Ron frowned. "Charlotte doesn't speak for me."

Scot crossed his arms over his chest. "*You* told me, if I got one more point, I was gone. Made me sign a contract too. Remember that?"

Ron held up his hand to silence Scot. "I'm not gonna argue with you. I just wanted you both to know that I'm disappointed. I'm letting you off because I'm a good guy, *not* because Kyle *thinks* he has something on me." He motioned toward his office door. "Get back to work."

★★★

At the end of the workday, Scot clocked out and waited in the break room for his partner in crime. Anna breezed into the break room, noticeably happier than she'd been that morning.

Scot smiled as she approached. "You look ... happy."

Anna clocked out and said, "I am. The day's finally over, and I'm looking forward to our dinner. Let's blow this joint."

They had plans to make dinner together at Anna's house.

Ron walked into the break room, his shoulders slumped. He approached Scot and Anna. "Did you two clock out yet?"

"It's past four," Scot said. "We didn't clock out early."

"I'm not saying you did. It's, uh ..." Ron cleared his throat. "I really need some help. Four people called off for the second shift. We have shelves that need restocking tonight. Corporate's coming tomorrow. I can't have empty shelves and boxes in the aisles."

"I hope you find some help," Scot said, stepping past Ron.

Anna followed.

"Come on, guys. Please. I wouldn't ask if it wasn't an emergency," Ron said, desperation in his tone.

Scot and Anna turned back to Ron. Scot looked at Anna and asked, "What do you want to do?"

"I'd like to go home and have a nice dinner with you, but I could use the money."

Scot let out a breath. "Me too."

Ron grinned. "You'll do it?"

"Yeah," they said in unison, without enthusiasm.

CHAPTER 39

One Month Later ...

Scot sat at a table in the break room, checking the price of Bitcoin, his brown-bagged lunch on the tabletop. "Damn it," he said to himself.

Over the past month the price of Bitcoin had slowly eroded. During that time, he'd purchased another ten Bitcoin, hoping to lower his average buy price, expecting the cryptocurrency to rally. But the price kept dropping. Scot did the math in his head. The current price was $225.38. He had purchased thirty-five Bitcoin at an average buy price of $280. *I've lost over $1,900. I'm so fucking stupid.*

His phone buzzed with a text.

> **Marie:** Just touching base to confirm dinner on Sunday at five. I can't wait to meet Anna! FYI Frank just told me that he's not going out of town this weekend.

Scot groaned and texted back.

> **Scot:** Frank will be at dinner?
> **Marie:** Yes but he'll be fine. I promise. You better not bail on me. I haven't seen you in months!
> **Scot:** We'll be there.

Anna approached his table, her eyes examining his expression. "What's wrong?" She set her Terraria-themed lunch box on the table.

Scot slapped his phone on the table. "My sister's stupid-ass husband will be at dinner on Sunday."

Anna sat next to him. "I'm sure it'll be fine."

"He's such a fucking douche."

"Don't let him ruin your time with your sister."

Scot blew out a heavy breath. "You're right."

Anna nudged him. "Cheer up. I'll be there with you. I'm really looking forward to meeting Marie."

"It's not just that. Bitcoin's down again."

"Is it down a lot?"

"It's only a few bucks, but it keeps going lower. It's down like fifty-five bucks over the past month." Scot hung his head. "I've lost almost two thousand dollars."

She covered his hand. "I'm sorry."

Scot leaned forward and banged his forehead on the tabletop several times, not hard. "I'm so stupid."

Anna rubbed his back. "That's not true."

Scot sat upright. "I'm thinking about selling, before I lose all my money."

"But you were so excited about it. What was that acronym you told me about? Hold on dearly."

Scot smirked. "HODL. Hold on for dear life."

"That's it."

Scot sighed. "I might as well hold on. I'm nowhere close to saving what I need to get back to school anyway. Maybe it'll come back."

Anna opened her lunch box. "I'm sure it'll come back."

CHAPTER 40

Sunday Dinner

"You are just adorable," Marie said, smiling at Anna in the open-plan kitchen.

Anna blushed. "Thank you. Scot told me so many nice things about you."

"I have my moments." Marie winked at Scot.

"Don't overcook the brisket," Frank called out from the living room.

"I should check the meat." Marie went to the double oven, checking the brisket with a fork and knife. Then she called back to Frank, "It's not ready yet."

"It smells delicious," Anna said.

"Come here, Scot," Frank called out. "Let the girls talk."

Scot walked to the family room, while Marie and Anna chatted like best girlfriends.

Frank lounged on his leather La-Z-Boy, a beer resting on his stomach, several empties on the end table next to him. A preseason football game was on the big-screen television. Frank gestured with his beer to the leather couch. "Have a seat."

Scot sat at the other end of the couch, as far away from Frank as possible.

"You want a beer?"

"No thanks. I'm driving."

"Smart man."

They watched the game in silence for a minute.

Frank pointed the remote, muting the television at the commercial break. Then he said, "Marie told me about you saving for school."

"I still have a ways to go," Scot replied, sitting upright on the edge of the couch, as if poised to bolt.

"You're learning the value of hard work."

Scot nodded.

"What are you doing with your savings? Money market account? Short-term treasuries? Please tell me that you don't have it in a bank account, collecting zero interest."

Scot cleared his throat. "I've been saving in Bitcoin."

Frank scrunched his face, as if he'd eaten a lemon. "*Bitcoin*? You can't be serious. It's a fucking Ponzi scheme."

Scot's face felt hot. "The blockchain is a revolutionary way to settle accounts without the banking—"

"I know all about the blockchain," Frank said, holding up his hand. "It's bullshit. It's a bubble. It'll eventually go to zero."

CHAPTER 41

Six Months Later ...

"It's up again?" Anna asked, standing next to Scot at the back of the break room.

Scot stared at his screen, a grin on his face.

Coworkers milled around them, waiting for the morning meeting. Many ate their sugar-filled breakfasts in the form of pastries, doughnuts, and leftover Valentine's Day candy.

Scot slipped his phone into his pocket. "It's on fire. Four-thirty-two."

"That's great," Anna replied.

Over the past six months the price of Bitcoin had nearly doubled. During that time, Scot had continued to save in Bitcoin and had continued to work as many hours as possible. He had purchased an additional forty Bitcoins at an average buy price of three hundred dollars. At the current price, with a total of seventy-five Bitcoins, Scot had $32,400 in savings. At this rate he'd easily have the $46K he needed for school in the fall.

"You should invest," Scot said. "Seriously. I can help you set up your wallet."

"I don't have the stomach for it," Anna replied. "I don't have that much saved up anyway. I just drained most of my savings fixing my car."

Anna's Honda Civic had recently failed inspection, requiring new brakes, new tires, and a new windshield. All wear-and-tear items, except for the windshield, which was bad luck. A truck had kicked up a rock on the way to work, the rock creating a small crack. Anna had no intention of repairing the windshield, but, since the crack was in her field of vision, she had to have it repaired per Pennsylvania State law.

Ron and Charlotte breezed into the break room. Charlotte took her place near the front of the crowd.

Ron faced the crowd of associates, holding a folder. "Good morning, everyone."

A few associates mumbled, "Good morning."

Charlotte said, "Good morning." Her boisterous voice was an attempt to liven the crowd.

Scot smirked at Anna.

"Come on, gang. Let's wake up. Let's get our squirm on," Ron said.

Groans came from the associates.

"Let's get squirmy!" Ron gyrated back and forth, his legs bending left and right. "Come on, everybody. Get your squirm on!"

A few associates wiggled back and forth.

Mercifully, Ron stopped dancing and said, "All right. Now that we're awake, I have an important announcement to make." He paused for a beat. "I'll be at the Big-Mart corporate conference this weekend, and I'm off on Monday, so I wanted to award the Associate of the Month for February a few days early."

The Big-Mart corporate conference was a two-day training session for Big-Mart general managers across the country, teaching leadership, inventory management, customer service, human resource management, and marketing.

Scot leaned over and whispered in Anna's ear, "You look pretty today."

She reddened and whispered back, "What are you smoking? My hair's stringy, and I didn't have time for any makeup."

Ron continued. "To be honest, I should've recognized this person sooner. He's an extremely hard worker."

Scot leaned over and whispered again, "I stand by my statement."

Ron said, "He's worked every day over the past six months. Not a single day off. I'm pretty sure that's a record."

"I think Ron's talking about you," Anna said.

Scot faced forward.

Ron continued. "He's done a fantastic job too, filling in wherever I need him to. He's worked in every department. Done just about every job without complaint. Congratulations, Scot Caldwell. Come on up here."

The room erupted with applause.

Scot stood stunned and slack-jawed.

Anna cheered the loudest.

Scot woke from his stupor and waded through the crowd. His fellow associates patted him on the back. The hardest smack on the back came from Kyle. As Scot walked through the crowd, he saw Charlotte out of the corner of his eye. She clapped too but with a stiff smile and dead eyes. Scot shook Ron's hand and accepted the printed certificate and the one-hundred-dollar Big-Mart gift card. He tried to be cool. He tried to hide it, but ultimately, he let his smile blossom. He wished Henry was there, but Henry had reduced his hours to give his legs more rest.

Scot returned to Anna, and Ron led them all in the daily cheer. For the first time, Scot participated.

At the conclusion of the meeting, Ron approached Scot and asked, "Can I see you in my office?"

Scot sat across from Ron at his desk.

"First of all, congratulations again on being the associate of the month," Ron said.

"Thanks, Ron," Scot replied.

"I know we've had our differences in the past, but you've shown me that you're a team player. I hope that we can have a positive working relationship going forward."

Scot nodded. "So do I."

"I also wanted to let you know that I'm giving you a raise. Fifty cents more an hour. It may not seem like much, but it adds up."

Scot sat up straight, doing the math in his head. Given that he had been working seventy hours per week, with overtime, that was an extra $42.50 per week. "It definitely adds up. Thank you, Ron. I appreciate it."

Ron smiled. "Well, I appreciate all your hard work around here. If everyone was as reliable and hardworking as you, this place would be a breeze to manage."

"Thanks again." Scot paused, waiting for Ron to talk, but he didn't. "Is that it?"

"That's it."

Scot and Ron stood from their seats.

As they shook hands over the desk, Ron said, "I'm glad you've accepted your place."

"Thanks." Scot left the office, thinking about what Ron had said. *I've accepted my place? What does that mean?*

CHAPTER 42

That's Love

Henry slumped into a chair at his kitchen table, coughing, his breathing elevated.

Scot and Anna stood from the table.

Anna rushed to his side. "Are you okay?"

Henry didn't answer for several seconds, until his coughing stopped and his breathing slowed. "I'm fine, dear. I get a little winded is all."

"You sit. Scot and I will get the food."

"We got it, Henry," Scot said, going to the sink to finish filling the water glasses.

Henry tried to rise, but Anna placed a hand on his shoulder. "I'm serious. You relax."

Scot and Anna finished preparing the dinner and setting the table, like an old married couple. They were already intimately familiar with Henry's kitchen. Dinner at Henry's had become a weekly ritual.

They sat at the table, eating lasagna, salad, and garlic bread.

Midway through the meal, Henry had eaten very little of the small portion on his plate. He said, "I'm so happy you two found each other."

Anna smiled. "Me too."

Scot swallowed some lasagna. "Me too."

"I met my Alice in 1966," Henry said. "She was a social worker in Harrisburg. It was my first year teaching at HACC. She was teaching

Intro to Social Work at night to make a little extra money. I was teaching Philosophy of Religion at the same time." Henry addressed Anna. "You remind me of her. Like you, she was so special. She made the people around her want to be better."

Anna blushed, stabbing lasagna with her fork. "I don't think I'm like that."

"She's exactly like that," Scot said.

Henry winked at Scot. "It took me the whole semester to ask her out. I changed which way I walked, so I could run into her. We talked in little bits of time here and there. On the way to class. On the way to the parking lot. I was so nervous." Henry chuckled to himself. "I had good reason to be nervous, mind you. When you're a short man like me, you get rejected quite a lot."

"It shouldn't be like that," Anna said.

"Well, it all worked out in the end."

Scot leaned forward, his elbows on the table. "What happened when you asked her out?"

"I had planned to ask her out several nights in a row, but I chickened out every time, telling myself that I'd ask her out the next night. Then it was the last day of the semester, and she told me that she wasn't going to teach again. She felt like it was interfering with her cases. So I knew it was now or never. We walked slower than usual to the parking lot. My hands were sweating profusely. My mouth was like cotton. I couldn't swallow. By the time we got to her car, I was hanging by a thread. I thought I might pass out. That's when she said, 'Would you like to go to dinner with me?'"

Everyone laughed.

"Plato once said, 'Every heart sings a song, incomplete, until another heart whispers back. Those who wish to sing always find a song. At the touch of a lover, everyone becomes a poet.'"

"That's deep," Scot said.

"That's love," Henry replied.

CHAPTER 43

The Flame Still Burns?

Late on Saturday night, Scot moved the pallet jack under a shrink-wrapped pallet of cereal as tall as him. He cranked the jack, lifting the pallet. Then he pulled the pallet of cereal off the truck and into the warehouse.

Scot watched Kyle expertly maneuver the forklift, lifting the last pallet, then loading it on a rack. He parked the forklift and hopped off the machine. Scot walked to Kyle, taking off his work gloves.

Kyle removed a glasses case from his pocket. "I'm gonna make the rounds, see what kinda freaks we got tonight."

Scot shook his head. "Be careful. Someone might sue you for harassment."

Kyle opened the case, removing a pair of dark-rimmed glasses with clear lenses. He slipped on the glasses and grinned. "Don't worry about me. I'm incognito."

"That's not much of a disguise."

Kyle touched the side of the frames. "I just took your picture."

Scot squinted at the glasses, seeing a little red light in the corner of the frames. "It's a camera?"

"That's right, my man. Check you later." Kyle left the warehouse.

Scot returned the pallet jack to its spot in the corner. Then he headed for the store to help stock shelves. Charlotte entered the warehouse, letting the metal door shut behind her. Scot froze like a deer in headlights.

"I won't bite," Charlotte said.

Scot swallowed and continued toward the door and Charlotte. "What are you doing here so late?"

"End of the month paperwork."

Scot nodded, his gaze dropping to her nipples protruding through her red polo.

Charlotte hugged herself. "It's so cold in here."

Scot was still warm from the manual labor and his Big-Mart sweatshirt. "The door was open for the truck."

Charlotte nodded. "Right. The delivery."

"I should get back to work." Scot started past Charlotte, toward the warehouse exit.

She grabbed his arm. "Wait a second. I feel like we haven't talked in forever."

Scot stopped and stared at her hand on his arm. "That's because we haven't."

Charlotte released his arm. "Congratulations on associate of the month, by the way."

"Thanks."

"You like working here now?"

Scot shrugged. "It's a means to an end. I'm making the best of it." She inched close enough that Scot could smell her flowery perfume.

"Are you still planning to go back to Penn?"

"Yeah. I should have enough money by the end of the summer."

Charlotte smiled. "Good. That's great."

"What about you? You like working here, now that you're a manager?"

She rolled her eyes. "*Assistant* manager."

"Right. Still."

"It's okay. The salary and benefits are decent. It's a lot of work though. Sometimes I miss being a cashier. I feel like I have no life outside of Big-Mart. Even with Ron. All we talk about is Big-Mart."

"I should go." Scot brushed past her.

"I think about you."

Scot turned back to Charlotte, his heart pounding in his chest.

"Do you ever think about me?" she asked.

"Not really." He walked away, thinking about Charlotte.

CHAPTER 44

Another Six Months Later ...

Anna plopped on her single bed, sitting cross-legged, wearing shorts and a T-shirt. "What's the big news?"

The television blared through the paper-thin walls of the trailer. Anna's roommate, Felicity, watched a reality TV show in the living room.

Scot stood in front of Anna, his hands on his hips like Superman. "I'm not going back to school."

Anna knitted her brow. Her hair danced in the breeze of the stationary fan. Apart from the fan, the metal trailer provided little relief from the summer heat. "I don't understand. You saved more than enough money."

Patches, her calico cat, jumped on Anna's bed and flopped next to her, also enjoying the mechanical breeze.

Scot asked, "You know how I've been waiting until the last minute to sell my Bitcoin to pay for school because Bitcoin keeps going up?"

Anna petted her cat, her gaze on Scot. "Sure."

Scot spoke with his hands, excitement in his voice. "Well, I started thinking about whether I'd be better off with the Bitcoin or with an engineering degree. I can always go back to school to get an engineering degree, but I think Bitcoin is a once-in-a-lifetime opportunity."

"But ... what if it isn't?"

"The blockchain is like the internet in 1985, and Bitcoin's like Google or Apple or Microsoft.

Anna nodded. "I hope you're right."

"I've already made $22,000 this year. Pure profit for doing *nothing*. If I keep buying as much as I can, in a few years, I won't have to work anymore. Lots of analysts think Bitcoin will go to a million dollars. I don't know if that'll happen, but $100,000 is realistic. If that happens, I'll have ten million dollars. Can you imagine? Ten *million*."

Over the past six months, Scot had continued to purchase Bitcoin with his savings. He now held one hundred Bitcoins, valued at $578.16 each.

Anna pursed her lips. "It seems so risky. You worked so hard to get back to school. What if ..."

Scot drew back. "I thought you'd be happy. Sounds like you want me to leave."

"No. It's not that. I thought you really wanted to be an engineer."

Scot sat next to her on the edge of the bed. "I don't know if that's what I want anymore. My grades weren't that great anyway. And I don't want to leave you."

Anna shook her head. "Don't put this on me. If I had the money to go to school, I'd go in a heartbeat."

"And leave *me*?"

"It's not like we'd never see each other again."

"Why aren't you happy for me?" Scot asked, his voice rising.

Patches scurried from the bed and hid behind her dresser.

"You're upsetting Patches." Anna stood from the bed and faced Scot.

Scot stood from the bed too and asked again, this time in a calm tone, "Why aren't you happy for me?"

"I am. I'm just ... I'm just surprised."

"I'm right about Bitcoin."

"I'm sure you are."

Scot shook his head. "Don't patronize me. If you thought I was right, you would've invested in Bitcoin too. You know how much money you lost leaving your money in the bank?"

Anna crossed her arms over her chest. "I didn't lose any money."

"You didn't make any either. You know what I mean."

"It wasn't that long ago that you lost a bunch of money and wanted to sell all your Bitcoin."

"You still think I'm wrong about Bitcoin."

"I didn't say that."

"You didn't have to."

Anna rolled her eyes.

Scot glared at her. "Why did you just roll your eyes?"

Anna threw up her hands in disgust. "Because you're being ridiculous."

Scot crossed his arms over his chest. "Oh, I'm ridiculous. You're just jealous."

Her face reddened. "*Jealous*? I can't believe you'd say that to me."

"I can't believe you're not being supportive. It's not like this was an easy choice for me."

"You drop this bomb on me, and I have to immediately support it? I haven't even had time to think about it. You're being irrational."

"Oh, so I'm ridiculous and irrational?"

Anna pressed her lips together.

"If I'm ridiculous and irrational, you're jealous and petty."

"I'm done with this. Go home, Scot."

"Good idea." Scot left, slamming the door behind him.

CHAPTER 45

Regret

Late on Saturday night, Scot sat in the deserted break room, checking the price of Bitcoin. It was down ten bucks. Scot had lost $1,000 that day. He hung his head, thinking about his fight with Anna. They hadn't spoken or even texted in twenty-four hours. Scot had thought she'd at least send him an apology text. He thought about the last thing she'd said to him. *I'm done with this. Go home, Scot. What did she mean by I'm done with this? Was she talking about the argument, or was she talking about our relationship? Did she break up with me? The same shit happened with Charlotte.*

Scot rubbed his aching temples.

"You look like you've had a rough day," Charlotte said.

Scot raised his gaze to his ex-girlfriend, half-wondering if his thoughts had conjured her out of thin air. "I guess you could say that."

Charlotte sat across from him at the table.

"You're here late. End of the month paperwork again?" Scot asked. It was August 27, 2016.

"Every day's starting to feel like the end of the month," Charlotte replied.

Scot nodded.

"What's going on with you? Why are you down in the dumps?"

He almost told her what was really bothering him. "I lost $1,000 today."

Charlotte leaned forward. "How? What happened?"

"Bitcoin's down ten bucks."

"That sucks."

Scot shrugged and sat up straight. "It's up and down. I need to stop letting it bother me."

"How many Bitcoin do you have now?"

"A hundred."

"How much are they worth?"

"About five hundred and seventy dollars."

Charlotte cocked her head. "Each?"

Scot nodded again.

"Oh my God, you have like $500,000."

"No. It's like $57,000."

Charlotte giggled. "That's embarrassing. I'm *so* bad at math."

"You just added an extra zero."

"Fifty-seven thousand is still really great. I assume you're going back to school soon? Ron didn't mention anything about you putting in your notice."

Scot glanced around, making sure they were alone. "I'm not going back to school. I didn't want to sell my Bitcoin. I think it might go to a million."

"*Really*? Like one million dollars for one Bitcoin?"

"Yeah."

"*Wow*. You'd be seriously rich."

"Nobody knows if it'll get that high, but I think $100,000 is very realistic."

"That would still be a lot. You'd have like a hundred million dollars."

"Ten million."

She giggled again. "Extra zero."

Scot smiled. "Right. Extra zero."

"This is why you're gonna be a millionaire, and I'm not. You're smart."

"You're smart too."

Charlotte frowned. "I barely made it through high school. I think this is it for me."

"Don't sell yourself short. You're very talented."

She smiled wide. "You're sweet."

"I guess I should get back to work." Scot stood from the table.

Charlotte stood from the table. "You wanna see my new office? I took Gary's old office." Gary was the Hardware Department manager. He had recently transferred to a Big-Mart closer to his home.

Scot hesitated for a long beat, then said, "Yeah, okay."

Charlotte led Scot down the employee hallway to the managers' offices. His heart thumped in his chest.

She gestured to her open door. "Check it out."

Scot stepped into the office. The walls were bare, except for a poster of a kitten hanging from a branch with the message, *Hang in There*, scrawled across the bottom in goofy cursive. A metal desk dominated the room, a leather swivel chair behind it. A few cardboard boxes with office supplies sat on the floor. It smelled like her flowery perfume.

Charlotte shut the door behind them.

Scot turned to her, his entire body buzzing.

"I still have some decorating to do, but it's a lot bigger than my old office," Charlotte said. "What do you think?"

He gestured to the kitten on the wall. "Nice poster."

She smirked. "I got that here. I can get you one, if you want."

"That's not necessary. You know me. I have tons of kitten posters."

Charlotte laughed.

Scot laughed.

She stopped laughing and inched closer, close enough to kiss. "I've missed you."

Scot put up his hands in defense, accidentally grazing her breasts. "I don't know about this."

She bit the lower corner of her lip. "You don't know about what?"

Scot leered at her cleavage.

She gave the smallest of smiles, as if she knew she had him in the palm of her hand. She pressed her curvaceous body against his and kissed him, her tongue swirling in his mouth. He wrapped his arms around her and reciprocated. While they kissed, she undid his belt and fly and slipped her hand into his pants, squeezing his erection.

Scot groaned in response.

Charlotte squeezed again, Scot on the border between pain and ecstasy. Then she retracted her hand, undid and unzipped her own khaki pants, exposing pink cotton underwear. Scot slid his hand between her legs, under the cotton. She shuddered from his touch and moaned in his ear. His fingers slickened as he touched her.

Then she whispered, "I want you to fuck me."

He trembled in anticipation.

She slid her pants and underwear down to midthigh, exposing a neat triangle of dark hair. Then, she turned around and bent over her desk. Scot's hands shook as he pulled his boxer briefs and pants down to mid-thigh. A dreamlike haze covered him, like thick fog. Every molecule of his being screamed, *Keep going.*

He gripped her hips and pushed inside her. The best idea in the world. The necessity of the act. The animal magnetism. The overwhelming desire. It all disappeared thirty seconds later with his orgasm. The regret settled on him like a ton of bricks, while he was still inside her, bathed in the glow of the cold fluorescent light.

He pulled out and whispered to himself, "What have I done?"

Charlotte turned around and pulled up her pants, a crooked smile on her lips.

Scot pulled up his pants and shook his head. "I'm sorry. This was a mistake." He pivoted and opened the door.

"Scot, wait," Charlotte said.

He fast-walked down the hall, buckling his belt.

Kyle entered the hallway from the break room. "What up, Scotty?"

Scot rushed past him, tucking in his shirt, not making eye contact.

CHAPTER 46

Face the Music

Morning sun filtered between the blinds, warming Scot's face. His eyes fluttered and opened. He grabbed his phone from the bedside table and checked his text messages.

Anna: Call me as soon as you get up.

He sat up in bed, his stomach turning. *She knows. Shit. Kyle must've told her.* He thought about avoiding her, but he wanted to get it over with, like ripping off a Band-Aid. He tapped Anna's contact, his heart thumping. She answered on the first ring.

"Hey," she said, her voice even.

"Hey," he replied.

Anna hesitated for a moment. "I'm sorry about the other night. I should've been more supportive. I guess I thought you wanted to go to school. I thought we had that in common. It was a shock, and I didn't handle it as well as I should've."

Scot exhaled, relieved. "I'm sorry too."

"Thanks." She paused for an instant. "I was thinking that, just because it's my dream to finish college and vet school, doesn't mean you have to have the same dream. If you don't want to go to college, and you want to be a Bitcoin investor, that's fine with me. I just want you to be happy."

Scot swallowed the lump of guilt in his throat. "I love you."

"I love you too. Let's never fight again."

"Sounds good to me."

"What time do you have to work today?"

"Noon."

"You want to go hiking before work?"

Scot stood from his bed. "Sure. Memorial Lake?"

CHAPTER 47

Careful What You Wish For

"We're going hiking at Memorial Lake," Scot said, sitting at the kitchen table, a bowl of sugary cereal before him.

"That'll be nice," Laura replied, sitting across from him, sipping her coffee.

Scot nodded, chewing his sugary cereal.

"I really like her."

Scot swallowed. "Me too."

Laura set down her coffee mug. "Treat her right. Don't be like your fathers."

Scot stared at the multicolored rings floating in milk, suddenly losing his appetite.

"I'm so proud of you and Heather," Laura said. "Your sister has thirty thousand followers on Instagram. Did you know that?"

Scot swirled his spoon in his cereal. "That's great."

"And you've been working so hard, saving your money. You were a little saver, even when you were little. Do you remember?"

Scot raised his gaze. "With my birthday cards?"

"That's right. You saved every dollar from those cards."

When Scot was twelve, he had asked his mother to hold his money, when they went to the shore on a family vacation. It was the money he'd saved from years of birthday cards. He had thought he might want to buy something on the boardwalk, but he never did, and Laura never returned his money. When Scot had asked for it back,

Laura had told Scot that she had used the money buying things for him, but, to his recollection, she hadn't bought him anything.

Laura continued. "You'll be a wealthy man one day. I'm sure of it."

Scot shrugged. "We'll see."

"Don't downplay your accomplishments. You will be. A mother knows these things."

Scot stood from the table. "I should get ready."

Scot dumped his remaining cereal down the garbage disposal and went upstairs to get ready. He brushed his teeth, then went to his room to change.

As he slipped his T-shirt over his head, a knock came at his door. "Come in," Scot said, figuring it was Anna.

Charlotte entered his bedroom, wearing short shorts and heavy makeup.

Scot drew back, his eyes bulging. "What are you doing here?"

She shut the door behind her. "I need to talk to you about last night."

He gestured to the door. "You need to leave. Anna will be here soon."

Charlotte pouted. "I don't mean anything to you, do I?"

He spoke rapidly. "You'll always have a place in my heart, but I'm with Anna now, and you're with Ron. Our time is over."

"What if I don't want it to be over? What if I miss you? What if I still love you?"

Before Scot fell in love with Anna, he had fantasized about Charlotte wanting him back, but it wasn't a fantasy now. It was a nightmare. He nudged her toward his door. "I'm sorry about last night, but I'm with Anna now. I really need you to leave."

Her eyes filled with tears. "*Fine.*" She whipped open the door, rushed down the stairs, and left the townhome.

Shortly thereafter, Anna appeared in his open doorway. "I think I saw Charlotte's red Camaro."

"Really?" Scot asked, not making eye contact.

Anna spoke in an ominous tone. "Maybe she's stalking you."

Scot forced a laugh.

As they drove to Memorial Lake, Scot thought about coming clean, his stomach in knots. His gut knew the truth. Such a confession would end with Anna never wanting to see him again.

CHAPTER 48

One Year Later ...

Scot sat at a table with Anna in the otherwise empty break room. Henry wasn't working that day. He only worked two days a week now, given his aching legs.

Scot gaped at his Coinbase account balance on his phone. "This is unbelievable. At this rate I'll be a millionaire by the end of the year."

Anna nodded, nonplussed. Over the past year, she'd heard it many times. He was ecstatic when Bitcoin hit $1,000. Elated at $1,500. Thrilled at $2,000. Overjoyed at $3,000. And now he was positively euphoric at $4,400.

Kyle entered the break room, just as Scot said, "My account balance is $532,759.20. Can you believe that?"

"That's great," Anna replied in monotone.

Kyle walked to the vending machine, glancing at them as he went.

Scot lowered his voice. "Bitcoin only went up like forty-five dollars since yesterday, but I still made over five hundred bucks in one day."

Kyle grabbed a Snickers bar from the vending machine and walked over to their table. "You guys talkin' about Bitcoin?"

Nobody answered.

"I bought two last week." Kyle gestured to Scot. "I heard about this guy gettin' rich, always talkin' about Bitcoin. How many do you have?"

Scot suppressed a grin. "A hundred and twenty."

"Holy shit! That's like half-a-million bucks. Why the fuck are you still workin' *here*?"

Charlotte entered the break room and marched to Kyle. "Can you keep it down, Kyle? I heard you use the F-word. A customer might hear."

"Fuck that."

Charlotte frowned. "Don't be a dick."

Kyle opened his candy bar, a smirk on his face.

Charlotte turned to walk away.

"You know your ex is rich now." Kyle took a big bite of his Snickers bar.

"Shut up, Kyle," Scot said in a hushed whisper.

Charlotte turned around.

Kyle spoke with his mouth full. "He has over five hundred grand in Bitcoin." Kyle swallowed and grinned.

Scot dipped his head.

Kyle continued. "Ron won't see five hundred grand in his whole fuckin' life."

Charlotte stomped away.

Anna glared at Kyle. "Was that necessary?"

Kyle chuckled. "Girls love guys with big fat … wallets." He pumped his eyebrows at Scot. "You know what I'm talkin' about, don't you, Scotty?"

Anna rolled her eyes.

CHAPTER 49

Sex Sells

Scot drove home from work, Anna in the passenger seat next to him, passing strip malls, big-box stores, and fast-food joints. Scot glanced from the road to Anna. "Mind if we stop by my house real quick? I need to change. Get rid of the Big-Mart smell."

"We'll be late for the movie."

"I'll be quick."

Anna looked down at her rumpled khakis. "If you're changing, I want to change too."

Scot stopped his car at a stop sign. "That's fine. If we can't make the movie, we can see something else, or we can just go out to eat."

"Okay."

Scot flipped down the sun visor, shading the afternoon sun. He drove through the intersection.

"What do you think Kyle meant when he was talking about girls liking fat wallets?" Anna asked.

"Probably just that girls like guys with money."

"But he said you'd know what he was talking about. What does that mean?"

Scot shrugged. "I don't know. It's Kyle. All he does is talk shit."

Anna pursed her lips, thinking for a moment. "You think he thinks I'm with you because you have money?"

Scot looked from the road to Anna, his brow furrowed. "No way."

She held out her hands. "Then what? Is it Charlotte?"

Scot turned right onto a two-lane road. "*Charlotte*? What are you talking about?"

They drove past a mix of working-class neighborhoods and run-down farms.

Anna said, "Charlotte obviously didn't like what Kyle was saying about you having money. I think she regrets breaking up with you."

Scot forced a laugh. "Charlotte hates my guts."

"Maybe."

Scot turned on the radio. Anna turned to the passenger window.

Shortly thereafter, Scot turned into his neighborhood. He parked in a visitor spot near his mother's townhome. A brand-new BMW with thirty-day tags was parked in the driveway.

"I wonder who's here," Scot said.

Scot and Anna walked to the townhome, admiring the red BMW on the way. Inside, shopping bags were stacked at the bottom of the stairs. They walked into the kitchen. Laura and Heather ate Mexican takeout at the kitchen table. Laura had a burrito and tortilla chips. Heather had a huge plate of nothing but black beans.

Laura set down her burrito and smiled at them. "Hey, you two. Did you see Heather's new car?"

"That's yours?" Scot asked, with raised eyebrows.

"Yep." Heather shoved a large spoonful of beans into her mouth.

"Congratulations," Anna said.

Heather nodded to Anna, still chewing.

Laura held up her hand, showing off the gold watch on her wrist. "Look what your sister bought me. Isn't it beautiful?"

"It is," Scot said.

"That's so nice of you, Heather," Anna said.

Laura leaned over and kissed Heather on the cheek. "I have the best daughter in the world."

Heather beamed.

Scot thought about his older sister, Marie. He wondered how Heather and Laura were so close, yet Marie hadn't talked to Laura in years.

Anna tugged on Scot's shirt and whispered, "We need to get moving."

"We should get going," Scot said. "We're headed to the movies, and we're running late."

"Have fun," Laura said.

They went upstairs to Scot's bedroom. Scot changed his work khakis for a pair of jeans.

Anna sat on the edge of his bed. "Your sister makes all that money from Instagram?"

Scot buckled his belt. "I guess. She has like one hundred thousand followers."

"How did she get so many followers?"

"Cleavage and ass shots."

CHAPTER 50

Skeletons

Every other Friday, paychecks were placed in the associates' mailboxes inside the break room. About half of the Big-Mart associates had direct deposit, but they still received a physical pay stub. The mailboxes were cubbyholes, labeled by name and open to all. Scot had never heard of anyone having their paycheck stolen from their mailbox. A thief wouldn't be able to cash the check.

Scot and Anna grabbed their paychecks. A few other associates stood nearby, scowling and comparing their paltry earnings. Managers steered clear on payday, as associates were often disillusioned and disappointed with their pay, sure the tax deductions were wrong or they had actually worked more hours. Scot opened the envelope, glanced at his pay stub, then shoved it into his back pocket.

Anna gaped at a piece of paper.

"What is it?" Scot asked.

She glared at him. "This was in my box."

Scot moved closer to her, so they were side by side. He read the printed note.

SCOT FUCKED CHARLOTTE IN HER OFFICE LAST YEAR.

"This is bullshit. It has to be a prank," Scot said, a flush spreading across his face. He remembered Kyle seeing him in the hallway, immediately after it happened.

Anna stared at Scot for a long beat. "Is it?"

"*Yes,*" he replied, his voice going higher.

CHAPTER 51

Liars

On Saturday afternoon, Scot confronted Kyle in the warehouse.

"What up, Scotty," Kyle said, as he hopped off the forklift.

Scot spoke in a hushed whisper, "Did you give Anna that note?"

"What note?"

Scot looked around, making sure they were alone. They were. "The note about me and Charlotte."

Kyle gave him a crooked grin. "I knew you were hittin' it. My man. Way to get back at Ron." Kyle held up one finger. "Remember. It's just sex. Don't turn this shit into a relationship."

Scot frowned. "You're not listening. Did you write a note telling Anna about this?"

"No. Why would I do that?"

"Anna got a letter in her box yesterday, saying that I had sex with Charlotte last year."

Kyle drew back. "Whoa. That's crazy. Wasn't me."

"You sure?"

"Dude. I wouldn't do that. I know I'm an asshole, but I have my limits." Kyle stroked his blond beard. "It's weird that this is happenin' now."

"Weird? Why is that?"

"I heard Ron asked Charlotte to marry him, and she said no."

Scot pressed his lips together, processing the information. "I need you to keep all this to yourself."

Kyle smirked. "Don't worry about me."

Scot left the warehouse. He fast-walked to the front of the store. He caught a glimpse of Anna at her cash register, waiting on a customer. Scot slipped into the employee-only area, without Anna noticing. He marched down the hall and knocked on Charlotte's open office door.

She looked up from her laptop.

"Can I talk to you for a minute?" Scot asked.

She pursed her lips, then gestured to the plastic chair in front of her desk. "Sure."

Scot shut the door behind him and sat in the chair, feeling a powerful sense of déjà vu. He stared at the metal desk, remembering their tryst from a year ago.

"What is it?" Charlotte asked, ice in her tone. "I'm pretty busy."

He raised his gaze and asked, "Did you put a note in Anna's mailbox?"

"A note? About what?"

"It said that we had sex."

Charlotte scowled. "That was so long ago. Why would I do this now?"

"I don't know."

"It has to be Kyle. He saw you. Remember?"

Scot shook his head. "He denied it."

"And you believe him? He's a liar."

CHAPTER 52

The Truth

After their shift, Scot and Anna left Big-Mart together, the summer sun muted by dark clouds. They walked toward the back of the lot, where they had parked next to each other.

"You want me to come over?" Scot asked. "I don't have to work until twelve tomorrow. We could stay up late, watching eighties' movies."

Anna didn't look at Scot as she replied, "I'm really tired. I should go to sleep."

Scot dipped his head, disappointed. "Okay."

When they arrived at their cars, Anna said, "You're telling me the truth, right?"

Scot furrowed his brow.

"About Charlotte."

Scot took her hand and squeezed. "I'm telling the truth."

She nodded, her hand limp in his. Then she went to her car, and Scot went to his. He sat in the driver's seat of his Hyundai, watching her drive away. *I'm such a piece of shit.*

CHAPTER 53

OnlyFans

Scot unboxed cheesy DVD movies and placed them in the bargain bins. Scot had picked up an extra shift on Sunday night, not because he needed the money but because Anna didn't seem enthused about spending time with him.

Kyle sauntered toward him.

Scot continued to stock the DVDs.

Kyle lifted his chin. "What up, Scotty."

"Kyle."

"You take care of your problem?"

Scot looked around, making sure they were alone. "As long as you keep your mouth shut."

Kyle frowned. "It's not me that you have to worry about."

"Who do I have to worry about? Charlotte?"

Kyle gaped over Scot's shoulder. "Holy shit. Incomin'."

Scot turned to see Heather strutting toward them, wearing short shorts, a V-neck T-shirt, and flip-flops.

"What are you doing here?" Scot asked Heather.

Kyle stared, his eyes bulging.

Heather rested one hand on her cocked hip. "I need a new webcam."

Scot pointed to the electronics section. "They're in the third aisle, one over from the laptops."

"You gonna introduce me?" Kyle asked.

Scot gestured to Kyle. "This is Kyle. He works in the warehouse."

Kyle moved closer to Heather, his eyes crawling over her. "I'm an internet entrepreneur. I don't need this job."

Heather ignored Kyle, making a who-the-fuck-is-this-douchebag face at Scot.

Scot shrugged in response.

"See ya later," she said to Scot, purposely ignoring the disheveled hipster.

Kyle leered at her bubble butt as she walked away. "I wish I was wearin' my camera glasses."

Scot glared at Kyle. "Don't even think about it."

"Think about what?"

"You know what."

Kyle turned his attention to Scot. "How do you know her?"

"She's my *sister*."

Kyle drew back. "Oh, shit. She's ..." Kyle cleared his throat. "I should get back to work."

Kyle's work suggestion made Scot suspicious. "Hold on a second. You were about to say something about her."

Kyle looked away. "It's nothin'."

"What is it, *Kyle*?"

Kyle hesitated for a moment. "She's Hot Heather on Instagram."

Scot held out his hands. "Yeah. So?"

"You ever been to her page?"

"A long time ago. I know she posts some bikini shots, but that's her business."

Kyle shook his head. "She uses Instagram to get guys to sign up to her OnlyFans."

"What the fuck's OnlyFans?"

"It's a subscription-based platform for fans to get special content."

Scot thought about Heather's new BMW. "Okay. So, what?"

"The special content is usually ..." Kyle winced. "Porn."

Scot lifted one side of his mouth in disgust. "You think she's selling porn?"

"She sells a lotta shit. It's not all porn. She's *huge* on OnlyFans. I heard she makes ten grand a week sellin' her farts in a fuckin' jar."

"Now I know you're full of shit. Selling *farts*?"

Kyle removed his phone from his pocket. "I'm dead serious." He tapped on his phone. Then he shared his screen with Scot. "Check it out."

A video of Heather in her room, wearing lacy red underwear, played on Kyle's phone. Heather used her hands as she spoke. "For my best fans, I want *you* to have the full Hot Heather erotic experience. What does that mean? It means that I will engage *all* of your senses. By subscribing here on OnlyFans, you can see *all* of me. You can make special requests, such as certain poses, certain sex acts ..." Heather winked. "Or even just to talk, giving you that special girlfriend experience.

"I wanna connect with you guys on a deeper level. Not only do I want you to see me and hear me, I want you to *smell* me." She bent forward, showing her cleavage, and grabbing something from behind the camera. In one hand, she showed a signed picture of herself, without a stitch of clothing. The other hand held a white handkerchief.

Thankfully, the nude image was so small that it was barely discernable on the phone screen.

"For a short time, anyone who orders a signed picture will also receive an official handkerchief with my personal perfume." *Only $29.99 with free shipping in the US lower 48* appeared on the bottom corner of the screen. "I have to say, I've been *so* impressed by all the tributes I've received on my beautiful face." Heather kissed her own picture. "Keep 'em *coming*." She giggled.

Scot cringed and turned away.

Kyle cackled and smacked Scot on the back. "This is the good part. Watch this."

Scot looked at the screen again, his face contorted, as if he'd eaten a lemon.

Heather put her hands between her legs and moaned. Then she tittered and said, "How would you like to have these panties? I've been wearing them *all day long.*" *Only $39.99 with free shipping in the US lower 48* appeared at the bottom corner of the screen. She ran her tongue over her upper teeth. "Exercising. Sweating. Touching myself." Heather winked. Then she turned around, revealing her thong underwear and bare ass. She smacked her rear end, her curvy butt cheek rippling in response.

A customer, an older woman, walked past, giving them the evil eye.

Kyle led Scot out of the aisle, into the relative seclusion of the Home Goods Department.

Heather faced the camera again, a knowing smile on her lips. Then she reached forward and grabbed something else from behind the camera. Heather presented an empty jar with her logo on the side, Hot Heather, written in black, with a hot pink background. She grinned. "This is only for my really *dirty* boys out there. You know who you are." Heather put her hand over her heart. "I'm a lady in every way. Let's not get it twisted, but even ladies have occasional gas. When I do, I save my gas in these jars, special for my *dirty* boys." *Only $49.99 with free shipping in the US lower 48,* appeared at the bottom corner of the screen.

"I have to go for now. I love you guys." Heather blew a kiss toward her admirers.

CHAPTER 54

Hot Heather

Scot returned home from work after midnight. Laura lay on the couch snoring, the television flickering in the darkness. Scot covered his mother with the blanket draped over the back of the couch. She stirred but didn't wake. Then he turned off the television and went upstairs.

On the way to his bedroom, he noticed a sliver of light from under Heather's bedroom door, along with the sound of mouse clicks. He showered and changed into his pajamas. He flipped off the light and lay in his bed, thinking about Heather's video. He grabbed his phone from the bedside table and tapped his way to Instagram.

Scot found Heather's Instagram page. She had well over one hundred thousand followers. Her latest post was a selfie of her sitting in her car, wearing a zip-up hoodie and no bra, the zipper tantalizingly low. Under the picture was the message, *Wanna see more? Click here.*

Scot clicked the link, which took him to Heather's OnlyFans page. Here, he was encouraged to subscribe for $9.99 per month. Scot scrolled through Heather's posts, which were often identical to her Instagram posts. In addition, many posts had an image of a lock, where the picture or video should've resided. Underneath was a blue button with a message that read SUBSCRIBE TO SEE USER'S POSTS. These locked posts had alluring headers, such as *I show way too much in this one* or *I can't believe I did this* or *Too HOT to handle.*

He set down his phone and thought about the situation. *If Mom knows about Instagram, she must know about OnlyFans. Maybe. Maybe not. She's not the most attentive parent. Heather is eighteen. Who cares if she's doing porn? But she's only eighteen. This could ruin her life. What if she decides she wants to go to college and be a teacher or something? What if she wants to get married and have kids? She probably wouldn't even tell her husband. If he ever found out, it would be a disaster. Or worse, what if her child found out?* Scot cringed, thinking about how he'd feel if he found out Laura had done porn.

Scot hoped that Heather was only sending racy pictures and not performing sex acts for all the internet to see, although her video mentioned sex acts specifically. Earlier that evening, he had called Anna about it during his break. Anna had suggested that he ask Heather about it. She had encouraged him to approach Heather with empathy and understanding.

Scot rolled out of bed and went to Heather's door. The sliver of light still came from the bottom of the door. He knocked lightly.

Tapping on the keyboard stopped, followed by light steps on the carpet.

Heather opened the door, wearing a T-shirt, and pink pajama pants. "What do you want?"

"Can I talk to you for a minute?"

She lifted one shoulder. "Yeah, I guess."

Scot followed her into her room. It was dominated by a four-poster bed with a lacy white canopy.

Heather turned her swivel chair at her desk to face Scot, then sat and asked, "What is it?"

Shopping bags from various boutiques stood next to the closet. Boxes and packing materials were piled next to the desk. A few dozen empty jars were stacked next to the packing materials.

Scot said, "You know that guy at Big-Mart that you met earlier, Kyle?"

She swiveled a little back and forth, reminding Scot of her as a child. "What about him?"

"He said you're on OnlyFans."

She scowled. "So what? It's not a crime. Celebrities are on Only-Fans."

"He said you're doing porn."

"That's none of your business."

Scot showed his palms. "I know. I'm not trying to be up in your business. It's just that you're young. You can do anything you want in life. You can *be* anything."

Heather shook her head. "That's bullshit. You of all people should know that's bullshit. Look at you. You're smart enough to get into Penn, and you're working at Big-Mart. What chance do I have? I'm fucking stupid."

"Don't say that. You're not stupid." Scot meant this. Her sales pitch had been quite smart, albeit cringey for Scot.

Tears welled in her eyes. "It's true. So I'm using my assets while I have 'em."

"You can do so much better. Look at me. I got kicked out of school, but I worked and invested, and now I'm doing pretty good."

She stood from her seat, tears slipping down her face. "You're such a hypocrite. You think you're better than me because you bought some fucking nerd coin?"

Scot stepped back. "I don't think—"

"You think you're the only one who gets to be rich? I actually have to work for a living. You just bought some imaginary coin."

"Look. I just—"

"Who the fuck are you to judge me? I'm an entrepreneur."

"Selling sex."

She pointed to the door, her face tear-streaked. "Get the fuck out."

CHAPTER 55

Good Guy?

On Monday, Scot ate lunch with Anna and Henry in the Big-Mart break room. Henry had made homemade meatball subs, bringing one for Scot and Anna.

"You're not eating?" Anna asked.

Henry sat at the table, his back hunched, his skin pale. "I'm not hungry."

"Are you not feeling well?"

"I'm just old."

Scot swallowed a big bite of his sub. "I can cut mine in half."

Henry waved him off. "You eat your sub. I'm going home soon anyway."

Ron entered the break room and marched to their table. His hair and clothes were disheveled. His eyes were bloodshot. He pointed at Scot and said, "In my office. *Now.*"

"What's this about?" Henry asked, with the authority of a protective parent.

But Ron didn't stick around to answer.

"What's going on?" Anna asked.

"I don't know." Scot stood from the table and wrapped his half-eaten sandwich, using the wax paper it came in. "I'll be right back."

Scot left the break room and walked to the end of the managers' hallway, his anxiety increasing with each step. He thought of possible reasons for the summoning. *Did Charlotte tell him about what they did? Why would she do that over a year later? Or maybe it's about Kyle taking those pictures for his website. Maybe I'm just a witness.*

Scot entered Ron's open office.

"Shut the door."

Scot shut the door behind him and sat in the plastic chair across from Ron at his desk.

Ron glowered at Scot. "If we weren't at work, I'd …"

Scot swallowed hard.

"You're fired."

"For *what*?" Scot's voice went up an octave.

Ron clenched his jaw. "You know what. Don't make me show you the security cam footage."

"I don't know what you're talking about." That was a lie.

Ron turned around his laptop. Scot and Charlotte having sex in her office was paused on the screen.

Scot winced and looked away.

Ron shut the laptop and pushed a paper and pen across the desk. "Sign this and get the fuck out of my sight. We'll mail your final check."

As Scot signed the termination paperwork, Ron said, "You had me fooled. I thought you were a good guy, but you're just another piece of shit."

Scot set down the pen and left the office, not making eye contact with Ron. His heart thumped in his chest, and his stomach felt queasy, as he walked back to the breakroom. Scot hesitated outside the break room, trying to compose himself, and trying to figure out what to say. *I'll tell them that I got caught smoking with Kyle.*

Scot entered the break room. Henry still sat at the table, but Anna stood ten feet away from Henry, staring at her phone. Scot stepped toward Anna, like he was walking through a minefield. "What is it?"

Anna looked up from her phone. Her face was red. Her eyes were glassy. She glared at Scot for a split second, then slapped him across the face. "Don't ever talk to me again."

Hurricane Anna left the break room, reducing Scot's edifice to rubble.

CHAPTER 56

Fate?

Scot stood, stunned, his left cheek stinging.

"Scot?" Henry asked, from the table ten feet away.

Scot pivoted and ran from the break room and into the store, searching for Anna. She glanced his way, just before entering the women's bathroom, her face streaked with tears of disappointment. Scot left the store and fast-walked toward his car, fighting his own tears.

Along the way, he passed Charlotte's Camaro. She held her face in her hands. Scot composed himself and tapped on her window. Startled, she then recognized Scot, and powered down her window.

"You okay?" Scot asked.

She shook her head, pouting. "He fired me."

"Me too."

"This is just my fucking luck."

Scot exhaled. "I'm sorry. I didn't want this to happen."

Charlotte lifted one shoulder. "Well, it did."

Scot nodded, a lump in his throat. "Yeah. It did. I'm sorry again." Scot pivoted to walk to his car.

"You wanna go for a ride with me?"

Scot turned back to Charlotte. "I should go home. Figure things out."

"Come on. You've never ridden in my car. I won't have it much longer, if I can't make the payments."

PHIL M. WILLIAMS

Scot hesitated for a moment. "Yeah, okay."

Charlotte drove them across town, zipping in and out of traffic like a race-car driver. Scot gripped the armrest, wondering if he'd make it back to his car in one piece. Charlotte drove them to Memorial Lake, Anna's favorite hiking spot. Scot tried not to think of her, worried about breaking down in front of Charlotte.

Charlotte parked her Camaro in a lonely parking lot, overlooking the lake. "Ron took me here last weekend."

Sunlight reflected off the blue water, like starbursts. A gaggle of geese ate grass near the shoreline.

Scot almost mentioned Anna.

"I don't know what I'm gonna do," Charlotte said, staring at the lake.

"Me either," Scot replied.

She turned from the lake to face Scot. "At least you have money. I'm gonna lose this car. My condo. I'll have to move back home."

"You bought a condo?"

"I'm renting. I was so sick of living at home, and Ron wasn't ready to live together."

Scot wondered if this was a lie or if Kyle was mistaken about Charlotte rejecting Ron's marriage proposal.

They sat in awkward silence.

Scot felt compelled to fill the silence. "I'm sorry about everything. We never should've ..."

She turned in her seat toward Scot again. "Do you ever think things happen for a reason?"

"What do you mean?"

"Maybe this was supposed to happen. I didn't appreciate you, and I lost you, but I never stopped loving you. *Never.*"

Scot opened his mouth to speak, but nothing came out.

Charlotte turned back to the lake. "I know you'll never love me again, but I don't regret what we did. I would rather have that one night with you than never being with you ever again." Then she hung

160

her head and cried.

Scot started to reach for her, to comfort her, but retracted his hand. After several excruciating minutes, listening to her moan and wail, Scot checked her glove box, finding some napkins. He handed Charlotte a stack of them.

She took the napkins, the crying finally subsiding. She sniffled, wiped her face, and turned to Scot again. Her face was a blotchy mess, with smudged mascara. Her voice quivered. "I wish I could go back in time and do it all over. I'd treat you the way you deserve to be treated. I'd be the best girlfriend." She sniffled again. "I know I sound stupid." Charlotte exited the car and walked to a vacant bench.

Scot exited the car too, feeling responsible for Charlotte's demise. He walked to the bench and sat next to her, the geese honking in the foreground. She scooted closer to him and leaned her head on his shoulder. The bright sun warmed their faces in a way that the fluorescent lights of Big-Mart never could. They sat together, staring out over the lake for a long moment.

Charlotte placed her hand on his upper thigh and tilted her head upward. He turned to her, staring at her full lips, inhaling her flowery perfume. She closed her eyes, and he pressed his lips to hers.

Then Scot pulled back and said, "I'm sorry. I can't."

CHAPTER 57

Purpose

Scot knocked on the door of the wisest person he'd ever met.

Henry opened the door.

"I need to talk to you," Scot said, before Henry could speak.

Henry stepped aside. "Come in." He led Scot into the living room and gestured to the couch, the cushions worn and depressed. "Have a seat."

Scot sat at the end of the couch.

"You want something to drink?" Henry asked.

"No thanks," Scot replied.

Henry swiveled his Barcalounger toward Scot and sat with a groan, his legs shaking.

"Your legs hurt?" Scot asked.

Henry waved him off. "It's fine. I'm assuming you're here to talk about Anna."

Scot nodded. "I really messed things up."

"Appears so."

Scot dipped his head, embarrassed, hoping for something more philosophical from the former philosophy professor. When he raised his gaze to Henry, he asked, "What am I supposed to do?"

Henry let out a ragged breath. "Depends on what you did. For Anna to hit you the way she did, I imagine it was pretty bad, not that I condone violence."

Scot swallowed hard, his throat dry. "A year ago, I was with Charlotte." Scot spoke rapidly, as he clarified his indiscretion. "It was one time. It didn't mean anything. I wish I could take it back."

"Well, it obviously meant something to Anna."

"I know. How do I fix it? Tell me what to do. I'll do anything to get her back."

Henry didn't speak for several seconds, pondering Scot's request. "Anna's a virtuous person. I think you know that."

Scot nodded.

"Above anything, that's what she wants in a partner. Virtue."

"So, I have to be a good person, and she'll eventually come around?"

Henry shook his head. "That's not how virtue works. You have to be virtuous *because* it's the right thing to do. If there's an ulterior motive, such as winning back your girlfriend, it's not virtue. It's just manipulation."

"So I'm supposed to be this great person and not expect anything in return?"

"What you do or don't do is entirely up to you."

Scot rubbed his temples, brooding over the futility of it all. "So what you're telling me is that I'm screwed."

"Not necessarily." Henry peered through Scot, as if deep in thought. "Some couples do recover from these transgressions."

"Did you ever cheat?"

"No, but my wife had an affair."

Scot sat up straight. "Why?"

Henry stared at the mustard-colored carpet for a long time. Then he looked up and said, "When Alice got pregnant, I was thrilled. I asked her to marry me on the spot. She wasn't quite as sold on me as I was on her though. You have to understand. She was a beautiful woman, with many suitors. Her family wasn't sold on me either. I was too quiet, too awkward, and very small for a man. But, with the baby coming, we were married within the month. Then …" Henry pressed his lips together, his eyes misty. "Then … he died. Charles Henry

Rogers. That would've been his name."

"I'm sorry, Henry."

Henry wiped the corners of his eyes with his handkerchief. "It was a long time ago." Henry paused again. "After the miscarriage and Alice's hysterectomy, I think she was lost. I think we both were. Then she met a man at work. They connected at a time when we were having problems. He was much more physically attractive than me." Henry sighed. "Biology's a powerful thing, even for the most virtuous."

"But you forgave her. You guys worked it out."

"I did. We did. But, apart from the death of our child, it was the hardest thing I've ever endured. She told me the day after it happened. Had she not done that, I don't think I could've continued the marriage. I wouldn't have been able to trust her."

"I didn't tell Anna." Scot's throat tightened. "I held this lie between us for over a year, like the selfish coward that I am." Scot sniffed. "Now she'll never forgive me."

"You don't know that, and neither do I, but, either way, you have to put one foot in front of the other and try to be better."

Scot slumped his shoulders, his eyes glassy. "I don't know how to do that. I feel … empty, like I have no reason for being here. What difference does my life make?"

"You're a hard worker. A good son and brother. You're a good friend to at least one old man."

Scot forced a smile that quickly evaporated. He blinked, and a tear slipped down his face. "I don't think I matter at all."

Henry stood from his Barcalounger, sat next to Scot, and hugged him.

Scot dissolved into tears, his head on Henry's bony shoulder.

Henry patted Scot's back, letting him cry.

When the tears subsided, Scot sat upright, and Henry let go. Scot wiped his face with his T-shirt.

"Everyone has a purpose," Henry said. "Not everyone lives their purpose, but everyone can."

Scot smirked. "Even me?"

Henry smiled. "Especially you."

"What's my purpose?"

"Aristotle thought our purpose was to serve others and to do good. Emerson said, 'The purpose of life is not to be happy, but to be useful, to be honorable, to be compassionate, to have it make some difference that you have lived and lived well.'"

"What do *you* think?"

Henry rubbed the white stubble on his chin. "I think if you can tell the truth. Do your best, even if you're a lowly Big-Mart greeter." Henry winked at Scot. "And be kind to others; you'll live a life of purpose."

CHAPTER 58

Done

Scot parked behind Anna's Honda Civic. Thankfully, Anna's room-mate wasn't home. He thought about what Henry had said in response to his assertion that Anna would never forgive him. *You don't know that, and neither do I.* Scot exited his Hyundai and took several deep breaths, trying to calm his nerves.

The night air was cool. The first hints of autumn. He walked to the front door of her single-wide trailer and knocked. He wiped his sweaty hands on his khakis.

Anna opened the door, her face a hard mask. "What do you want?"

"Can we talk inside?" Scot asked.

Anna shook her head. "You're not coming inside."

Scot cleared his throat. "I'm really sorry. I didn't mean to hurt—"

"How many times?"

"Only once."

"Were you with her today?"

Scot hesitated. "No—"

"*Liar.*" Anna crossed her arms over her chest. "Kyle saw you two drive away in her *stupid* sports car."

Scot held out his hands like a beggar. "She wanted to show me her car. That's it. I didn't have sex with her."

"Did you kiss her?"

He hesitated again.

"I'll take that as a yes."

"It didn't mean anything."

"It means *everything*!"

Scot flinched, startled by her voice.

Anna raised one side of her mouth in disgust. "Go back to Charlotte. It's who you've always wanted."

"That's not true. I want you."

"We're done." She slammed the door in his face.

CHAPTER 59

The Fairy Tale

The next evening Scot paced in his room, thinking about what to say to Anna. He sat on his bed and picked up his phone from the bedside table, checking the time—*4:21 p.m. She's probably home from work now. Maybe she'll pick up this time.* He tapped Anna's contact. His call went to voice mail after two rings. It was his sixth call that day. All of them had gone to voice mail.

Her familiar greeting said, "You've reached Anna Fisher. Leave me a message, and I'll call you back. Or just send me a text. Thanks."

After the tone, Scot said, "I really need to talk to you. Please, Anna. Call me back. I love you." He disconnected the call.

Then he sent Anna another text. It was the twelfth one that day. None of them had been returned, but they had been tagged as *Delivered*, so Scot knew she was receiving them.

> **Scot:** This is the worst thing I've ever done, and I did it to the person I love the most. I'm so sorry. I'll do anything to make it up to you, to earn your trust back. Please talk to me. I can't live without you.

Scot sent the message. He stared at his screen, waiting for the *Delivered* tag, but it never came.

The doorbell chimed downstairs. Scot figured it was probably some guy for Heather.

He called Anna again. This time a quick busy signal was followed by his call being dropped. He tried again but had the same result. He hung his head and rubbed his temples. *I can't believe she blocked me.*

A knock came at his bedroom door.

"Who is it?" Scot called out.

"It's me," Charlotte replied.

Scot hesitated. "Come in."

Charlotte stepped into his bedroom, wearing tight jeans and a V-neck T-shirt. She shut the door behind her and offered a tentative smile.

"What are you doing here?" Scot asked, still sitting on his bed.

She sashayed to his bedside, bringing her floral perfume with her. "I wanted to check on you. How are you?"

Scot looked up at his ex. "I've been better."

She sat next to him on his bed. "Talk to me."

Scot tilted his head. "Really?"

"I know there's no chance for us"—she placed her hand atop his and squeezed—"but I'll always love and care about you. Even if we're not together."

"Thanks."

She retracted her hand.

Nobody spoke for several seconds.

Charlotte elbowed him playfully. "You gonna talk to me?"

"I don't think …" Scot exhaled. "I doubt you want to hear about my problems. I'm sure you have your own stuff."

"I do, but I'd like to be a friend to you. A *real* friend." She pursed her glossed lips. "Anna won't talk to you, *huh*?"

Scot turned his upper body toward Charlotte. "How did you know that?"

"I know girls like her."

Scot frowned. "What's that supposed to mean?"

Charlotte frowned back. "You want my help or not?"

"Sorry."

"I'm guessing Anna hasn't had many boyfriends."

"She had one in high school for a few months, and she had a few dates after high school."

"Exactly. She hasn't had much experience. She still believes the fairy tale."

"What fairy tale?"

"That she found her perfect Prince Charming and her happily ever after."

"*Me?*" Scot touched his chest. "You think she thinks that about me?"

"She did, until you showed her that real people make mistakes and ruined her fairy tale. She wasn't ready for that. Real love is about forgiveness."

Scot's shoulders slumped. "You don't think she really loves me?"

She placed her hand on his thigh. "It's not your fault. I just don't think she was ready for real love. You have to have some experience."

"What if she forgave me?"

"Then I'd be wrong."

"Maybe she just needs some time."

Charlotte shook her head. "I doubt it. How do you get close to someone?"

Scot thought for a moment. "Spending time with them?"

"Exactly. If she won't talk to you, you're drifting apart."

"I need to try harder."

Charlotte removed her hand from his thigh. "I agree."

Scot forced a smile, already thinking about the best way to approach Anna. "Thanks for listening."

Charlotte stood from the bed and faced Scot. She bent over, showing her cleavage, and kissed Scot on the cheek. "Anytime. I'll see ya."

Scot watched her round hips rock back and forth as she left his bedroom.

CHAPTER 60

One More Chance

The next day Scot drove into the Big-Mart parking lot, scanning the lot for Anna's Honda Civic. He parked his Hyundai two rows away but with a clear view of Anna's car. He glanced at the clock on his radio—*3:51 p.m.*

He powered down both front windows to allow a breeze inside his car. Despite the airflow, it was warm from the bright sun overhead. His palms and underarms were wet with sweat. He watched customers come and go, with their plastic bags and shopping carts.

At just after four, he saw various Big-Mart associates leaving the big-box store. He stepped out of his car, acquiring a better vantage of the Big-Mart entrance and exit. Anna walked with purpose, her keys in hand. Scot made a beeline for her, intercepting her as she arrived at her car.

Her eyes bulged. "Get away from me."

"Please, Anna," Scot said, his hands shaky, and his speech rapid. "I love you. I made a mistake, but I'll never do it again. You have to forgive me. Please. Love is about forgiveness."

A few customers rubbernecked as they walked past.

Anna scowled. "I don't *have* to do anything."

Scot showed his palms. "You're right. I know that."

Anna pressed her key FOB, unlocking her car. She opened her car door.

"Please, Anna. I love you."

She turned from her open door. "Do you really love me?"

"More than you can imagine."

"You *broke* my heart. Do you understand that?"

Tears welled in his eyes. "I know. I'm so sorry."

"If you really love me, you'll leave me alone."

"Please give me another chance."

"*No.*" Anna pointed at Scot. "You need to understand that I *don't* love you anymore. You *disgust* me."

Scot opened his mouth to speak, but nothing came out.

Anna climbed into her car, slammed the door, started the engine, and drove away, leaving Scot in the empty space.

CHAPTER 61

An Old Beginning

Scot lay under his covers in the darkness, the sobs dissipating, but Anna's last words still playing in his head. *You disgust me. You disgust me. You disgust me.*

A soft knock came at his door, but Scot didn't answer. Instead, he sniffled and wiped his eyes, not wanting to explain to Laura or Heather why he was crying. Laura would say he was just like his fathers, and Heather would probably say something unhelpful like, "Sucks to be you."

His door creaked open and then shut again. He peered into the darkness, only a faint glow from the streetlights filtering between the blinds.

Charlotte floated toward him, glowing in her white peasant dress.

She sat at his bedside, touched his cheek, then leaned in and kissed him softly on the lips. Scot breathed in her flowery perfume, her mouth tasting like mint.

When they separated, Scot sat up and asked, "What are you doing here?"

"I came to check on you," Charlotte said. "Are you okay?"

Scot shook his head.

"Anna won't forgive you."

"It's definitely over."

"It wasn't meant to be."

"Because I fucked it up."

"Maybe. Maybe not."

Scot swung his legs out of bed and stood. "I should turn on the light."

Charlotte grabbed his hand. "Don't." She pulled him back to a sitting position next to her on the bed. "Do you ever think about me?"

Scot hesitated. "Sometimes."

"Do you remember when we had sex in your car?"

"How could I forget?"

They had driven around that night, searching for a place to park, finally finding an abandoned logging trail. They had only driven far enough for the trees to conceal them from the highway. It was summer, and Charlotte had dressed especially for the occasion. It was only their third time together. They'd climbed into the back seat. Charlotte had hiked her skirt with a crooked smile.

Scot had been shocked by her surprise. They had been to dinner and a movie, all the while Scot had no clue that Charlotte had nothing under her short skirt. Scot had been quick and overexcited, but Charlotte hadn't complained, and they'd done it twice, the second time better than the first.

Charlotte chewed on her bottom lip. "You were the best I've ever had."

"Really?" Scot asked, surprised, as he had always felt inadequate with Charlotte, too fast and too small. Not that night in the car but many times afterward, when she didn't seem that into it.

One time he had asked Charlotte if she wanted him to stop, and she'd said that it didn't matter. He had stopped, hoping she might encourage him to keep going, but she hadn't.

"Yes. *Really*." Charlotte stood from the bed and faced Scot. She kicked off her sandals, her eyes laser-focused on Scot. She slipped the straps of her dress off her suntanned shoulders. Scot watched, his mouth ajar, his heart thumping in his chest. Charlotte let her peasant dress fall to the floor revealing nothing underneath. Scot sucked in a sharp breath.

Charlotte stepped closer to him, the V of dark hair at his eye level. She placed one bare foot on the bed, her legs wide open. Scot took the obvious hint, contorting his neck and licking her clitoris. Charlotte moaned, just loud enough for Scot to hear, encouraging him to continue. Her fingers ran through his hair. She gripped his head, tighter and tighter, as she neared her climax.

When she was dripping and close, she stepped back, bent over, and whispered in his ear, "I wanna come with you inside me."

Scot removed his boxer briefs and T-shirt like they were on fire. Charlotte straddled him and rode to ecstasy in less than sixty seconds. Scot climaxed immediately after.

She collapsed on him, still straddling him, her head on his shoulder. He held her, still inside her, for a long moment. Then she pecked him on the lips and said, "I love you."

He wasn't sure if he still loved her after everything that had happened, but he said it anyway. How could he not? He couldn't stomach another woman's disappointment.

Charlotte dismounted and asked, "You wanna watch something on Netflix?"

"Sure. Let me get my laptop," Scot replied.

Charlotte slipped her dress back over her head, and Scot put on his boxers and T-shirt. He grabbed his laptop from his desk and returned to bed. They propped the pillows against the wall and snuggled into bed, as the laptop loaded. Then Charlotte did something truly surprising.

"What do you wanna watch?" she asked.

"Whatever you want," Scot replied. They had always watched what she wanted.

She kissed him on the cheek and said, "You pick."

CHAPTER 62

Hint, Hint

The waitress set their cocktails on the table, a blue lemonade gin concoction for Charlotte and a dark and stormy mule for Scot.

"Thank you," Scot said.

The blonde smiled. "Your appetizers will be out shortly."

Charlotte sipped her cocktail. "This is *so* good."

Scot drank from his copper cup. "Mine's good too."

Charlotte scanned the dining area from their booth. Tables and booths were mostly occupied. Dim yellow lighting warmed the wooden tabletops. Soft popular music played in the background. "This is nice." She locked eyes with Scot. "Thank you for taking me out. I'm so lucky to have you."

Scot blushed. "I don't know about that."

"*I* do. I know I didn't appreciate you before, but I do now. So, thank you."

Scot smiled. "You're welcome."

Charlotte sipped her cocktail, then set her glass on the coaster. "I think we're both better this time, don't you think?"

"Yeah. Definitely less fighting. Less stress." Scot sipped his mule.

"I think you've really grown up."

Scot nodded.

Charlotte pursed her lips. "I've always loved you, but I think before I was worried that you couldn't commit."

He tilted his head. "I was committed."

"I mean like really committed. Like marriage, a house, kids, the whole thing."

Scot leaned forward. "Is that what you want?"

"More than anything in the world."

CHAPTER 63

Two Blissful Months Later ...

A knock came at Scot's bedroom door.

He set his phone on his bedside table and called out, "Come in."

Charlotte stepped into his room and shut the door behind her. This wasn't a surprise. She had texted him fifteen minutes ago.

Charlotte: I need to talk to you. It's an emergency

Scot: What is it?

Charlotte: In person

She moved tentatively, like she might step on a snake. Her eyes were red and puffy.

Scot stood from the edge of his bed. "What's wrong?"

Charlotte wrapped her arms around him.

Scot hesitated for a beat, then reciprocated. "What is it?"

She sniffled and shook her head.

"What is it?" he asked again. Scot stepped back, holding her shoulders, trying to get a read on her face, but she hung her head. "What is it? You're worrying me."

She lifted her gaze and said, "I'm pregnant."

He let go of her shoulders. "What?"

She sat on the edge of his bed, her shoulders slumped. "I'm pregnant."

He sat next to her. "Are you sure?"

She nodded.

"What are you going to do?"

Charlotte turned to him, her face a mask of barely controlled fury. "I thought you were ready for commitment."

Scot showed his palms. "That's not what I meant. I just meant that it's your choice, and, whatever you choose, I'll support that choice."

She narrowed her eyes. "You want me to get an abortion, don't you?"

"I don't, ... uh ..."

"You don't what? You don't care?"

"*No.* I'm sorry. I know I'm saying all the wrong things."

She crossed her arms over her chest. "That's for fucking sure."

"What do *you* want?"

She took a deep breath. "I want you to take care of me and our baby."

"I *will.* Of course I will."

She dropped her hands to her lap. "I'm scared, Scot."

Scot hugged her. "We'll figure it out."

She pushed him away. "What does that mean?"

"It means you're not alone."

Charlotte stood from the bed. "This isn't figuring out what to watch on Netflix or where to go to dinner. This is a baby—your baby growing inside me."

"I know."

"Do you?"

"*Yes.*"

"Then what are you gonna do when the baby comes? Are we gonna put the crib in your room? Or my mom's trailer?"

"We'll figure it out—"

"Am I just gonna be your baby mama?"

Scot stood and took her hands. "What if we got married? What if I started looking for a house?"

Her eyes bulged. "You mean it?"

Scot hesitated for an instant. "Yes."

"You have to ask."

"What do you mean?"

She rolled her eyes. "If you want me to marry you, you have to ask."

"Oh. Right. Sorry." Scot cleared his throat. "Will—"

"Not like that." Charlotte snatched her hands from his grasp. "You have to get down on one knee."

Scot grimaced. "Shit. Sorry." He went down on one knee and looked up at Charlotte. His voice quivered as he asked, "Will you marry me?"

She beamed and said, "Yes."

CHAPTER 64

One Expensive Month Later ...

"I still can't believe it," Charlotte said, grinning like a Cheshire cat. "Bitcoin's over $16,000 today."

Scot forced a smile, sitting across from her at a corner booth. He spoke without enthusiasm. "Yeah. It's crazy."

Charlotte frowned. "What's wrong? Aren't you happy?"

Scot shrugged and slid out of the booth. "I'm going to the bathroom. If the waiter comes, can you order me a burger?"

"A *burger*? This isn't McDonalds."

"That's what I want."

Charlotte huffed.

Scot left the booth, walking through the dimly lit restaurant to the bathroom. While he peed at the urinal, his phone buzzed in his pocket. After he washed his hands, he checked his phone. It was another voice mail from Henry. Scot played the message.

Henry said, "Hello, Scot. I hope you're well. I'm sorry to keep bothering you, but I have something important to talk to you about. Please call me back."

Scot deleted the message. He hadn't spoken to Henry in three months, not since asking for his help with Anna, after Scot had been fired from Big-Mart. Not having contact with Anna was her choice, but Henry was Scot's choice, collateral damage from his breakup with Anna. Simply put, it hurt too much. Scot's friendship with Henry had always included Anna and now ...

Scot slipped his phone back into his pocket and returned to the booth. Charlotte sipped a hot tea. Her left hand rested on the tabletop, her diamond ring sparkling despite the dim light. They'd shopped for the ring together, spoiling some of the magic. They had settled on the two-carat diamond that had cost him a single Bitcoin.

"I ordered your stupid burger."

Scot frowned. "Thanks."

She set down her mug, the tea splashing, nearly spilling over the edge. She leaned forward and said in a hushed whisper, "What is your problem?"

Scot flashed his palms. "I'm sorry."

"Can we try to have a good time?"

"Yeah. Of course."

For the rest of the meal, Scot feigned happiness, listening to Charlotte speculate about the future price of Bitcoin, and what *they* might spend *their* growing wealth on. Despite Scot's mask of happiness, he couldn't shake the anxiety deep in the pit of his stomach.

After Scot paid for their expensive meal, Charlotte drove them in her Camaro back toward Lebanon, pop music on the radio.

Scot reached over toward the car radio. "Can I change it?"

"*No.* I like this song," Charlotte replied, turning up the music.

Scot had paid the last three months of her car payment. Neither of them had worked a day since they were fired from Big-Mart, and Scot was the only one with substantial savings.

As they entered the suburbs of Lebanon, Scot pointed to Briarcliff, a new community of McMansions built on half-acre lots. "Can you turn in there?"

"What for?" Charlotte asked, annoyance in her voice. "You told me that they were too expensive."

"Please."

They had been house hunting over the past month, since Charlotte became pregnant, or more accurately since she took that pregnancy test. Charlotte had been pushing to buy a house in

Briarcliff, but Scot thought they were too expensive. Two weeks ago, out of frustration, she had said, "Just do what you want. You don't listen to me anyway."

Scot had relented, calling the real estate agent in secret. His lack of spontaneity was also on Charlotte's list of complaints. He figured he was killing two birds with one stone. He figured he was being a man. Taking charge. That was what she wanted.

Charlotte jerked the wheel, nearly missing the turn. "If I get a nail in my tire, you're paying for it."

As if there was any question. "I know."

Many houses were under construction. Some were empty lots with wooden stakes. Others were wooden skeletons, awaiting their skin. Scot told Charlotte to park in the driveway of a completed stone-faced McMansion with multiple peaks and a three-car garage. The young grass was straw-colored, dormant from the first few frosts.

Charlotte parked the car and beamed at Scot, finally understanding why they were there. "Is this what I think it is?"

Scot smiled and shrugged. "Maybe."

Charlotte exited the car and ran up to the front door, like a child on Christmas. "This is the one I wanted!"

Scot walked after her, impressed at her speed in heels.

The house that Charlotte wanted had been built for another couple, but they had walked away once the house was complete, losing their deposit in the process. The real estate agent had been thrilled with Scot's all-cash offer. Scot had been surprised by the ease and swiftness of the transaction—likely the result of his cold hard cash.

"Why wait?" the real estate agent had said. "It's just sitting there empty."

Charlotte tried to open the door, but it was locked. She bounced, her hands clasped together as if in prayer. "Tell me this is our house."

Scot shrugged again, still smiling. "Might be." He reached into his pocket for his keys. "Let's see if this works." He found the key, turned the dead bolt, and opened the door.

Charlotte stepped into the dark house.

Scot shut the door and flipped on the chandelier in the foyer. He flipped another switch, illuminating the recessed lighting in the living room.

Charlotte gaped at the empty open-plan home. Shiny wood floors covered the first floor. A spiral staircase wound upstairs. A stone fireplace stood on the north wall, dormant.

"We can move in whenever we want," Scot said.

She hugged Scot, squeezing him tight. "Thank you, thank you, thank you."

When they separated, Scot said, "I have another surprise."

He led her upstairs, to the master bedroom. It was the only room that had any furniture—a king-size bed covered in rose petals, along with his and hers dressers.

Charlotte smirked at Scot. "Look at you with the romance."

"I'm not always clueless."

Charlotte wrapped her arms around him and kissed him open-mouthed for a long time. When they came up for air. Charlotte glanced at the bed and said, "You wanna break it in?"

Scot grinned and removed his jacket, dropping it on the carpet.

Charlotte led him by the hand to the bed, then pushed him on his back. She removed her faux fur coat, kicked off her heels, and hopped on the bed, standing over him. He tried to rise, but she said, "Stay right there. I have something for you too."

She swayed to an imaginary beat. She slipped off her cardigan and tossed it on Scot, with a giggle. Then she moved the straps of her blue cocktail dress off her shoulders. Charlotte tugged the top half of her dress slowly down to her hips, revealing her black bra.

The swaying had to stop for a moment to push the dress beyond her curvy hips. She kicked aside her dress, now swaying in her underwear. She turned around, leaning on the bedpost, revealing her thong underwear and her heart-shaped rear end. She bent forward and moved her thong to the side, showing more.

Blood rushed to Scot's penis. He fumbled with the buttons of his shirt, as Charlotte slid her thong down her legs. Still with her back to Scot, she stood upright, and unclasped her bra. Scot took off his pants, his eyes glued on Charlotte. She tossed her bra to the floor and turned to Scot, her long wavy hair covering her breasts. With great aplomb, she flipped her hair behind her shoulders, revealing her D-cup breasts.

Scot gaped at her, just like she'd gaped at his McMansion.

She dropped to her knees and crawled like a cat to Scot. He still wore his boxers, T-shirt, and socks. A few weeks ago, Charlotte had mentioned that he needed to lose a few pounds. He hadn't removed his shirt since, and she hadn't asked him to.

Charlotte rubbed the outline of his penis over his boxer shorts. Then she pulled his penis through the hole in his boxers, exposing his erection. He groaned, as she took him in her mouth.

After a short time, he tugged her head, signaling that he was close, but she kept going, taking him deeper in her mouth, until he did the thing he had been forbidden to do.

Scot basked in the afterglow. Charlotte kissed him on the lips and cuddled next to him. Had he thought about it, he might've shied away from her kiss.

Instead, he thought about why he had been so uptight at dinner. Five days ago, he had sold half of his Bitcoin to close on the house and to set aside some more cash for bills. Prior to the sale, he had been a Bitcoin millionaire, his Coinbase account valued at over 1.3 million dollars. In those five days since, the price of Bitcoin had risen from $11,180 to over $16,000 today. Scot had calculated that, by selling, he had missed $250,000 in gains. As it stood, he was still wealthy beyond his wildest dreams. He still owned sixty Bitcoins, currently valued at $963,000, and he owned his own home, the nicest house he'd ever entered. Scot glanced at her left hand, resting on his chest, the engagement ring sparkling in the light.

He kissed Charlotte on the cheek. *Maybe it was worth it.*

CHAPTER 65

Last Chance to Get Off

Scot moved his clothes from his mother's old suitcase to his new dresser. The master bathroom door opened, and Charlotte padded toward him, her head bowed.

He turned toward her. "What's wrong?"

She looked up with glassy eyes. "I got my period."

He furrowed his brow.

She wiped the corners of her eyes. "I'm not pregnant."

"I thought the test …"

"A few weeks ago I had some bleeding, but it wasn't much. I didn't think …" She chewed on the lower corner of her lip.

Scot embraced her, squeezing her tight.

She cried in his arms for a long time.

He rubbed her back, whispering over and over again, "It's okay. It's okay."

When her crying ended, she sniffled and asked, "Do you still wanna marry me?"

He drew back, looking into her eyes. "Of course I do."

CHAPTER 66

Another Year Later ...

Scot stared at his laptop, his stomach queasy. Bitcoin and consequently his Coinbase account were down again, the numbers all in red. He currently had forty Bitcoins, valued at $3,292.09, for a total of $131,683.60. Over the past year, he had liquidated twenty Bitcoins to cover their bills, as neither Charlotte nor him were working—although Scot claimed to be a professional cryptocurrency trader, which sounded much better than an unemployed loser who got lucky with Bitcoin.

What if it goes to zero? Peter Schiff, a perpetual crypto skeptic and gold bug, had made that very case in a YouTube video Scot had watched that morning. *Fucking boomers. Why would anyone buy gold? It hasn't done shit for nine years.*

Charlotte strutted into his office, standing just inside the doorway, resembling a pirate, with her jeans tucked into her long black boots.

"Would it kill you to put on a pair of jeans and a decent shirt?" Charlotte asked, scowling at the sweatsuit Scot had been wearing for three days. "Danielle and David will be here soon."

They were going Christmas and Hannukah shopping.

Scot looked up from his laptop. "What difference does it make? I'm not going."

"You could go," Charlotte said.

"I have to work." That was a lie. He had planned to do what he did most days. Masturbate to busty women on Pornhub, then play Halo.

Charlotte placed one hand on her hip. "They'll still see you when they come in."

"They don't have to."

"Don't be difficult. David likes you. He'll wanna say hello. You know, he's disappointed that you're not coming."

"Can you go easy on the spending today? Your Discover bill was over five grand last month."

"It was stuff we needed. We're married now. We can't live like we still work at Big-Mart."

Scot huffed. "I can't keep selling Bitcoin to cover our bills."

"How else are we supposed to live? You're not working."

"I'm trading crypto. It's a full-time job."

Charlotte rolled her eyes. "Are you making any money trading?"

Scot opened his mouth to speak, but nothing came out.

"That's what I thought."

The doorbell chimed.

Scot stood from his desk. "I'll run up and change."

Charlotte went to the front door, while Scot ran upstairs, breathing hard from the exertion.

Scot changed, then walked back downstairs, wearing jeans and a fleece. Dr. David Levin and Danielle Levin chatted with Charlotte in the living room. They all turned to Scot, as he descended the spiral staircase. David was a small pasty-white man, with dark curls and delicate hands. Danielle was two inches taller than David, her skinny jeans accentuating her muffin top and flat ass. The late-thirties couple was always a little too thrilled to hang with Scot and Charlotte, like befriending a young couple made them cool. David often used slang incorrectly, and Danielle stuffed herself into the latest fashion trend.

David and Danielle lived two streets over. Charlotte and Danielle had met at the community gym, and they'd hit it off. David and Scot were along for the ride, although David was always keener than Scot.

"There he is," David said, grinning.

Scot stepped to the trio, with a forced smile. "You guys are going

Christmas shopping, *huh*?"

Charlotte frowned at Scot. "Hannukah shopping too."

"I was hoping you'd change your mind and come with us," David said. "I'll have to carry two purses." He chuckled.

Danielle and Charlotte laughed too.

"Sorry. I have to work," Scot replied.

"You're no fun," Danielle chided.

David did an impression. "All work and no play makes Scot a dull boy."

Scot tilted his head, confused.

"That's from *The Shining*. Stephen King."

Scot nodded. "Oh. Right."

Charlotte lifted one shoulder. "Never heard of it."

David touched Charlotte's forearm. "You have to see it. It's so good. Better yet, I'll lend you the book. Read the book first."

Danielle stared at her husband's hand.

David retracted his hand, as if he'd been caught in the cookie jar.

"I guess we should go," Danielle said.

Scot escorted the shopping-trip trio to the door. He shut the door behind them, then watched as they walked toward David's Mercedes, which had a vanity plate that read *ENT DOC*. Both women were in front of David. The good doctor wasn't looking at Danielle's flat ass.

CHAPTER 67

While the Cat's Away

Later that evening Scot paused his game and went to the kitchen. He grabbed a half-eaten bag of sour-cream-and-chive potato chips from the cupboard and returned to his office. The roar of David's AMG Mercedes came from the driveway. Scot split the blinds, confirming his suspicion. He shoved a few fistfuls of chips into his mouth, then stuffed the bag into the bottom drawer of his desk. As he chewed, he saved his game, closed Halo, then navigated to Coinbase.

The front door opened and shut.

Scot wiped his face with his sleeve, erasing the evidence. Charlotte didn't like him eating junk food or playing video games. Scot expected Charlotte to come to his office. Instead, he heard her footsteps climbing the stairs. Scot left his office for the spiral staircase. Charlotte had reached the top and disappeared into their bedroom. She held as many bags as one person could possibly carry.

Scot followed Charlotte to their bedroom, finding her in her walk-in closet, hanging a blouse, the shopping bags at her feet. "You said you weren't going to spend too much."

Startled, Charlotte faced Scot. "Oh my God. You scared me."

"Why did you buy so much? You know Bitcoin's in a bear market."

She glared. "I didn't buy that much. You should've seen how much crap Danielle bought. David didn't even flinch."

Scot frowned at the shopping bags. "Looks like a lot to me."

"It was all on sale."

"I thought you were buying Christmas presents. It looks like this stuff is all for you."

"Yeah. I'm buying *my* Christmas presents. Why are you being so cheap?"

"I'm not being cheap. I'm trying to be smart. What happens if Bitcoin keeps going lower?"

"It won't."

"But what happens if it does?"

Charlotte shrugged. "I don't know. You're the *professional* crypto trader."

Scot held out his hands. "What if I was broke tomorrow? Seriously. What would you do? Would you stay with me?"

She pursed her lips. "Your responsibility as my husband is to support me. If you can't do that …"

"If I can't do that, what?"

She shrugged again. Then she removed a dress from one of the shopping bags, holding it to her body, and placing one foot forward, as if trying it on for size.

CHAPTER 68

Contingency Plans

The next afternoon Scot parked in Heather's driveway. Her mansion was fancier than Scot's, with a brick and stucco facade, several acres of land, and seven thousand square feet of interior space. Scot called it the House That Farts Built. He exited his Hyundai, immediately shivering in the winter wind. The clouds cast everything in a dirty gray.

He peered into the garage window. Only Laura's BMW was inside. It was a 2018 Five Series, a gift from Heather for being such a great manager. Laura had been Heather's manager over the past year. Previously, Heather's platform had grown beyond what she was capable of managing, so Laura had offered to help.

Scot walked to the front door and pressed the doorbell. Thirty seconds later, Johnny Black answered the door. Scot doubted that was his real name. Johnny had sleeve tattoos, piercings, jet-black hair, and a plethora of bracelets. His deep wrinkles and paunch didn't quite fit his rocker image. Laura had met the former-blackjack-dealer-turned-musician six months ago in Vegas, while attending a content creator conference. Scot had always wondered if it was a porn industry conference.

Johnny lifted his chin. "Scot. What's up, man?"

"I need to talk to my mom," Scot replied.

"She's in her office."

Johnny escorted Scot to Laura's first-floor office, as if he owned the place.

Laura sat behind her laptop, typing, her reading glasses on the end of her nose. She wore a low-cut shirt and heavy makeup, conforming to the image of the wannabe rocker girlfriend.

"Babe," Johnny said. "Scot's here."

Laura looked up from her screen and smiled. "Hi, honey. This is a nice surprise."

"I need to talk to you."

"Sure. Of course."

Johnny loitered in the doorway in his ass-tight leather pants.

"Alone," Scot added.

Johnny showed his palms and frowned. "I can take a hint." He walked away.

Scot shut the door and sat across from his mother at her desk. "Where's Heather?"

"Probably with some scumbag." Laura shook her head. "That girl will be the death of me. She's out of control. Out all hours of the night. A different boyfriend every week. Success has gone to her head. It's a struggle just to get her to show up for a photo shoot. To make matters worse, we've had problems with subscribers stealing content and posting it on the internet. Our subscriber base has stopped growing. Why pay when you can get it for free?"

"I'm sorry to hear that. Maybe this isn't the healthiest profession for Heather."

Laura held out her hands. "This was her choice. Not mine. I tried to talk her out of it, but she's an adult. I thought, by being her manager, I could protect her. I'm doing my best, but I'm not sure I'm doing a good job."

"I'm sure you're doing a good job, Mom."

"I don't know." Laura sighed and set her glasses on the desktop. "You didn't come here to listen to my problems. What do you need, honey?"

Scot removed an envelope from his inside jacket pocket and handed it to his mother.

Laura took the envelope. "What's this?"

"A check for $46,000. I made it out to you because I need you to hold it for me."

Laura opened the envelope and stared at the check. "I don't understand."

Scot took a deep breath. "I'm worried about my marriage. Charlotte's spending too much money, and I'm not sure what's going to happen. If it goes bad, I'd like to at least have enough money to finish my degree."

"Oh, honey. I'm so sorry. I didn't know you were having problems with Charlotte."

"To be fair, it's not just her. Bitcoin's in a bear market, and I'm afraid, if I don't set aside this money, I might be tempted to blow it on another cryptocurrency. I need to know that I have another option, if everything goes to shit."

On the way home, he drove by Anna's neighborhood. It wasn't exactly on the way. Her car wasn't in her driveway.

CHAPTER 69

Secrets

After talking to his mother, Scot returned home and entered his house through the garage. Pop music came from the whole-house speaker system. He found Charlotte in the master bathroom, at the double sink, working her curling iron, and singing along with the music. She wore a little black dress that left little to the imagination.

Scot turned down the music at the keypad.

Charlotte made a face in the mirror.

Scot appeared in the mirror next to Charlotte. "You're going out?"

She didn't even glance at Scot in the mirror, nor slow her hairstyling. "So?"

"You've been going out a lot lately."

Charlotte sighed. "We've been through this. You never take me anywhere. What am I supposed to do? Sit at home?"

"Who are you going out with?"

"Danielle, Gretchen, and Leah, not that it's any of *your* business."

"I *am* your husband."

"And I'm your wife, but you have your little secrets."

Scot knitted his brow. "What are you talking about?"

"You *know* what I'm talking about. I can hear you. The vent from your office goes right to our bedroom."

"What the hell are you talking about?"

She set her curling iron on the counter and scowled at Scot. "I can hear you jerking off."

Scot was speechless.

"It's fucking disgusting."

Scot's face felt hot. "I'm not, … uh …"

"Don't even try to lie. I don't care. You do you."

"What am I supposed to do? We haven't had sex in months."

She snatched the curling iron plug from the socket. "Be the man I married, and you might get some." She walked away, her hips swishing back and forth.

CHAPTER 70

Late Night

Scot tossed and turned in bed, thinking about his recent obsession with pornography. It had coincided with Charlotte's lack of interest in sex. What the hell am I supposed to do? I have needs. He wondered if Charlotte told her friends about catching him. Of course she did. He imagined the four women laughing at his expense. It won't end there either. They'll tell their husbands. The whole neighborhood will know. Scot rolled to his back and stared at the white ceiling. What difference does it make? She doesn't want me. Like she said, she doesn't care. Scot grabbed his phone from the bedside, checking the time—3:19 a.m.

"Shit," he said out loud. "Where the hell is she?"

As if on cue, the roar of a motor came from his driveway. A car door opened and shut. Scot lay in the dark, listening to Charlotte carefully open and close the front door, then tiptoe up the stairs and enter their bedroom. She snuck past their bed, headed for the bathroom.

If he hadn't been awake, he wouldn't have heard her, and he wouldn't have smelled the trail of alcohol and men's cologne.

CHAPTER 71

Halo

The next afternoon Scot immersed himself in Halo, sustaining himself with soda and junk food. With his headphones on, he didn't hear Charlotte knock on his office door. He didn't notice her either, not until she was only a few feet from his desk. Scot was startled, then clicked and tapped frantically, downsizing Halo, then upsizing his crypto-trading platform.

Charlotte smirked, still wearing her pajamas, her hair disheveled. "What are you doing?"

"Working," Scot replied.

"Yeah, right."

Scot frowned. "I'm not jerking off, if that's what you think."

"I know what you're doing. You're playing video games."

He turned his laptop screen to Charlotte. "I'm working."

She glanced at the screen and rolled her eyes. "I can see the Halo tab."

"I just play when I'm taking a break."

"You must take a lot of breaks. You click a lot when you're playing video games. I can hear it upstairs through the vent. It wakes me up."

Scot glanced at the clock on his laptop. "It's after one. Maybe it's time to get up."

Charlotte pressed her lips together.

"How was your night last night? You got in late."

"It was fine."

"You going out again tonight?"

Charlotte lifted one shoulder. "Maybe. It is Friday."

CHAPTER 72

On the Prowl

As soon as Charlotte left the house, Scot ran to the garage, entering from inside the house. He rushed to the garage window, catching a glimpse of Danielle's Mercedes as they drove away. Scot hopped into his Hyundai and raced after them.

Earlier Scot had asked, "Where are you guys going?"

While doing her makeup, Charlotte had replied. "I don't know yet."

Under the cover of darkness, Scot followed Danielle's Mercedes into Harrisburg, doing his best to allow one car between them most of the time. They parked in a large parking lot near a club called XL Live Harrisburg. Scot parked a few rows away, hidden by other cars. He lost them behind several groups of people headed for the club.

The west wall of the club featured a massive mural of Jimi Hendrix playing the guitar, surrounded by blotches of neon green, giving the painting a trippy feel. Scot waited in a long line, condensation spilling from his mouth and funky music coming from the club entrance. Groups of scantily clad women shivered in the cold night. He felt self-conscious as the only single attendee, surrounded by groups of women and groups of men. He scanned the line for Charlotte and her friends, but he didn't see them. Most of the people were likely in their twenties, but there were some older people too—forty-something men with paunches and a little gray, and forty-something women with heavy makeup and puffy faces.

When he made it to the door, the beefy bald-headed bouncer said, "Your ticket."

"Can I buy one from you or the ticket window?" Scot asked.

People in the crowd snickered.

Someone said, "Fuckin' dumbass."

The bouncer scowled. "Box office is closed. Move aside."

Scot stepped out of line, processing the situation. *If tickets are required ahead of time, Charlotte was lying about not knowing where they were going. Why lie? I need to get into this club.*

Scot walked alongside the line and asked, "Anyone have a ticket to sell? Does anyone have a ticket to sell?"

Near the end of the line, a greasy man wearing a black leather jacket said, "How much you willin' to pay?"

Scot faced the man. "A hundred bucks."

The greasy man chuckled. "Five hundred."

Scot twisted his face in disgust. "That's crazy. Two hundred."

"Three hundred."

Scot let out a heavy breath. "Fine." He paid the man with nearly all his cash, then took his place at the back of the line.

Twenty minutes later, he entered the club. Inside, Bad Fish covered the nineties alt-rock band Sublime. A throng of people danced by the stage, the crowd extending almost to the bar at the opposite end of the rectangular building. A mezzanine level ran along the left side, also packed to the gills. The club had a warehouse feel, with black furniture and shiny metal accents.

Scot stood near the bar, checking the crowd for signs of Charlotte, Danielle, Leah, or Gretchen. Nothing. The music and ambient chatter was loud enough that the bartender leaned toward his patrons to hear their drink orders. Scot left the bar area, headed for the metal steps to the mezzanine level. He thought he might find them from above, but, if they were on the mezzanine level, it was likely they'd see him. It was a risk he was willing to take.

Scot climbed the metal steps, slipping past a line of people on their way down. He found an open spot along the railing. From his vantage point, he scanned the crowd, searching in a grid pattern. He found Danielle kissing a red-faced chubby Paul Bunyan look-alike. The man was the complete opposite of her husband, David. Gretchen and Leah stood nearby, flirting with a group of forty-something men, with lots of leaning in, incidental touching, and flipping of their hair.

Scot continued to scan the crowd from the mezzanine, but he didn't find Charlotte. *Maybe she went off with some guy her own age.* Scot descended the stairs from the mezzanine. Foot traffic brushed against him, coming and going. He moved toward the wall, underneath the mezzanine, just to get out of the way. Then he saw Charlotte leaning against one of the mezzanine posts, smiling, a handsome twenty-something leaning perilously close.

Scot moved behind a group of women, worried that Charlotte might spot him. He lost sight of her, as the women blocked his view. He moved away from the women, craning his neck for a better view, locating Charlotte and her handsome friend again. Now they were kissing open-mouthed.

A muscly guy shoulder-checked Scot and said, "Watch where you're goin'."

Scot dipped his head. "Sorry."

When he looked up again, Charlotte and her man were gone. Scot left the club in a daze, shocked but not shocked at the same time. He sat in his car, with the engine running, his eyes glassy. *She doesn't give a shit about me. I don't think she ever did. Why would she?*

Scot had moved his car for a better view of the parking lot exit. He waited for an hour, curious as to whether Charlotte would go home in Danielle's Mercedes or with her handsome suitor. Danielle, Leah, and Gretchen walked from the club to the parking lot, escorted by the same group of forty-something men they'd been flirting with in the club.

At Danielle's Mercedes, each of the married women kissed a man who wasn't her husband. They bantered, exchanged cell phones and presumably phone numbers, then they left. Shortly thereafter, Charlotte exited the club, holding hands with her handsome suitor. He was tall, rugged, and well-built, a man's man—the opposite of Scot.

Her rugged suitor led her to a white pickup truck. Scot followed them away from Harrisburg, through Hershey, Palmyra, and Cleona, finally reaching a run-down townhome community in the suburbs of Lebanon. Scot parked on the corner, gripping his steering wheel, watching the man lead Charlotte inside the townhome.

Scot had seen enough. He turned his car around and gunned the engine. He drove home wildly, far exceeding the speed limit, pushing his little Hyundai to the limits of its engine and suspension. He unbuckled his seat belt and thought about yanking the wheel and hitting a tree head-on.

But he didn't have the courage.

CHAPTER 73

The Beginning of the End

Scot didn't know exactly what time Charlotte had come home. It had to be after 4:00 a.m. He had had trouble sleeping, his body coursing with adrenaline, but he had finally fallen asleep around four. When he woke up in the late morning, she wasn't in bed with him. He found her snoring in a guest bedroom. He had spent the morning distracting himself with Halo, but even immersive video games didn't stop his mind from wandering and replaying the events from the night before.

At lunchtime, Scot sat in the breakfast nook of his kitchen, eating sugary cereal. Faint footsteps came from the spiral staircase, then across the hardwood. Charlotte appeared in the kitchen, bleary-eyed and disheveled. She went straight to the Keurig coffeemaker, loading a K-Cup of vanilla coffee, and starting the machine.

When she turned from the counter, Scot said, "Long night again."

"So?"

Scot stood from the breakfast nook and marched to his wife. "Who was the guy you fucked?"

Charlotte twisted her face in anger. "Who the hell do you think you are, talking to me like that?"

"Answer the *fucking* question."

"Fuck you." Charlotte marched from the kitchen.

Scot followed her to the living room.

She plopped on the couch.

"The fact that you won't answer the question tells me a lot," Scot said.

Charlotte flipped on the television.

"I know what you did."

Charlotte turned up the volume as high as possible, then set the remote on the armrest.

Scot reached to grab the remote, but Charlotte snatched it first, holding it tight to her body. Scot walked over to the television and ripped the plug from the wall, silencing the reality TV show. He pivoted to Charlotte and said, "I know what you did last night."

Charlotte sneered. "You don't know shit."

Scot stood in front of Charlotte, his arms crossed over his chest. "Really? I saw you making out with some douche at XL Live in Harrisburg. I saw you go home with him in his white pickup."

Charlotte was slack-jawed, her eyes wide.

"I never should've married you."

Charlotte huffed and stood from the couch. "It's the other way around. I never should've married *you*." She gestured to Scot's ratty sweats and chubby body. "Look at you. You're disgusting. If it wasn't for Bitcoin …"

"If it wasn't for Bitcoin, what?"

Charlotte rolled her eyes.

"You never would've married me, right?"

"I can't deal with you anymore. You're fucking pathetic." She left the living room, headed for the spiral staircase.

Scot followed her upstairs. "I might be pathetic, but at least I'm not a gold-digging bitch."

On the upstairs landing, she turned and slapped Scot across the face.

Scot drew back, his hand on his face.

"You're a fucking loser." Charlotte went to the guest bedroom.

He followed her inside the room.

She grabbed her handbag from under the bed. Charlotte opened the handbag and retrieved a stack of papers, with a few little yellow tabs sticking out from the sides. She faced Scot and said, "I was planning to wait until after Christmas, but I can't do this anymore." She thrust the papers at him.

Scot took the papers. "What the hell is this?"

"I want a divorce. Sign at the yellow tabs."

Scot flipped through the papers, searching for anything pertaining to the division of assets. Charlotte was asking for the house, her car, $5000 per month in alimony for ten years, half of their bank account, and half of his Bitcoins.

Scot threw the papers across the room, the stack hitting the wall. "I'm not fucking signing this. You had an affair. The court won't take your side."

She put her hands on her hips. "Can you prove it?"

He opened his mouth to speak, but nothing came out.

"That's what I thought."

CHAPTER 74

Les

On Monday afternoon, Scot sat across from Les Herman, a weaselly divorce attorney with a combover.

"I doubt she'll get alimony," Les said. "You haven't been married long enough. A judge will likely split all your assets down the middle."

"Even stuff I had before we got married?" Scot asked.

"Depends on the judge, but that's probable. If you want, I can draw up a counter to their proposal."

CHAPTER 75

Christmas Eve

For the next six days, Scot and Charlotte avoided each other, with Charlotte gone most of the time. Scot had seen Charlotte's Camaro parked at Danielle and David's for much of that time. Until Christmas Eve.

Charlotte appeared in Scot's office. She stepped to his desk and placed her hands on her hips.

Scot paused his game.

She said, "I need you to *not* be here tonight."

Scot stood from his desk. "Where the hell am I supposed to go?"

"I don't care. I've given you the space to be here for the past week. The least you can do is give me tonight."

"It's Christmas Eve."

"No shit. We invited my mother and *my* friends for dinner. Remember?"

Scot vaguely remembered having a conversation about a Christmas Eve get-together. "I'm not leaving. They're my friends too."

Charlotte shook her head. "Not anymore. Nobody wants you here."

Scot crossed his arms over his chest. "I didn't do anything. You're the one who's having an affair."

"You're delusional, and nobody likes you. Nobody wants you here."

"Fine. I'll stay upstairs."

"No. It'll be awkward, and, if my mom finds out you're here, you'll regret it."

Scot held out his hands, his voice whiney. "I don't have anywhere to go."

"Go see your mother."

"She's in Vegas with Johnny."

"Not my problem."

CHAPTER 76

What Could've Been

Scot drove around the suburbs of Lebanon, looking at Christmas lights, and imagining himself at a Christmas party. He steered his Hyundai into Anna's neighborhood, as if his hands were controlled by someone else. Anna's trailer was dark, no cars in the driveway.

Scot drove to Henry's house a few miles away. He parked across the street. The lights were on. A Christmas tree stood in the bay window. Anna's Honda was parked in the driveway. Scot imagined how his life would've been different, if he hadn't fucked it all up. He would be with Anna and Henry right now. Henry probably made eggnog and Christmas cookies. He probably had some gift for Anna that suited her perfectly.

Since their breakup, Henry had tried to stay in touch with Scot but had ultimately given up with Scot's lack of reciprocation.

Scot called his mother, but she didn't pick up. He didn't leave a message. He called Heather, but she didn't pick up either, which wasn't surprising. She was much more likely to respond to a text message. Laura had said that Heather was spending Christmas with some new boyfriend.

He called his older sister, Marie. She was in New York with Frank's family.

She answered on the fourth ring. "Scot?"

"Merry Christmas, Marie," Scot said, his voice strained.

"Thanks. Merry Christmas to you too."

A few seconds of awkward silence passed.

"Are you okay?" Marie asked.

"I'm fine," he replied.

"You don't sound fine."

Scot forced an upbeat tone. "No. I'm great. I won't keep you. I just wanted to wish you a Merry Christmas."

"Thanks. What are you and Charlotte doing for Christmas?"

Scot hadn't told anyone about the impending divorce. "We're having her mother and some friends over for Christmas Eve dinner."

"That's great. Sounds fun."

In the background, Frank asked, "Who are you talking to?"

"Hold on a second." Marie covered the receiver, but Scot still heard their muffled voices. "Scot," she said to Frank.

"We're having dessert."

"I'll be there in a minute."

"*Now*," Frank said.

Marie came back on the line. "We're having dessert. I should go. Call me when you get a chance though. I feel like we haven't talked in so long."

"Yeah, okay," Scot replied.

"I gotta go. Tell Charlotte I said Merry Christmas."

"Okay. I love you, Marie."

But she had already disconnected the call.

Scot sniffed and cleared his throat. Then he called his stepfather. He hadn't spoken to Eric since his wedding to Janine. There wasn't animosity between them. They were simply living separate lives.

Eric answered. "Hey, Scot."

A cacophony of jubilant voices and Christmas music played in the background.

"Hey, Dad. Merry Christmas," Scot said.

"Thanks. Merry Christmas to you too," Eric replied.

"Sounds like you're at a party."

"Oh, it's just Janine's parents and her sister and her husband."

"How's the baby?"

Eric had married his girlfriend, Janine, one month before Scot had married Charlotte. They already had a two-month-old baby boy. Scot couldn't remember the child's name.

"Lucas is doing great. Thanks for asking," Eric replied. "How's Charlotte doing?"

"Uh, … she's great. We're having some friends over tonight for Christmas Eve."

"That's wonderful. That's what Christmas is all about. Family and friends."

"Yeah. Well, I should let you go."

"It was good to hear from you," Eric said.

"Yeah. See ya, Dad." Scot disconnected the call.

Scot rested his head on the steering wheel. His throat tightened, and tears welled in his eyes. A door shutting caused Scot to lift his head. Anna stood on Henry's porch, looking in Scot's direction. He put his car into Drive and sped away.

He went to the one place he knew he could park in peace. He parked a few spaces away from a camper in the back of the parking lot, near the free-standing Big-Mart sign. He peered up at the sign, reading the slogan, *Big savings. Big selection. Big smiles.*

Scot crawled into his back seat. He lay on his side, pulled his knees to his chest, and wrapped his jacket around him like a blanket.

He cried himself to sleep.

CHAPTER 77

The End of the End

Scot skimmed the divorce settlement. It was exactly as they had agreed. Charlotte got the house and household items but no alimony. They split their meager bank account, and all outstanding bills. Scot kept his remaining Bitcoin, his car, and personal items.

Over the past four months, Charlotte had run up their credit cards, adding to her wardrobe and jewelry box, in addition to antique furniture for *her* house. After paying the credit cards and his divorce attorney, Scot only had thirteen Bitcoin left, currently valued at $5,454.45 each. His divorce attorney, Les Herman, wanted to fight for the house, but Scot wanted it to be over, knowing Charlotte would fight until the bitter end, bankrupting him just for spite. Besides, he'd already disobeyed Les and had diminished his claim to the house by moving into an apartment.

Scot glanced at Charlotte, sitting across the shiny mahogany table. She sat ramrod straight, mean-mugging Scot. He signed his name to two copies of the divorce settlement and scribbled the date, 4-24-2019. He slid the documents to Les, sitting next to him. Les glanced at the signature page, then handed one copy across the table to Charlotte's divorce attorney.

Charlotte's divorce attorney, an impeccable woman dressed to the nines, scanned the signature page, then whispered to Charlotte. They stood in tandem.

Les groaned as he stood. Scot stood too.

"I guess that's it," Les said, holding his hand out to Charlotte's attorney.

The attorneys shook hands.

Scot shoved his hands into the front pocket of the hoodie he'd been wearing for the past four days.

Charlotte looked at Scot as if he were a cockroach perched on her filet mignon. "I can't believe I married you. Biggest mistake of my life."

Scot stared back at her, playing his part as the cockroach. "There never was a baby, was there?"

She lifted one shoulder. "You'll never know." Then she pivoted and left the room, her attorney following in her wake.

"That went well," Les said, his tone upbeat.

Scot frowned. "Yeah."

Scot left the attorney's office. House sparrows chirped overhead. Scot squinted into the bright blue sky. Not a cloud in sight. He walked along the Lebanon city rowhouses, headed for his car. Many of the brick-and-stone rowhouses had been converted to offices for lawyers, architects, dentists, doctors, and various consultants.

Along the way to Scot's car, Dr. David Levin's AMG Mercedes drove past, recognizable by the *ENT DOC* vanity plate. Scot caught a glimpse of a long-haired passenger. The Mercedes stopped at a nearby red light. Scot ran toward the car, on the sidewalk, trying to get a view of the passenger.

Just before the light went green, Charlotte turned her head, glaring at Scot. Then she was gone.

CHAPTER 78

A Screaming Buy

Scot sat on his single mattress, his back against the wall, watching a video on his phone. The tiny room was nearly empty, except for his mattress, an old suitcase filled with his clothes, and a wooden desk with an inkjet printer. The walls were bare except for his dartboard.

On his phone, Carlton Thatcher, with his slicked-back hair said, "Aeron uses blockchain technology to track pilot logs and aircraft maintenance. It's currently building a decentralized database, hosting data on pilots, aircraft, and flight schools, which will make aviation safer for everyone. Aeron isn't simply a cryptocurrency. It's a blockchain solution for aviation record keeping. This crypto could easily break triple digits by the end of this year. At thirty-nine cents, it's a screaming buy."

The video ended. Scot navigated to Instagram and tapped his way to Anna's page. Still the same two images. One with her roommate, Felicity, and another with her cat, Patches. Anna hadn't posted in two years, and her Facebook page had been deleted. Scot wished he still had pictures of her on his phone. A few months after he'd gotten back together with Charlotte, she'd found the images of Anna on his phone and had deleted them.

He thought about what Charlotte had said to him earlier. *I can't believe I married you. Biggest mistake of my life.* Scot stared at Anna on his phone, smiling, and holding Patches like a baby. The caption read *My Baby!* The image was unfiltered, her face free from makeup, and her hair in a ponytail. He placed his index finger near her face but not touching the screen, imagining her soft skin. *I agree. Biggest mistake of my life too.*

CHAPTER 79

Speculation

"*Shit.*" Scot scowled at his laptop, sitting on the old couch that Marie had given him when he'd moved into his one-bedroom apartment. "I should've sold yesterday."

Bitcoin had dropped nearly three hundred dollars. He pecked and clicked on his laptop, checking Aeron crypto, ticker symbol ARNX. The price held steady at thirty-nine cents. He thought about what the analyst had said. *This crypto could easily break triple digits by the end of this year. At thirty-nine cents, it's a screaming buy.*

Scot took a deep breath, then signed into his Coinbase account. He sold his remaining Bitcoin for $5,160.54 each, for a total of $67,087.02. Then he purchased 40,000 ARNX coins at thirty-nine cents each.

Not wanting his buying to boost the price of the thinly traded crypto, he made several buys over the course of the week, ultimately purchasing a total of 159,500 ARNX coins, with an average buy price of forty-two cents each.

If Aeron can just get to ten bucks, I'll be a millionaire again.

CHAPTER 80

Okay, Boomer

One month later Scot sat at his kitchen table, playing Halo on his laptop. Three empty soda cans and two candy bar wrappers littered the table. His kitchen table had lived a former life as a card table. He'd snatched it out of the apartment Dumpster two weeks ago. It was the last time he'd left his apartment.

His cell phone chimed on the tabletop. Scot paused his game and answered the call. "Hey, Marie."

"Hey, little brother," Marie replied. "I was just calling to check on you. I haven't heard from you in a while. How are you?"

"I'm great."

Marie hesitated. "Really?"

"Yeah, why wouldn't I be?"

"With the divorce and all …"

Scot leaned back in his plastic chair. "It was the best thing for me."

"I'm glad you have a good outlook. Have you found a job yet?"

Scot spoke, excitement in his voice. "Don't need it. I bought into Aeron, which is a blockchain database for the aeronautical industry. I've already made twenty-three grand this month. Can you believe it?"

Marie hesitated again. "That's great. Just be careful, okay? Frank says that cryptocurrencies are a big Ponzi scheme."

Scot chuckled. "Boomers don't understand crypto. And Aeron isn't exactly a cryptocurrency. It's a blockchain solution with real-world applications."

CHAPTER 81

The Day After Christmas

Scot threw his phone at the wall in his bedroom, nearly striking the bull's-eye on his dartboard. "Fuck!"

Over the past seven months Aeron had ground lower, reaching just thirteen cents that afternoon. His Coinbase account had dwindled to $15,600.

He paced in his bedroom, talking to himself, the floor littered with dirty clothes. "This is why they say, *Hold on for dear life*. It's just a cycle. It'll come back. You need to relax. It'll be fine. Just stay the course."

His cell phone chimed. He walked over to the dartboard and picked up his phone, which was still intact, partly because of his weak throwing arm and partly because of the protective case. It was his mother. He sent the call to voice mail. He slipped his phone into the front pocket of his hoodie and went back to pacing.

"I never should've sold Bitcoin. It's outperformed Aeron. I'm such a fucking dumbass. I can't go back now, not with Aeron at fire-sale prices. If I liked it at forty-two cents, I should love it at thirteen cents. Nothing's changed except for the price."

His cell phone chimed again. Marie, for the third time that day. He sent her call to voice mail too. Laura had been in Las Vegas over Christmas with her boyfriend, Johnny, but Marie had invited Scot over to her house for Christmas dinner. Scot had lied, telling her that he was going to Cancun over Christmas with a girl he'd met and wouldn't be back until the twenty-sixth. The last thing Scot wanted to hear was an I-told-you-so from Frank about the cryptocurrency crash.

What a ridiculous lie though. Scot wouldn't be caught dead at a beach with his pasty-white gut for all to see. Scot hadn't been on a scale, but he figured he was about forty pounds overweight. Marie had been happy about his new "girlfriend," wanting to know everything about the girl. Scot had been vague, telling his sister that it wasn't serious.

His cell phone buzzed with a text.

> **Marie:** Why aren't you answering my calls? I'm worried. You said you'd be back from Cancun today. For all I know, you were kidnapped by a drug cartel. If I don't hear from you in five minutes, I'm coming over.

Scot blew out a breath and called Marie. When she picked up, he said, "I'm fine. I was sleeping. I'm a little jetlagged."

"Sorry to bother you. I was worried," Marie said.

"Don't worry. I'm doing great."

"Are you sure?"

"Of course."

"How's Anita?"

Anita was the name he'd given Marie for his fake girlfriend. He'd almost said, Anna, changing course midsentence, ending up with Anita.

"I don't think it's going to work out," Scot said.

"I'm so sorry to hear that. Are you okay?" Marie asked.

"I'm fine. It wasn't serious. It's not a big deal."

Marie hesitated for a beat. "Okay. I'd like to see you soon. We haven't gotten together in forever."

"Yeah. Sorry. I've been busy trading. It's been crazy. Good crazy, but crazy."

"Okay. Well, give me a call when you have time."

"I will." Scot disconnected the call.

He went to the kitchen and opened the refrigerator. It was mostly empty, except for half-a-loaf of bread, ketchup, and a twelve-pack of soda. He grabbed a soda and sat down to his laptop at the kitchen table. An open bag of chips was on the table. He shoveled handfuls of sour-cream-and-chive potato chips into his mouth and washed them down with soda.

Scot burped, wiped his greasy hands on his sweatpants, then put on his headphones and immersed himself in the world of Halo.

CHAPTER 82

Rock Bottom

Scot sat at his desk in his bedroom, staring at his laptop screen, both of his hands pulling at his greasy hair. "Fucking Covid."

Over the past eleven weeks, Covid-19 had run roughshod over Wuhan, then China, then the global economy and the crypto market. Aeron was now trading at seven cents. His Coinbase account was down to $7,250. He only held 100,000 Aeron coins because he had had to sell some to pay for rent and food.

Scot clicked over to YouTube, scanning the crypto channels. He played Carlton Thatcher's latest from the Crypto Speculator.

"This is how fortunes are made," Carlton said, resembling a Wall Street trader, with his suit and slicked-back hair.

Scot wondered if he was wearing pants, given that he was only visible from his chest up.

"You have to buy when there's blood in the water, but you also have to know when to cut your losses," Carlton said. "Aeron, ticker symbol ARNX, is one of those cryptos where it's time to cut your losses."

Scot gritted his teeth. "God damn it!"

Carlton continued. "At the same time, I love Litecoin and Bitcoin Cash. I'd double down on both of those."

Scot stopped the video and hung his head. *What the hell am I supposed to do?* A few minutes later, Scot raised his gaze and said, "Fuck it. I'm out." He opened his Coinbase account and sold all

100,000 of his Aeron coins. Then he setup a wire for $6,000 to add that much-needed cash to his bank account.

He still had $1,200 in his Coinbase account. He thrummed his fingers on his desk, thinking about what to do. The idea made him smile for the first time in weeks. He clicked his way to a Coinbase list of all the cryptocurrencies that traded on their exchange. He made the font on the list as small as possible, then printed the top five pages.

He snatched the pages from the printer and walked over to his dartboard, tacking the pages up with several darts. Then he took several steps away from the dartboard and turned to face it again. He closed his eyes and threw a single dart in the general direction of the dartboard. When he opened his eyes, the dart stuck into the lower corner of the dartboard, hitting one of the crypto lists. Scot walked to the dartboard and cackled to himself.

"I can't get away from this douche." The dart had punctured the L in Litecoin. Scot went to his computer and used roughly $400 to purchase eleven Litecoins. He was still pissed at Carlton Thatcher for his pump and dump of Aeron, but Scot did like Litecoin. It was almost identical to Bitcoin in architecture but with much faster transaction speeds.

Then he threw another blind dart. The second dart hit Ethereum. Another crypto Scot liked but had never owned. Ether could be used to settle contracts. *Could be a good one.* Scot went back to his laptop and spent $375 to purchase three Ether.

He threw his final dart, opened his eyes, and walked to his dartboard. He laughed so hard that he doubled over and fell to the floor. When his laughing fit subsided, he went to his computer and purchased the cryptocurrency that was started as a joke—Dogecoin. It was trading at .0017, a fraction of a cent, so he purchased 235,294 Dogecoins for $400.

A knock from his front door startled him. He padded to the living room in his sweats and stocking feet, but he stayed back from the door, not wanting to see anyone. His living room was littered with junk-food wrappers, pizza boxes, and soda cans.

Another knock came at the door. "Scot. It's me," Marie said.

Scot stood like a statue, hoping his sister would leave. Scot had been avoiding everyone for months, but she'd been the most persistent with her calls and texts.

Marie knocked again. "Scot. Open up. I know you're in there. Your car's in the parking lot."

Scot still stood silent. It was quiet for several seconds. Scot breathed a sigh of relief. Then his phone chimed.

Marie banged harder. "Open up, Scot! If you don't open this door, I'm calling the police. I just need to know you're okay."

Scot slumped his shoulders, silenced his phone, and padded to the front door. He spoke through the door. "I'm fine, Marie. Just go home."

"No. I'm not going anywhere until I see you. I haven't heard from you in months. Something's wrong. I know it."

"You're hearing from me now. I'm fine. Go home."

"Absolutely not. Open the door, or I'm calling the cops. I'll tell them you're suicidal."

"Fine." Scot opened the door but blocked the doorway.

Marie winced at the sight of him. Then she shook her head. "Oh, Scot. What have you done to yourself?"

"I'm fine. You can go home now." Scot tried to shut the door, but Marie wedged her boot into the doorway, then forced her way inside.

Marie followed Scot to the couch. He flopped onto it. Marie surveyed the dark and dingy apartment, her face twisted in horror. She stood in front of Scot. "What is going on here?"

Scot shrugged, not looking at his sister.

She sat next to him. "Talk to me. Please."

He hung his head and swallowed the lump in his throat. "I lost everything."

"What do you mean, you lost everything? Are you talking about that cryptocurrency?"

"I'm talking about everything." Tears welled in his eyes. "I'm a broke loser, and nobody will ever love me." Tears slipped down his face.

Marie put her arm around him. "That's not true."

"It is." Scot leaned on his sister's shoulder and sobbed.

Marie wrapped her arms around him, rocking him, and rubbing his back. "It's okay. It'll be okay. I'm here."

She held him until he was out of tears.

Scot finally sniffled and sat upright.

Marie let go of her brother.

"I don't know what to do," he said.

"One thing at a time. Let's get you cleaned up first." Marie escorted him to the bathroom. She glanced at the wrinkly towel on the floor. "Is that towel clean?"

"Kind of," Scot replied.

"Get cleaned up, and I'll see if I can find you some clean clothes."

Scot nodded. "Thanks, Marie."

"You're welcome." She smiled. "You know you're wrong though."

"About what."

"Nobody ever loving you. I love you, and I always will. Don't forget that."

Scot nodded again. "I love you too." It was then, in the bright fluorescent light of the bathroom, that he noticed the heavy makeup around her left eye.

She smiled again. "Get your dirty butt clean." Then she shut the door, leaving him in the bathroom alone.

CHAPTER 83

What's Past is Prologue

The next day Scot sat at his desk, scrolling through job openings at Indeed.com. His room smelled like lemon from the cleaning products Marie had purchased. He wore a clean pair of sweatpants and a fleece. With Covid-19, there weren't many job openings and none outside of retail that he was qualified for.

He closed Indeed.com on his laptop, picked up his phone, and opened Instagram. He went to Anna's page. Still the same two pictures. He stared at the one with her and Patches. He fantasized about running into her and rekindling their relationship. *Is that crazy? It's been a long time. Maybe she's forgiven me. Maybe we can start over. But I can't just show up at Big-Mart, assuming she still works there, or at her house. She might slap me again. She might have a boyfriend. He might smack me. I need to find out if I even have a chance.* Scot thought for a moment, then said it aloud, "Henry."

Scot grabbed his phone but then hesitated. *How long has it been?* The last time they'd talked was the day he was fired from Big-Mart and Anna broke up with him. *That was two-and-a-half years ago. And then I call him out of the blue because I want info on Anna? I'm a fucking asshole.* Scot then used his power of rationalization to overcome his conscience. *What would Henry want? He wanted me to call him before. I'm sure he'd want to talk to me now. Obviously, I owe him an apology, but I'm sure he'll want to talk to me.*

Scot tapped Henry's contact.

"Hello?" Henry answered.

"Henry, this is—"

"Scot. It's so good to hear from you." Henry sounded excited.

Scot cleared his throat. "I'm sorry that it's been so long. The past few years haven't gone that well for me."

"Shakespeare wrote, 'What's past is prologue. What to come, in yours and my discharge.'"

"I'm not sure I understand."

"The past has merely set the stage for the next act. What you choose next is up to you."

Scot thought about Henry's statement. Instead of asking about Anna, Scot asked, "How are you doing?"

"I'm doing okay. Thank you for asking. It would be nice to get together and catch up. I actually have something I need to talk to you about in person."

"Sure, yeah. When?"

"Are you free tonight?"

"Yeah. In case you're worried about Covid, the only person I've been around is my sister."

"I'm not worried."

★★★

Henry opened the door, with a huge grin. "It's great to see you, Scot. Come in."

Scot smiled and stepped inside. "It's great to see you too. Thanks for having me over."

"You're welcome anytime."

They walked through the dim living room. It was still a 1970s' time capsule. They entered the kitchen. The smell of cooking hamburger and French fries made Scot's stomach rumble. The kitchen table was set for one. A small salad sat on the tabletop.

Henry opened the oven. "Fries are ready."

The burger warmed on the covered skillet, the burner on low.

"Smells great," Scot said, taking off his jacket. "You need any help?"

Henry waved him off. "I got it. You sit."

Scot sat at the table, feeling self-conscious about his gut when sitting, not that Henry was one to judge.

Henry filled Scot's plate with a burger and fries. "I'm sorry. I had to cook the burger on the stovetop. My grill rusted out."

"It's okay. Looks great."

"Let me get you some ketchup."

On the way to the fridge, Henry gripped the edge of the table, nearly toppling.

Scot rose to his feet. "Are you okay?"

Henry slumped in the seat opposite Scot, out of breath. When his breath regulated, Henry said, "I'm fine. Sorry. I get tired so easily these days."

"You sure you're okay?"

"I'm fine."

"I'll get the ketchup," Scot offered.

"Thank you."

Scot went to the fridge, grabbed the ketchup, then returned to his food. He stared at Henry, with his hunched shoulders and pale face in the fluorescent light.

"Eat your food. It's getting cold," Henry said.

"You're not eating?" Scot asked.

"I'm not hungry."

Scot raised his eyebrows.

Henry frowned. "I'm fine. Eat your food."

Halfway through his meal, Scot wiped his mouth and asked, "Are you still working at Big-Mart?"

"No. I had to quit last year," Henry replied. "My legs hurt too much to stand all those hours. I suppose it's for the best, although I do miss seeing people."

"Do you see Anna at all?" Scot shoved two fries into his mouth, hoping his eating showed nonchalance.

"At least once a week. Sometimes twice, depending on her schedule."

Scot swallowed, his stomach fluttering. "How's she doing? Is she still working at Big-Mart?"

"She's doing fine. She's at Target now."

Scot nodded. "Is she still saving for vet school?"

Henry let out a ragged breath. "She doesn't talk about it anymore, if that tells you anything. It's a struggle for her to make ends meet."

Scot nodded again. He took a bite of his burger, chewed, and swallowed. He didn't look at Henry when he asked, "Does she have a boyfriend?"

"I don't think so."

Scot suppressed a smile. "I really miss her. Do you think there's any chance for me to, uh, … get her back?"

Henry shook his head. "I'm sorry, Scot. I think that ship has sailed."

Scot slumped, like a deflating balloon. "I'll do anything."

"You broke her heart."

"I know. I screwed it all up. How do I make it right?"

Henry leaned forward, resting his elbows on the table. "I don't know that you can make it right with Anna. It depends."

"Depends on what?"

"Anna loved you because you were kind and hardworking and honest. Is that who you are now?"

Tears welled in Scot's eyes. "No. I'm lazy, selfish, and a liar."

Henry reached across the table and covered Scot's hand with his own. "That was honest. You have so much goodness inside you. I've seen it." He paused, out of breath. "Maharishi Mahesh Yogi once said, 'The important thing is this—to be able, at any moment, to sacrifice what we are for what we could become.'" Henry retracted his hand.

Scot discreetly wiped the corners of his eyes, not wanting to cry in front of Henry.

Henry coughed and wheezed.

"You okay?" Scot asked again.

"Don't worry about me. It's just a cough. It's not Covid either."

"That's a relief." Scot took a deep breath. "I'm sorry about bringing up all this Anna stuff. I don't want you to think I came here just for that."

"I understand."

"You said on the phone that there was something you needed to tell me."

Henry clutched his chest, wheezing again, but louder.

"Henry?"

Henry toppled to his side, falling from his chair to the linoleum floor.

Scot rushed to his side, kneeling. "Henry! Oh my God."

Henry said one barely audible word, "Help."

"I'm calling an ambulance." Scot fished his cell phone from his pocket. His hands trembled as he dialed 9-1-1.

"Nine-one-one, what is your emergency?" the operator asked.

"I think my friend's having a heart attack. He needs an ambulance."

Scot gave the operator Henry's name and address.

Henry's hand rested on his chest, no longer clutching. His wheezing slowed.

"Is Henry still breathing?" the operator asked.

"Yes, but I think barely. Please hurry," Scot replied.

"They're on their way."

Scot held Henry's hand, still holding the phone to his ear with his other hand. The old refrigerator rattled in the background.

CHAPTER 84

In Case of Emergency

Scot paced in the waiting room at the hospital. A handful of people sat in chairs near the television. Two of them wore surgical masks.

Anna appeared in the waiting room, wearing her uniform from Target—khakis and a red polo. Scot gaped at her, wondering how she knew about Henry. Anna scanned the waiting room, narrowed her eyes at Scot, then marched his way.

Scot met her along the north wall, near the vending machines.

"What happened?" Anna asked.

"He had a heart attack. How did you know he was here?" Scot asked.

"The hospital called me. I'm his *in case of emergency* person."

"Oh."

"You need to tell me exactly what happened."

Scot told her everything he could remember about what had happened.

She bit her lower lip, her eyes glassy.

Sensing her distress, Scot highlighted the positive. "I'm sure he'll be fine. The paramedics got there really fast. He was alive when they took him. He even seemed a little better when they loaded him into the ambulance. He gave me a thumbs-up."

A female doctor entered the waiting room. "Anna Fisher. Anna Fisher."

Anna pivoted and fast-walked to the doctor. Scot followed close behind.

"I'm Anna Fisher," she said.

"Let's talk in the hall," the doctor said, ignoring Scot.

Anna and the doctor left the waiting room and walked down the hall. Scot stepped into the hallway, watching them, but staying out of earshot. From his point of view, he could see Anna's face and the back of the doctor's head.

The doctor talked, her head bobbing slightly. Anna's face reddened. She turned, using the wall to brace herself. Anna held her face in her hands and sobbed. Scot rushed to Anna, putting his arms around her.

Anna shoved him, her face blotchy and streaked with tears. "Don't *touch* me."

Scot staggered backward, wide-eyed, the doctor and Anna glaring at him. He turned and walked away, holding back tears.

CHAPTER 85

Funeral One

The funeral home had various rooms and even their own chapel to help the living deal with death. Four days after Henry's death, Scot sat in the second row of one of those rooms. Wooden folding chairs were arranged in neat rows, facing a podium. A table next to the podium featured flowers, an urn, and a large photo of Henry smiling so wide that his eyes were mere slits. Anna stood near the podium, talking to the funeral director.

Scot glanced back at the empty chairs behind him, incredulous. He had purposely arrived thirty minutes early, sure that Henry's death would attract a packed house. Just as Scot thought it would only be him and Anna, a middle-aged man entered the room, sitting in the back row, followed by two elderly women, one wearing a curly black wig, the other with hair as white as snow.

The two women sat in the front row near Scot. The black-haired woman turned in her seat and held out her hand. "I'm Delia Russo. I used to work with Henry."

Scot shook her hand. "I used to work with him too. I'm Scot."

Delia narrowed her dark eyes, the action magnified by her thick glasses. "You look awfully young to have taught with Henry."

"We worked at Big-Mart together."

"That's right. He was a greeter."

Scot nodded.

The other woman turned in her seat too. She waved at Scot. "I'm

Edith. I taught with him too."

Scot waved back. "It's nice to meet you both."

Anna took her seat in the front row, as far away from Scot as possible. The funeral director went to the podium. He was wiry, with jet-black hair and a sunken face, like he himself had one foot in the grave. Scot wondered if it was like how dog owners often resembled their pets.

The funeral director droned on about death, speaking in vague platitudes. Scot snuck peeks at Anna, the funeral director's words going in one ear and out the other. Until he said, "I met Henry a year ago. I was very impressed with his outlook on life and death. In fact, I think he turned me into an amateur philosopher. I quite liked his descriptions of the Stoic teachings of Marcus Aurelius and Epictetus." He smiled briefly. "But I'm sure you'd rather hear from someone very close to Henry." He motioned to Anna, letting her take his place at the podium.

Anna stood at the podium, wearing a long black dress, her eyes red rimmed. She unfolded a piece of paper and checked the small audience, her gaze on the women in the front row. "Henry gave this note to Mr. Danvers for me to read, so that's what I'm doing." She cleared her throat. "*I imagine not many people will attend my funeral. When Alice got sick, I lost touch with my friends and former students. Alice was my everything, and all my focus and attention went to her care. I learned the hard way that death comes for us all. Even the best among us, like Alice. So, for my few friends who made it to my funeral, despite my neglect, I thank you from the bottom of my heart. Please know that I love you, even if I didn't always show it.*"

Edith blotted her eyes with a handkerchief.

Delia smiled, her eyes glassy.

Anna continued reading Henry's note. "*In 399 BC, Socrates was tried and found guilty of corrupting the youth of Athens. He was given the choice to quit teaching and to live in exile or to be executed by poison. Socrates chose death over exile because he believed it would be an injustice to his beliefs. I hope I mustered a fraction of his courage when I died.*"

Scot thought of the thumbs-up that Henry had given as he was loaded into the ambulance. Scot's throat tightened, thinking that, like Socrates, Henry *was* courageous in death.

Anna read the last of Henry's note. "*I'll leave you with the words of Marcus Aurelius. 'Think of yourself as dead. You have lived your life. Now, take what's left and live it properly. What doesn't transmit light creates its own darkness.'*"

At the conclusion of the funeral, the middle-aged man who sat in the back approached and said, "Scot Caldwell?"

"Yes?"

"I'm Larry Boyd, Henry's probate attorney."

CHAPTER 86

The Will

A few days later, Scot and Anna sat across from Larry Boyd in the conference room of Boyd, Platt, and Associates. The urn containing Henry's ashes sat between them on the mahogany table, along with a tattered paperback.

The day before, Governor Wolf had placed a Stay at Home order on several Pennsylvania counties, due to Covid. Thankfully, Lebanon County was still open.

Larry Boyd read directly from Henry's will. "*Anna, I love you as much as I could ever love my own child. You are a daughter to me, and you always will be. I bequeath my ashes to you to do with as you wish. Spread them someplace nice or keep them on your mantel. It doesn't matter to me. Whatever gives you comfort.*"

Anna smiled, her eyes glassy.

Larry glanced at Scot, before reading again. "*Scot, I know you've lost your way, but you have a good heart, and you'll eventually find and live your purpose. I bequeath to you my old copy of* Meditations *by Marcus Aurelius. I think it will help you to find your way, as it often did for me during my life.*

"*For the rest, I can't think of two better young people to leave my meager assets to. I leave my house, my bank account, my car, and all possessions inside my house to Scot and Anna to be divided evenly. Prior to liquidating my assets, I would like Scot and Anna to live in my former home for a period of no less than three months, not necessarily as romantic partners but as roommates and hopefully friends. This is simply a request and only to be enforced by the good consciences of Scot and Anna.*" Larry looked up from the will. "Henry's bank account is currently $2,890.23."

Anna stood from the table, her face scarlet. "I can't live with *him*." She pointed to Scot, while looking at the attorney.

"It isn't a legal requirement. The cohabitation was simply a request," Larry said, without emotion. "You and Mr. Caldwell may liquidate the assets and go your separate ways."

"I'm not going against Henry's wishes," Scot said.

Anna glared at Scot. "I don't want *anything* to do with you." She grabbed the urn from the table and addressed the probate attorney. "He can have it all."

Scot stood from the table. "That's not necessary, Anna. I'm sure we can figure it out."

"*No.* We can't." She pivoted and walked away, Henry in the crook of her arm.

CHAPTER 87

Meditations

Scot drove straight from the attorney's office to Henry's house. Technically, it was Scot's house now, although it didn't feel like it. Scot parked in the driveway behind Henry's 2011 Mercury Milan, also now technically Scot's.

He exited his Hyundai, carrying the worn copy of *Meditations*, as he walked to the front door. Along the way, Scot surveyed the house and property with fresh eyes. The cracked concrete walkway, the peeling paint on the window frames, the overgrown hedges were now Scot's responsibility.

Scot fished the key ring from his pocket, unlocked the front door, and let himself inside. He was greeted with the familiar mustard-colored carpet, worn furniture, and wood paneling of the living room. For the first time, with sunlight streaming through the bay window, he noticed several carpet stains, not to mention a thick layer of dust on every surface.

He purposely bypassed the kitchen and padded down the hall. He peered in each room: the guest bedroom with a single bed, the hall bathroom with tropical fish on the moldy shower curtain, the office loaded with books, and the master bedroom with the unmade queen-size bed. Scot returned to the office, scanning the overburdened bookshelf, still holding the worn copy of *Meditations*. A wide variety of philosophy books dominated the shelves: Aristotle's *Nicomachean Ethics*, Plato's *The Republic*, Jean-Paul Sartre's *Existentialism Is a*

Humanism, Viktor Frankl's *Man's Search for Meaning*, and hundreds of others.

Scot stared at the copy of *Meditations* in his hand.

Of all these books, Henry chose this one.

Scot left the office and the hallway, freezing just outside the kitchen, as if prevented from crossing by an invisible force field. He took one tentative step into the kitchen. Then two more. The refrigerator hummed in the background. The faucet dripped. Scot stared at the linoleum floor, remembering Henry's heart attack. The last word Henry had said to him was *help*. He thought about the fact that Henry had lived in this house, struggling to keep up with the maintenance, yet Scot had never helped him. Scot had never even *offered* to help. Toward the end, Henry couldn't even stand for more than a few minutes. *How the hell was Henry supposed to mow the grass or to clean the house? I'm a selfish asshole.*

Scot set his paperback on the kitchen table and slumped into a chair, his head hanging. *What am I supposed to do now?* He let out a ragged breath. *Henry's the only person who might have the answer.* He picked up the worn paperback, thinking about what Henry had said about the book in his will. *I think it will help you to find your way, as it often did for me during my life.* Scot opened *Meditations* by Marcus Aurelius.

In the first few pages, Marcus Aurelius gave credit to all the people who taught him and served as positive role models. *From my grandfather Verus, I learned good morals and the government of my temper. From the reputation and remembrance of my father, modesty and a manly character. From my mother, piety and beneficence and abstinence, not only from evil deeds but even from evil thoughts—and further, simplicity in my way of living, far removed from the habits of the rich.*

Scot wondered what he had learned from his family. He thought for a long time, staring at the tabletop. *I don't know.* He flipped past Book I, pausing on a highlighted passage in Book II.

Since it is possible that thou mayest depart from life this very moment, regulate every act and thought accordingly.

Scot set his book faceup on the tabletop. He went to the refrigerator, found some turkey, cheese, bread, and mayo, the expiration dates still good. He made himself a sandwich and continued to read as he ate. When he reached Book III, he found another highlighted quote, one he read several times.

If thou workest at that which is before thee, following right reason seriously, vigorously, calmly, without allowing anything else to distract thee, but keeping thy divine part pure, as if thou shouldst be bound to give it back immediately; if thou holdest to this, expecting nothing, fearing nothing, but satisfied with thy present activity according to nature, and with heroic truth in every word and sound which thou utterest, thou wilt live happy. And there is no man who is able to prevent this.

CHAPTER 88

Back to Square One

The next day Scot drove Henry's car, a 2011 Mercury Milan. Not exactly a luxury automobile but much nicer than Scot's Hyundai. Not to mention it only had 26,321 miles, which is nothing for a nine-year-old car. A stench came from the farms along the roadside, their fallow fields black with manure.

That Marcus Aurelius quote stuck in his head. Not the exact quote, but Scot's personal translation. *If I work hard, doing honest work, fearing nothing, satisfied with the current task, I'll be happy.* The thought of working hard jogged his memory to something Henry had once told him. *Anna loved you because you were kind and hardworking and honest. Is that who you are now?* Scot turned onto US 422 and drove past strip malls, gas stations, and big-box stores. He gazed at Big-Mart on his right. Just before he missed the turn, he yanked the wheel, making a split-second decision, eliciting a honk.

He parked in the Big-Mart lot, feeling an eerie sense of déjà vu. He grabbed his phone from the cupholder and sent Anna a text.

> **Scot:** I'm sorry about yesterday. I know you don't want me to be a part of all this. If you want anything of Henry's, just say the word. You can have the house, the money, the car, everything. His car's pretty nice. It only has like 26k miles. Anyway, just let me know.

Scot exited the Mercury and walked into Big-Mart. A large A-frame sign stood near the entrance that featured a rendering of a camera with a fat line through it, accompanied by the message *Please don't take photographs of our customers.*

As he passed the sign, an elderly woman in a surgical mask said, "Welcome to Big-Mart."

Scot smiled at her. "Thank you."

Scot walked around the corner to the employee-only area. He walked down the hall to the managers' offices. One department manager sat at his desk, pecking on his keyboard. At the end of the hall was Ron's office. Scot knocked on the open door.

Ron looked up from his laptop, squinting at Scot. Then he shook his head. "Look what the cat dragged in."

"Hey, Ron. Could I talk to you for a minute?"

Ron hesitated, then waved him in. "Yeah. Come on in."

Scot walked into the office.

"You look like shit," Ron said, chuckling. "You got fat. Or maybe fatter. You were always a little chubby."

Scot blushed from embarrassment. "Yeah."

"Have a seat."

Scot sat across from Ron at his desk.

Ron moved aside his laptop. "What the heck are you doing here?"

Scot took a deep breath. "Look, uh, … I need a job. I was wondering if you had any openings. I'll do whatever."

Ron leaned back in his chair, bouncing a little like a child. "You really wanna come back here? I thought you were a Bitcoin millionaire?"

"Didn't last."

Ron's lip twitched, as he tried to suppress his smile. "Sorry to hear that."

Scot shrugged. "It is what it is."

"It's a lot different here since you left. It's a tighter ship now. Your buddy Kyle's gone."

"Where did he go?"

"I thought you two were tight."

Scot shook his head. "I haven't talked to him since I left here."

"His website, People of Big-Mart is huge now. He has people all over the country taking pictures of all the freaks who come into Big-Mart." Ron frowned. "Corporate's trying to sue him, but, from what I heard, we don't have much of a case. That's why we have the signs about not taking pictures."

"That's crazy."

"You don't even know the half of it. I'm just glad that degenerate's gone."

An awkward silence passed between them.

"I should, uh, apologize to you," Scot added. "I'm sorry about that whole mess with Charlotte. It was a big mistake. We're divorced now."

"I'm not surprised. You both did me a favor. I realize now that I dodged a bullet with Charlotte. If you two hadn't had an affair, I never would've met my wife, Grace." Ron turned around the picture frame on his desktop, showing a picture of a young mother, holding an infant.

"You have a kid?" Scot asked.

Ron nodded. "Brianna. She's six months old."

"Wow. Congratulations."

"So, as you can see, no need to apologize to me. As far as I'm concerned, it's water under the bridge. Sounds like you're the one with the short end of the stick."

"I never should've married her."

"When Charlotte found out you had some cash, one way or another, she was gonna get her hooks into you. I understand who she is now, but, back then, I was just another lovesick puppy like you. It took some real soul searching. I kept replaying everything in my mind, and the thing I couldn't understand was the security video. By the way, I almost puked on my computer when I saw that."

Scot looked away. "Sorry."

"For months I kept thinking about it, and the question I was stuck on was, why would it just show up after a year? So, I had the tech guy check the video to see if he could find more info on who sent it." Ron paused for effect. "Turns out Charlotte sent it."

"What? Why would she do that?" Scot thought about the video also being sent to Anna. "She must've sent it to Anna too."

Ron pointed at Scot with a finger gun. "Devious stuff."

Scot leaned back in his chair. "I can't believe she'd do that to me. She ruined everything."

"That's exactly what I said to myself. Be thankful you're done with her now."

"Yeah." Scot thought about how strong Charlotte had come on to him that night. *It was always about the money.*

"Did you hear that she got married last week? Ugly dude, but I guess that doesn't matter when you're a doctor."

"I didn't know that." Scot thought about his ex-neighbor. "Did she marry David Levin?"

"Sounds right. It's on her Instagram."

"Better him than me."

Ron smirked. "I agree. Better him than me."

Another awkward silence passed between them.

Ron glanced at his watch. "Well, I should get back to work."

"Yeah. Of course. When can I start?"

Ron laughed. "You can't work here. It's company policy not to rehire someone who was fired."

Scot left Big-Mart, still thinking about what Charlotte did. *And I let her do it. I'm so stupid.* Scot climbed into the Mercury. Then he drove to the nearby Home Depot.

CHAPTER 89

A Single Step

Scot returned to his new home, after applying to Home Depot. He made himself another turkey sandwich. He sat at the kitchen table, eating and staring at Anna's Instagram photo on his phone. The fridge rattled in the background, and the faucet dripped.

He thumb-typed a text to Anna, knowing it wouldn't be returned.

Scot: I'm having dinner by myself at Henry's kitchen table, eating his food. The whole thing doesn't feel real. I miss him. I miss you. I tried to get my job back at Big-Mart. Ron laughed in my face. I guess I don't blame him. And I understand why you hate me too. I'm sorry for everything. I hope you're doing okay.

Scot regretted the text as soon as he sent it. He reread it several times, realizing that it sounded pathetic, like he was playing the victim, when his actions were the sole cause of his situation. He opened *Meditations*, reading to distract himself from the memories of his mistakes.

He pondered a highlighted passage in Book IV. *Be like the promontory against which the waves continually break, but it stands firm and tames the fury of the water around it.*

The fridge rattle and the faucet drip woke him from his thoughts. Scot rose from the table and went to the sink. He tightened the cold and hot knobs, but the spigot still dripped.

Scot grabbed his phone and tapped his way to YouTube, then thumb-typed *how to fix a leaky faucet*. He watched several videos, learning some basic plumbing and common causes of the leak, depending on the type of faucet. Henry had a ceramic disk double-handle faucet. The recommended fix was to replace the cylinders, aerator, and other internal parts in the spigot and handles.

As the video recommended, Scot turned off the water lines under the sink. Then he went to Henry's garage, which was packed to the gills with everything Henry and Alice had collected in their lifetimes. Wood flooring was stacked on a pallet. Empty cardboard boxes were thrown atop a wheelbarrow, a lawn mower, and two rusty bicycles. Scot imagined Henry not having the strength or the energy to break down the boxes. A stack of snow tires sat in one corner. A workbench sat in another corner. Miscellaneous boxes were stacked along the walls, labeled with black marker. Christmas decorations, household items, Halloween decorations, books, and clothes were among the labeled boxes.

Scot went to the workbench, finding a toolbox. Inside, he found wrenches, screwdrivers, a hammer, and a socket set. Scot took the toolbox inside and followed the instructions on the video to disassemble the handles and spigot, putting the internal parts in a ziplock bag.

He went to Home Depot with his parts to find new ones. After twenty-minutes of browsing the plumbing section, he asked for assistance. An older man helped him find what he needed.

As Scot drove home, he noticed several landscaping companies, spreading mulch around town, taking advantage of the beautiful spring day. Scot parked in his driveway. As he walked to the front door, he stopped and scanned the flower beds. Weeds grew underneath the overgrown hedges and choked the sporadic yellow flowers. At least Scot thought they were weeds, given his very limited knowledge of plants.

One thing at a time.

He went to the kitchen and reassembled the spigot and handles using the new parts. Then he turned on the waterline under the sink.

He stood and stared at the spigot, half expecting water to spray like a fountain. But it didn't. He turned on the hot and cold at the same time, then turned off the water. The handles felt tighter, and the drip was gone.

Scot smiled to himself.

CHAPTER 90

Another Step

The next morning Scot sat at the kitchen table, eating Henry's oatmeal and reading *Meditations*. With only five pages left, he found the final highlighted quote. *If it is not right, do not do it; if it is not true, do not say it.* Scot nodded to himself.

After breakfast, Scot pulled up a corner of the mustard-colored carpet in the living room, revealing the padding and subflooring underneath. He thought about the hardwood flooring in the garage. Henry had planned to replace the old carpet with the hardwood but had never gotten around to it.

Buoyed by his faucet fixing success, Scot went back to YouTube and watched several videos on removing carpet and installing hardwood flooring. After a few hours of research, Scot went back to the garage. He searched for a carpet knife or a utility knife. He found a box cutter that he thought might work.

He moved the furniture out of the living room. An hour later, he was dripping with sweat and out of breath. He collapsed on the end of the couch, which he had pushed into the kitchen. The kitchen table sat next to him. He had piled it atop the couch to make room. After catching his breath, he groaned as he stood, his back a little tight.

Scot peeled back the old carpet, rolling it from one end of the room to the other. He leaned against the wall, wheezing from the effort, his legs wobbly. He struggled with the carpet roll, dragging it outside, and dumping it in the driveway. He leaned on the Mercury, catching his breath again.

Once he had recovered, he returned to the living room, and removed the padding too. Then he collected the hardwood from the garage, stacking it in small piles, evenly spaced throughout the living room. For the rest of the day, he laid hardwood in the living room.

By the end of the day, his entire body ached, but he'd laid about half of the hardwood. The oak hardwood was beautiful, but it made the faux wood walls look uglier. Scot went back to YouTube and searched how to remove fake wood walls.

CHAPTER 91

Progress

In the afternoon of the next day, Scot stood on the living room hardwood, his hands on his hips and a big smile on his face. His back and kneecaps ached from working on his hands and knees for two days, and he was still an amateur at cutting the hardwood to fit corners and irregular edges, but he'd completed the job. He reached into his pocket and called Laura.

His call went straight to voice mail. "Hey, Mom. I was just calling to invite you over sometime this weekend. You still haven't seen the house. I just finished putting in new hardwood flooring. Anyway, I was hoping you could bring my college money with you. I'm thinking about going back in the fall, as long as Covid doesn't ruin that. If you can't make it this weekend, let me know. I can come by and pick up the check. Either way, call me back. Love you." Scot disconnected the call.

Scot couldn't help but grin at his prospects. *If I can fix up this place, I could rent it while I'm at school. With the extra money, I wouldn't have to work part-time. I could just concentrate on my classes. I could give half the rent money to Anna too.* He imagined graduating from Penn, living in Henry's fully renovated house, and working as an engineer. His fantasy took him to Target, where he would bump into Anna. She would be so impressed with his circumstances that she would ask *him* out.

Scot made another call.

Marie answered on the fourth ring. "Hi, Scot."

"Guess what I just did."

Marie exhaled. "I have no idea."

Scot paced on the new floor. "I put in new hardwood flooring, all by myself."

"That's great," she replied, unenthused.

"What's wrong?"

"It's nothing. Just this stay-at-home order. I miss my yoga class already."

Marie lived in Delaware County, Pennsylvania, which had been locked down for five days, since March 23.

"We're still open here," Scot said. "You should come over and check out the house."

"I heard Lebanon County will be locked down on April 1st."

"Come over tomorrow then. I'll order pizza."

"You know I don't eat that stuff."

"You can put lettuce on it." Scot laughed at his own joke.

Frank yelled in the background, his words inaudible.

"I'll be there in a minute," Marie shouted back.

More yelling came from Frank.

"I have to call you back." Marie disconnected the call.

CHAPTER 92

MIA

Marie and Laura hadn't called him back yesterday, but Scot had been so exhausted at the end of the day that he'd forgotten about them. Now he was in the garage, the door open, breaking down empty cardboard boxes and consolidating the cardboard. Every muscle in his body was sore from the past few days. He had only been working for an hour today, and he was already sweaty.

He thought about Marie as he worked. *Something's not right. She was upset. She said it was because of the stay-at-home order, but it felt like more than that.* Scot figured Frank now worked exclusively from home because of Covid. Scot thought about Marie being stuck with him in that big beautiful house. *I'd be upset too.*

In addition to the cardboard, Scot filled eighteen trash bags, with various garbage from the garage, and piled them in the driveway with the carpet and padding. He had a Dumpster coming on Monday.

After creating more space, he set about organizing the tools and workbench. He had purchased two sheets of pegboard and some hooks from Home Depot. When he drove a nail into the wall, it went into the drywall with little resistance. Scot figured that the nail would be much too loose to hold the pegboard. So he went back to YouTube and learned all about wall assemblies and how to find the studs.

Then he came back, tapped on the wall to find the stud, and drove the nail into the wood. He used multiple nails to hold each pegboard. The real joy came from hanging and organizing the tools on the wall.

When finished, he admired his handiwork for a moment, his stomach rumbling. He checked the time on his phone—1:07 p.m.

Scot went to the kitchen and made himself another turkey sandwich, with the last of Henry's lunchmeat. As he ate, he tapped on his phone, checking his texts and calls. Still nothing from Marie or Laura. He called Marie. It went to voice mail on the fifth ring.

After Marie's greeting, Scot said, "Hey. It's me. You never called me back yesterday. I'm a little worried. Call me back."

Scot then tried his mother. His call went straight to voice mail. "Hey, Mom. It's me. I called you yesterday. Not sure if you got the message. Call me back. It's important. Love you."

After showering, Scot dressed in the master bedroom, in front of the mirror over the dresser. Several sticky notes were arranged along the left edge of the mirror. Quotes from *Meditations*. He stared at his chubby upper body, before putting on his T-shirt. He pinched his love handles. There was a little less to pinch since he'd started working on the house.

He smiled at himself and slipped his shirt over his head. Then he did what he did every night before bed and every morning before breakfast. He read the quotes from the sticky notes, which were the same quotes Henry had highlighted. Scot thought Henry had highlighted those quotes specifically for him.

Scot turned out the lights and climbed into the queen-size bed. He was nearly asleep when his phone chimed. He groped for his phone on the bedside table. He glanced at the name, swiped right, and said, "Marie. Are you okay?"

She whispered into the phone. "I'm fine. Were you sleeping?"

"Not yet. I just laid down."

She still whispered, "I'm sorry. I'll call you tomorrow."

"I'm awake. What's going on?"

She hesitated. "I had a pretty bad argument with Frank."

Scot sat up in bed. "About what?"

"I was thinking about going back to school too."

A few days ago Scot had told Marie about his plan to return to Penn. "That's a great idea."

"Well, Frank doesn't agree."

"Fuck Frank."

Marie let out a breath. "Marriage is about compromise."

"What does he care? It's not like he can't afford it."

"He wants me here for him."

"What do *you* want?

She sounded more tired than Scot. "I don't know."

CHAPTER 93

Opportunity Knocks

By Monday, Scot had finished organizing the garage. He still hadn't heard from his mother, but he wasn't worried. It wasn't uncommon for her to disappear with her boyfriend, Johnny, for several days.

Scot had spent the morning loading the Dumpster with garbage, followed by watching YouTube videos, learning about small engine maintenance and repair.

After a trip to Home Depot for some parts, he spent the afternoon fixing the mower and the weed eater. The grass wasn't long yet, but it was growing, and he could collect the leaves and debris with the bag attachment. Plus he wanted to get the equipment running before he needed it. So he changed the oil and the sparkplug, sharpened the blade, cleaned out the carburetor, and filled the mower with fresh gasoline.

A Buick sedan parked along the street in front of his house, just behind Scot's Hyundai. Scot hoped it was someone who saw the For Sale sign in the Hyundai's window. With Henry's Mercury, Scot didn't need his Hyundai anymore. A familiar woman exited the car and waddled up the driveway. Scot stood from the mower and met her just outside the garage, bathed in bright sunlight. The *whirr* of a distant chain saw played in the background. It was the woman with the dark-haired wig from Henry's funeral, but Scot couldn't remember her name.

"Good afternoon, Scot." She smiled and waved. "I guess we're not supposed to shake hands anymore."

Scot waved back, still trying to remember her name. "Hi, how are you?"

"Do you remember me?"

"You used to work with Henry. I'm sorry. I'm so bad with names."

"Delia Russo."

"Right. I remember now."

"I heard Henry gave you his house and you were doing some big project, so I wanted to come by and see for myself."

Scot narrowed his eyes at the busybody. "How did you know all that?"

"Edith lives down the street. She saw you working in the garage. We were guessing that he gave you the house."

"Technically, he gave it to me and Anna, but that's …"

"Complicated?"

"Yeah."

Delia walked past Scot into the garage. "Wow. This looks great."

Scot followed her, keeping a polite distance. "Thanks."

"What else have you done?"

"I put in hardwood flooring in the living room, and I fixed the kitchen faucet. I need to do some landscaping too." He gestured to the mower. "That's why I'm working on the mower."

"You're quite the handyman."

Scot shook his head. "Not really. I'm learning."

"Don't sell yourself short."

Scot smiled.

"Are you planning to mulch those flower beds out front?"

"Yeah. I was planning to weed and trim the bushes first. I need to pick up some mulch from Home Depot. Not sure how much I can fit in my car."

"There's a tree company working around the corner, trimming trees off the powerlines. If you ask them, they'll give you wood chips for free."

"Really?"

She nodded. "Yes siree."

"Thanks for the tip."

"I'd love to see the hardwood. Henry had that godawful mustard carpet forever."

Scot led Delia inside, showing off his workmanship, which was average at best.

"You should really consider being a handyman," Delia said, standing in the living room, admiring the hardwood.

"I'm definitely not a professional."

"You should see some of these guys who call themselves professional. They're unreliable and lazy. I fired my last two handymen."

Scot forced a smile, wondering if the issue was the handymen or her.

"I would definitely hire you," Delia said.

"Thanks, but I'm not a handyman."

Delia dug in her purse, grabbing a pen and a notepad. "If you change your mind, give me a call. I would love for you to organize my garage." She scribbled on the pad, then handed Scot her phone number. "Think about it."

CHAPTER 94

Jump to Conclusions

Dark clouds moved in from the east, bringing a cool breeze. Scot pushed his wheelbarrow full of wood chips, dumped several small piles into the front flower beds, and spread them on his hands and knees. His entire body was still sore, with nearly a week of nonstop DIY projects. On the bright side, he'd cinched his belt one hole tighter that morning.

Scot stood and pushed his empty wheelbarrow back to the wood-chip pile on his driveway. He had been moving wood chips for five hours, and he was nearly done mulching the flower beds, but two-thirds of the pile remained. The tree guys had said fifteen yards of wood chips, but Scot had no idea what that meant. The tree guys had been busy at the time, with chain saws buzzing overhead and a chipper running nearby. Scot had agreed to the amount, not wanting to look like an idiot to the workmen, plus feeling pressured to make a quick decision.

He stared at the pile of wood chips, his hands on his hips, and a frown on his face. He thought about spreading the wood chips under the mature trees out back. Grass didn't grow there anyway, and it would cover the exposed roots.

His cell phone chimed. He took off his gloves, tossed them in the empty wheelbarrow, and fished his phone from the front pocket of his jeans. He was surprised to see his younger sister's name and number. Scot rarely talked to her, and, when they did talk, it was always by text.

He swiped right and said, "Hey, Heather."

She spoke rapidly, her voice frantic. "Have you heard from Mom?"

His heart rate increased. "No. I've been calling her, but she hasn't returned my messages. Is she okay?"

"I don't know. I think Johnny did something to her."

A few raindrops fell from the clouds.

"Where did she go?" Scot asked.

"She said she was going to Vegas with Johnny on vacation," Heather said. "It was a big road trip. Two weeks. They were supposed to be back three days ago, and now she's not returning my texts."

"It's only been three days. Disappearing for a few days isn't abnormal for them. I'm sure she's okay."

"No. She's *not*. My money's gone."

"*What?*" Scot fast-walked inside, as the rain began in earnest.

"I had a nail appointment, and I went to the ATM for cash, but I couldn't even get a hundred dollars."

Scot loosened and kicked off his boots, just inside the front door.

Heather sniffled. "I called PNC Bank, and they told me that my account was overdrawn."

Scot paced on his hardwood floor, thinking about his own money. "That can't be. Maybe Mom moved your money to another bank for better interest rates."

"She would've given me a new ATM card."

Scot wondered if Heather was overspending and if Laura had moved the money for Heather's own good. "How much money did you have?"

"I don't know exactly. Mom takes care of that." Her voice quivered. "I think Johnny killed her and took my money."

"Let's not jump to conclusions. First of all, unless Johnny's on your accounts, he can't take your money. If you have your bank statements, I can come over and take a look. Then we can try to figure out where they went."

Heather sniffled again. "Okay."

"I'll be there in twenty minutes. Try not to worry. I'm sure it'll be fine."

"Thanks, Scot."

"You're welcome. See you soon." He disconnected the call, then called his mother. The call went straight to voice mail.

Scot tried to leave a message, but a robotic voice said, "This inbox is full. Goodbye."

He felt sick to his stomach. *Maybe Johnny did do something to her.*

CHAPTER 95

The Tip of the Iceberg

Scot sat at his mother's desk, going through bank, credit card, and mortgage statements. He took a few notes and punched digits into the calculator on his phone, then scribbled some numbers next to his notes.

Heather paced in front of the desk. "What do you think?"

Scot shook his head. "A lot is going on here, and it's all bad."

Heather leaned over the desk, her eyes bulging. "What do you mean?"

"Don't you ever look at your bills?"

"That's Mom's job. She's my manager."

Scot let out a heavy breath. "Part of this is you. You overspend. You have an expensive car, house, makeup, clothing—"

"I have to look good."

"I'm just saying. But, the majority of the spending does appear to be Mom or Mom and Johnny. It looks like she ran up your company credit cards and was only paying the minimums."

Hot Heather was technically Hot Heather, Inc.

"That *fucking* bitch. What was she buying?" Heather asked, her hands on her hips.

"Lots of things," Scot said. "Restaurants. Airfare. Hotels. Shopping. Clothing for women *and* men. Jewelry. By far, the biggest charges come from various casinos in Vegas, Atlantic City, and online casinos too. It looks like most of the charges started when she met

Johnny, almost two years ago. I wonder if he's a gambling addict."

"That *motherfucker*. I knew he had something to do with this. How much do I owe?"

Scot read the total from his notes. "One hundred thirty-two thousand five seventy-three and some change."

"I'm gonna *fucking* kill him." Heather paced away from the desk, then back. "I'm so fucked." She slumped into the chair in front of Laura's desk. "What about my bank account? What happened to the money? My OnlyFans money is supposed to go there. I know it's been less lately, but it's still a lot of money."

"The OnlyFans deposits *have been* going into your bank account, but Mom—or at least her ATM card—has been withdrawing large amounts of cash from ATMs for almost two years, just like the credit card charges. These big cash withdrawals seem to coincide with the casino charges. Her last withdrawal was six days ago, immediately after your monthly OnlyFans deposit."

"This has to be Johnny. I knew he was a piece of shit."

"There's another problem."

Heather frowned.

Scot picked up a small stack of bills. "You're past due on your mortgage and your car payment."

"We need to find them," Heather said.

"I think we should go to the police," Scot replied.

CHAPTER 96

Missing Person?

"Was there any sign of a struggle?" the burly detective asked.

Scot and Heather sat across from Detective Gorman at his metal desk.

"What do you mean by that?" Heather asked.

"Did you find blood in her room or around the house?" Detective Gorman asked. "Furniture turned over. Broken glass. Anything that might be a sign of a struggle."

"No."

"Did you ever see any signs of abuse from the boyfriend?" The detective glanced at his notes. "This Johnny Black?"

"No, but I think he might be using my mom for money. He's a crusty old rocker who's just this leech. My mom's always cleaning up after him and making his meals. He does nothing."

"It's not a crime to be lazy. I doubt your mother's missing. I think she took the money and went to Vegas to have a great time with her boyfriend. You said she was prone to disappearing with him for days at a time."

Heather held out her hands. "What about my money?"

Scot wondered about *his* money too.

"Did you have a contract with your mother?" the detective asked.

"A contract? For what?" Heather replied.

"An employment contract. Anything that details the specifics of your business arrangement."

"She's my mother."

"According to your incorporation papers, she's also a 50 percent partner in your business. Her name's on your bank account and credit cards, which means she can legally spend that money."

Heather's face was beet red. "You're not gonna do anything, are you?"

"I'll open a missing person's investigation, but it'll be classified as low risk."

"What do you mean by low risk?" Scot asked.

The detective leaned back in his chair, resting his hands on his gut. "It means we don't have any reason to believe she's been kidnapped or is in danger, so less resources will be spent locating her."

"That means you're not gonna do shit," Heather said.

Detective Gorman scowled. "It's like triage at a hospital. We only have so many resources to allocate. I suggest you start by checking the local hospitals. And you might wanna hire an attorney, before she spends all your money."

Heather stood from the table, her face like stone. "Too late for that."

On the drive home from the police station, Heather said, "We need to go to Vegas, see if we can find Johnny."

"I don't think we can." The windshield wipers sluiced water back and forth, giving Scot split seconds of clarity, followed by split seconds of blur on an endless loop. "Covid lockdowns start tomorrow for Lebanon County, and I looked up Vegas. They're locked down starting tomorrow too."

"I'm so screwed."

"Maybe we could hire a Vegas private investigator. Do you know where they might be? Places they visit? Does Johnny have family in the area?"

"I have no fucking idea. I don't even think Johnny Black is his real name." Heather groaned. "What a fucking nightmare."

"Didn't he used to work at some casino as a blackjack dealer?"

"That's right. He did," Heather replied, excitement in her voice.

Scot stopped his Mercury at a stoplight. "Do you know which one?"

"He bragged about working at the biggest casino in Vegas, but it's probably a lie."

Scot glanced at his sister. "Maybe. Maybe not. The private investigator would figure that out."

"I can't afford a private investigator."

The light turned green. Scot drove through the intersection. "I can take care of it. My friend Henry left me some money, and I just sold my car."

"You'd do that for me?" Heather asked.

"Of course." Scot squinted into the rain, watching for brake lights. "This isn't totally altruistic for me."

"Altruistic? What does that mean?"

"It's like good or moral."

"Oh. Then why are you helping me?"

"Partly because you're my sister but also because Mom has some of my money too."

"How much?"

Scot stopped at another red light. He turned to his sister. "When I was going through my divorce, I gave Mom forty-six grand to hold for me. I was worried that Charlotte would spend it or that I might blow it on crypto. I'm hoping to go back to school this fall."

"Mom and Johnny might've blown it in Vegas."

Scot winced. "I hope not."

Heather's phone buzzed in her purse. She fished her iPhone from her purse and checked the text. She scanned the text and said, "It's Mom. Says they were at some desert resort with no cell service. Then she lost her charger."

"Sounds like bullshit. What about Johnny's phone?"

"She didn't say anything about it. Says they're trying to get home tonight before the lockdown."

"Don't say anything about the money. It's better if she doesn't know that we know."

CHAPTER 97

The Mask Comes Off

A pepperoni pizza sat on the coffee table, still in the Papa John's box. Scot and Heather sat a few seats away from each other on her black leather sectional, each with a plate and a slice of pizza. The massive LED television showed reruns of *House Hunters*. Scot ate his pizza, half-watching the show and half-thinking about whether or not his mother still had his money. The plan was to confront Laura and Johnny when they came home, hoping that the ambush might yield some truth.

Heather set her plate on the coffee table, most of her slice uneaten.

"You're not hungry?" Scot asked.

"I can't eat." She made a fist several times. "I'm so fucking pissed that my hands are shaky. I might punch them both in their fucking faces."

"Try to relax. Let's just ask them where the money is, and we'll see what they say. If we start out angry, I doubt they'll tell us anything."

Heather nodded. "If they try to lie, I'm gonna go off."

"Let's try to keep it together."

Heather took a swig from her diet soda and set it back on the coffee table.

Scot changed the subject, hoping to calm Heather before the confrontation. "Have you talked to Dad lately?" Scot was referring to Eric Manning, Scot's stepfather but Heather's biological father, and the man Scot considered to be his father, if not by blood.

"I haven't talked to him in a long time," she replied, her voice monotone.

"How come?"

She answered Scot's question with her eyes glued to the television. "He found out about OnlyFans. Freaked out and essentially disowned me."

Scot grimaced. "Shit. I'm sorry. I didn't know that."

Heather shrugged, but her eyes were glassy and still focused on the television. "I think it was just an excuse. We hardly talked since he left Mom for Janine anyway. It's like he wanted an excuse to dump me for his new family."

"He loves you. He'll come around."

"I don't even give a shit anymore."

Several hours later Scot slumped on the couch, his eyes heavy. Engine noise came from outside, followed by the rumble of the garage door opener. Scot sat upright. "I think they're here."

Heather set her phone on the coffee table. "Let's do this."

"Remember. Be calm."

Scot and Heather went to the kitchen. Johnny and Laura bickered about their luggage in the garage, their voices muffled by the wall separating them. The door from the garage opened, and Johnny and Laura moved past the laundry room, into the kitchen, rolling their designer suitcases behind them. For the first time since she went on disability, Scot saw his mother walk without a limp.

Laura startled at the sight of them, then smiled. "Hey, you two. You waited up for us."

"Hi, Mom," Scot said, his voice even.

Johnny lifted his chin, his eyes bloodshot. "I'm beat. Your mother made me do all the drivin'."

"What the fuck did you two do with my money?" Heather asked, her eyes laser-focused.

Scot nudged Heather, hoping she would tone it down.

Johnny stood up his suitcase, freeing his tattooed hands. "Don't talk to your mother like that."

Laura furrowed her brow. "What are you talking about?"

"You know exactly what I'm talking about," Heather replied. "Don't fuck with me."

Johnny pointed at Heather. "You need to watch your mouth, little girl."

"Don't tell her what to do," Scot said to Johnny. "You're not our father."

Johnny rolled his neck. "I'm too tired for this bullshit."

"I want my money," Heather said, through gritted teeth.

Laura shook her head, as if saying, *That's a shame.* "You spent it all. I tried to warn you about your spending problem, but you wouldn't listen."

Heather's voice went up an octave. "That's bullshit. You've been running up my credit cards and taking cash out for like two years." Heather gestured to Scot. "Tell her."

"It's on the bank statements," Scot said. "Just give her back her money. I want my college money too."

"I don't know anything about your college money," Laura said. "Ask your father. He was supposed to pay."

"I gave you forty-six grand to hold."

"I don't know anything about that." Laura's voice was cold.

Scot held out his hands, incredulous. "Why are you doing this to us?"

Heather stepped withing striking distance of Laura, her fists clenched. "I want my money."

Laura rolled her eyes, talking louder, as if performing for an audience. "Money, money, money. That's all you kids ever want. You buy a goddamn BMW, a mansion, designer clothes, and jewelry. What the hell did you expect?"

Heather reared back and punched Laura in the nose. Laura stumbled back, tripped over her suitcase, and fell on the hardwood.

Laura cried out from the floor, holding her nose, blood seeping between her fingers.

Johnny Black pushed Heather, causing her to fall on the floor. "What the fuck, little girl."

Heather scrambled to her feet, unharmed.

Scot stepped in front of Heather and shoved Johnny, causing him to stumble backward, but he regained his balance. "Don't touch her," Scot said to Johnny.

"I want my *fucking* money," Heather said, stepping forward.

Johnny went to Laura and helped her stand, her legs wobbly.

Laura touched her nose and looked at her bloody fingers. "You broke my nose," Laura said to Heather.

This was probably an exaggeration, as the blood wasn't excessive, and, from what Scot could tell, her nose didn't appear swollen or out of place.

"If you don't give me my money, I'll *fucking* kill you," Heather replied.

Johnny shielded Laura and said to Heather, "After everything she did for you? You ungrateful little bitch."

Heather pointed toward the garage. "Get the fuck out of my house! Both of you. You make me sick."

Laura sniffed. "If that's what you want. For the record, I tried to do whatever was best for you." Laura glanced at Scot. "Both of you. I can't believe my kids are so selfish."

"Fuck you," Heather said, her lower lip trembling, and tears welling in her eyes.

"Let's bounce," Johnny said.

Laura and Johnny went back to the garage, Laura still without a limp. They left in the Five Series BMW Heather had given Laura as a gift. Johnny left a streak of rubber on the concrete driveway on the way out.

Heather and Scot returned to the couch, shell-shocked. Heather lay in the fetal position, her knees pulled to her chest.

Scot hung his head, thinking about his mother and his options. *I can't believe she'd do this to us. She must be on drugs or something. Maybe that's why she wasn't limping. Fucking Johnny has her twisted. Even if she comes to her senses, I bet my money's already gone. If I can't get my money back, what am I going to do about school? I could sell Henry's house. It's not worth a lot, but it's paid for. I'm sure I could get at least one-fifty. Even if I gave half to Anna, it would still be more than enough to finish school.* Scot thought about the house and his DIY projects. *But it's my home.*

Tears slipped down Heather's face. Scot moved next to her and patted her back, as she sobbed. She stopped crying after a few minutes.

"Are you okay?" Scot asked.

She sat upright and shook her head. "What am I gonna do now? I have no money. I'm gonna lose my house, my car, everything. Where am I gonna go?"

"You can stay at my house. I have two extra rooms."

Heather wiped her face with her sweatshirt sleeve. "Nobody will ever want me now. Not after what I've done."

"That's not true," Scot said.

Heather turned to Scot. "It is. Why do you think I've gone through so many boyfriends? They only want me for sex, and they all think they're entitled to it, like I owe them the porn experience."

"What if you quit and started over? You're still young. You could go back to school. Do whatever you want."

She shook her head. "I'm Hot Heather. That's all I'll ever be."

CHAPTER 98

Sick

Scot woke late the next morning after his midnight confrontation with Laura and Johnny. In the aftermath, he had offered to stay over with Heather, but she had wanted to be alone.

He went to the bathroom, peed, washed his hands, and brushed his teeth. When he returned to his bedroom, he read his daily affirmations, words of wisdom written by Marcus Aurelius and chosen by Henry. He read the last one several times. *If it is not right, do not do it; if it is not true, do not say it. If it is not right, do not do it; if it is not true, do not say it. If it is not right, do not do it; if it is not true, do not say it.*

What if I don't know what's true?

As Scot dressed, he thought about his mother. *Is she a liar? A con-woman? A psychopath? Or is she sick? Did Johnny get her hooked on drugs?* He thought about what Marie had said to him. *At Temple, the same thing happened to her. Mom claimed that Ray was supposed to pay for her college, but Ray said he had already sent the check to Mom. I need to talk to Marie.*

Scot went to his bedside table, grabbed his phone, and tapped Marie's contact. His call went straight to voice mail.

After Marie's prerecorded greeting, Scot said, "It's me. I really need to talk to you. I think something's wrong with Mom. Maybe Johnny got her hooked on drugs or something. She stole Heather's money and my college money. They blew a shitload of money in

Vegas. I think she might have a gambling problem too. Call me back." Scot disconnected the call, then sent a text.

> **Scot:** I need to talk to you about Mom. It's an emergency.
> I'm coming over. Call me if you're not there.

Ninety minutes later, Scot drove through Marie's Villanova neighborhood of mansions on two-acre lots. He still hadn't received a return call or text from Marie. Scot parked in Frank and Marie's driveway. Lights were on inside. He exited his car and went to the garage window. All three cars were inside. He walked up the front walkway, guided by the landscape lighting, and rang the doorbell.

He peered into the sidelight window, but it was mostly obscured by the curtains, only a little patch of hardwood visible. Thirty seconds later, he rang the doorbell again, pressing it several times in a row.

Shortly thereafter, Frank moved the curtain and peered out from the sidelight window. His face was beet red, his jaw set tight. Frank yanked open the door. "What are you doing here?"

"I need to talk to Marie," Scot said. "Is she here?" Frank's left hand was on the door, and his right hand was on the doorframe, blocking the doorway like a sentry. Redness and a fresh cut on Frank's right knuckles caught Scot's attention.

"She's not feeling well. Call her tomorrow." Frank shut the door.

But Scot stepped forward, wedging his boot in the doorjamb. "I need to see her."

Frank opened the door again. "What are you doing? I said she was sick."

"I need to see her."

Frank shook his head. "No. Call her tomorrow."

Scot shouted, "Marie! Marie!"

Frank shoved Scot, not hard, but hard enough to move his foot from the doorjamb and back onto the stoop. "Be quiet. I have neighbors."

Scot narrowed his eyes at Frank. "What did you do to her?"

Frank raised one side of his mouth in contempt. "You need to go home."

"Did you punch her?"

"Who the fuck do you think you are, coming to my house and accusing me of abusing *my* wife?" Frank poked Scot in the chest. "You need to get the fuck off my property, before I call the police."

Scot stepped back. "Don't touch me."

Frank showed his palms. "You need to leave, before I call the police."

Scot removed his phone from his pocket. "That's a good idea. I'm calling the police myself." His phone chimed, before he had a chance to dial 9-1-1. It was a Villanova number, but it wasn't Marie's cell phone. Scot swiped right. "Hello?"

"It's me," Marie said, her voice weary. "I'm fine. Just not feeling well."

"Are you sure?" Scot glared at Frank, as he asked, "Did Frank do something to you?"

"No. Of course not. Call me tomorrow. I really need to go back to bed."

"Okay. I'll call you tomorrow. I hope you feel better."

"Thanks."

Scot disconnected the call.

"Satisfied?" Frank asked.

Scot nodded.

Frank went back inside and slammed the door.

CHAPTER 99

Fault Lines

The next day Scot called Marie and left her a message. "It's me. I hope you're feeling better. Please call me back as soon as you can. If I don't hear from you in the next few hours, I'm coming over." Scot then sent the same message in text.

Scot drove to Target and parked in the back of the crowded lot. His phone chimed. He glanced at Marie's name, then swiped right. "Marie."

"Sorry I missed your call earlier. I'm still feeling pretty rough," Marie said, sounding better than the night before.

Scot powered down the driver's side window, letting the spring air inside. "What's wrong? Do you have the flu?"

"I may have gotten food poisoning. You don't want details. Trust me."

"Sounds awful."

"It's beyond awful. So what's this about Mom running off to Vegas with everyone's money?"

Scot explained the situation, telling Marie about Heather's credit card bills and bank statements and then the confrontation. "What do you think? Do you think Johnny's got her hooked on drugs? Or maybe she's letting him gamble all the money?"

Marie hesitated. "I don't know."

"Do you think it's possible that this isn't Johnny's fault? Do you think it's possible that Mom stole our money?"

"It's not only possible, but it already happened."

"But we don't know if Johnny's behind it."

Marie exhaled.

"What?"

"You're always defending her. You gave her $46,000, and now it's gone. She was managing Heather's money. Now it's gone. Then she gaslights you both. I don't see how this is Johnny's fault."

"I don't think she would've done this without Johnny's influence. He must have a gambling problem."

"She stole my college money long before she met Johnny."

An awkward silence passed between them.

"You still there?" Marie asked.

"Yeah. I'm here," Scot replied.

"I understand what you're going through. It's hard to believe that our mother is a thief and a liar, but she is."

"But what if Ray never actually sent the check for your tuition? He didn't even try with me."

"If that's the case, how do you explain what she just did to you and Heather?"

"Like I said, Johnny—"

"I have to go," Marie said with ice in her voice. "I can't do this with you. Think what you want, but I can't do this."

"I'm sorry. I'm trying to figure it out."

"I have to go." Marie disconnected the call.

Scot set his phone in the cupholder and leaned his head on the steering wheel. He thought about his mother. *Is it her? Would she really do this? Or does she just make bad choices in men? Marie's making the same mistake. Frank's a total piece of shit.* Scot raised his gaze and took a deep breath. He exited his Mercury and walked into Target.

About half of the customers wore masks. Target was considered an essential retailer because of their medicine and food sections and, therefore, remained open on the first day of the stay-at-home order for Lebanon County. People were only supposed to go out if they were an essential worker or if they were shopping for food or medicine, although Scot doubted the cops were strictly enforcing the rule.

Scot didn't have on a mask, so he tried to keep his distance, as he made a lap around the store. As he walked by the registers, he surveyed the cashiers, their lower faces covered with masks. His heart nearly stopped when he spotted a cashier with a brown ponytail and the same build as Anna. The young woman turned from her register to the customer, giving Scot a better view. It wasn't Anna.

Scot's phone chimed in the front pocket of his jeans. He swiped right and said, "Hello?"

"Is this Scot Caldwell?" a man asked.

Scot nearly hung up, thinking it was a telemarketer. "Yes."

"This is Ted Armstrong from Home Depot."

CHAPTER 100

Cart Pusher Redux

A week later Scot pushed a train of shopping carts toward Home Depot. The hardware behemoth was considered an essential retailer and remained open during the stay-at-home order. A customer shoved their empty cart at him, the cart colliding with the train.

"Sorry," the customer said, wincing. "I'm in a hurry." She pivoted and fast-walked back to her SUV.

Scot grabbed the cart. A honk caused him to flinch.

A lifted pickup truck drove past, dangerously close. The driver hung out the window and said, "Watch out, dumbass." Then he gunned his engine, black smoke coming from the tailpipe. Scot turned his head after catching a face full of the acrid smoke. It was the first time he was thankful to be wearing a face mask. Scot added the errant cart to his train and pushed them inside the store, parking the train in the shopping cart receptacle.

Then he went back outside, helping customers load lumber, bagged concrete, PVC pipe, bags of mulch, and potted plants. He couldn't help but envy them, thinking about the projects he wanted to complete at his own house, like fixing and staining his deck, removing wallpaper, painting, and installing ceiling fans for the upcoming summer.

At lunchtime, Scot ate in his car. As he ate his bologna sandwich, he grabbed the phone number from his wallet. He stared at the number. *I need to do something different.* Scot finished the last of his sandwich, swallowed, and tapped the phone number.

"Hello?" Delia Russo answered.

"Hi, uh, this is Scot Caldwell. I'm not sure if you remember me—"

"Of course I do. You're the young man who's been fixing up Henry's old house."

"That's right. I was wondering if you were still looking for someone to fix up your garage?"

"As a matter of fact, I am. Do you want the job?"

Scot smiled. "Yes. Yes, I do."

"When can you start?"

"As soon as tomorrow."

After finishing his conversation with Delia Russo, Scot walked into Home Depot and went to his boss's office. He knocked on the open door.

Ted Armstrong looked up from his cell phone. "Scot. What can I do for you?"

Scot stepped into the office and set his orange vest and apron on Ted's desk. "I'm sorry. This isn't for me anymore."

CHAPTER 101

Scot's First Client

Scot hauled a trash bag from Delia Russo's garage, setting it on the driveway with the others.

Delia entered the garage from the house.

Scot hauled another trash bag.

Delia fast-walked to Scot, waving her arms back and forth. "No, no, no. What are you *doing*?"

Scot tilted his head, confused. "Moving the trash out, so I can organize the garage."

She crossed her arms over her chest. "And *what* do you plan to do with all this trash?"

"You said your trash comes on Wednesday."

"It does, but they won't pick it up here. You have to put it on the curb."

"I'll move everything to the curb before I go."

"No, no, no. You can't do that. The earliest the trash can go on the curb is the night before, so Tuesday night."

Scot exhaled, thinking about the fact that he'd only charged eighty dollars. "Okay, I'll come back on Tuesday to move them to the curb."

"Professional companies have a truck. They don't leave trash at the customer's house."

Scot thought, *Professional companies don't charge what I'm charging*. "I'm sorry, Mrs. Russo."

Her black wig was off-kilter, and sweat beaded along her hairline.

"Well, as long as you come back Tuesday night. I can't move all those bags by myself."

Scot stacked the trash on the driveway, then organized the garage, hanging pegboards, stacking storage bins, and moving the workbench. Scot had finished by lunchtime, figuring that, even having to come on Tuesday, he was still making more per hour than he had at Big-Mart.

But then Delia entered the garage.

Scot smiled. "What do you think? Looks great, *huh*?"

Delia surveyed her garage, with bins stacked neatly, the concrete swept, and tools hung and organized. She shook her head. "This won't do. The workbench should go along the west wall. And all those bins should go along the north wall." She pointed to the north wall, nearest the house. "I need those bins to be close to the house. It has my crafts and Christmas decorations. And don't stack them so high. They're too heavy when I have to reach over my head."

Scot spent the next hour moving everything to Delia's specifications.

Delia surveyed the garage again and frowned. "It looks too cluttered now. Put everything back the way you had it, but leave my crafts and Christmas decorations by the door."

Scot forced a smile, thinking about his profit margin going up in smoke.

★★★

At the end of the day, Delia admired her clean and organized garage. She handed Scot an envelope with two twenty-dollar bills and said, "I'll give you the other half when you move the trash to the curb on Tuesday."

"Thank you, Mrs. Russo," Scot said, forcing another smile.

"Before you go, make sure you put the trash bags in the garage. You can't leave them on the driveway. My HOA will fine me."

"Of course."

Scot spent fifteen minutes moving the trash bags back into the garage, so Mrs. Russo wouldn't get into trouble with her homeowner's association.

On his drive home, Scot called Marie and Heather. Neither of them answered.

CHAPTER 102

Stuck

The next morning, while eating his cereal, Scot's cell phone chimed. He glanced at the number, groaned, and swiped right. "Good morning, Mrs. Russo."

"Good morning, Scot," Delia Russo said. "I was just calling to tell you that I was very impressed with your work ethic and attitude. I know I can be particular."

"Thank you, Mrs. Russo. I'm happy that you're satisfied with my work."

"I have lots of friends who could use your services, but I wanted to ask you before giving out your number."

"Sure. That'd be great. Thank you."

"Make sure you come by tomorrow night to move the trash."

"Of course. It's on my calendar.

"See you then." Mrs. Russo disconnected the call.

Scot finished his breakfast; then he called his sisters again. Neither of them had returned his messages from yesterday. He wanted to see how they were doing and share about his new business venture.

Heather didn't answer his call, which wasn't abnormal, so he also sent her a text. Then he called Marie.

"Hi, Scot," Marie answered.

"Hey. I was just calling to see how you're doing," Scot replied, still sitting at the kitchen table.

"I'm fine."

"You're not sick anymore?"

"No. Thankfully, I'm all better. I wouldn't wish food poisoning on my worst enemy."

He leaned back in his chair. "So I started a new business."

"Really? What kind of business?"

"It's a handyman business."

"You know how to fix stuff?"

"I know a few things. I'm learning."

"That's great. You have any jobs yet?" A door opened and shut, the sound coming from Marie's phone. "I have to go."

"What? Why?"

"Frank doesn't like it if I'm on the phone too much."

Scot stood from the kitchen table. "Fuck Frank. That's bullshit. You're not a child."

"I really have to go. He gets mad."

"This isn't healthy. You shouldn't be afraid of your husband."

Frank's voice came from the background. "Get off that *fucking* phone."

Marie disconnected the call.

Scot called back, but his call immediately went to voice mail. He sent a text.

Scot: Are you okay? Text me, or I'm coming over.

Scot grabbed his keys and wallet from the kitchen counter and left the house. His phone buzzed with a text as he climbed into his Mercury.

Marie: I'm fine. Don't come over. I won't be home.
Scot: Where are you going? I can meet you for lunch later.
Marie: Another time. I don't have time today.

Scot thought about the last time he'd gone to Frank and Marie's house. Frank had abrasions on his knuckles, and he wouldn't let Scot see Marie. *I think he punched her. She probably made up the sickness, so I wouldn't see her face. He might be beating her right now.* Scot started his car and drove south to Villanova.

On the drive, he thought about what he should do. *I can't just knock on the front door, like last time. Frank won't let me in. Maybe I can walk around the house and look in the windows, see if I can get her attention.*

He parked down the street from Frank and Marie's house, not wanting Frank to see his car and be alerted to his visit. Then he walked into the backyard of their next-door neighbor and approached Frank and Marie's house from the back. Thankfully, it appeared that the next-door neighbor wasn't home.

Scot crept up to the walkout basement. A bank of glass doors lined the back of the house. Scot peered through the glass. Gym-quality machines and free weights were arranged in neat order. A flat-screen television sat dormant on the wall. He tried the door handle, but it was locked. He thought about breaking the window on the door, then reaching in and unlocking it.

Instead, he tiptoed around the right side of the house, stepping up the flagstone stairs to the first floor. He peeked in Frank's office window. It was empty. Barely audible but sharp voices came from inside the house. Glass shattered. Marie cried out. Scot ran to the backdoor, grabbed a rock from the landscaping near the patio, then smashed the windowpane next to the lock. He reached inside and turned the lock. Scot opened the door, and the alarm blared, like an air raid siren.

He sprinted through the gym, ran up the stairs, and into the first-floor living room. Frank tapped on the keypad, near the front door, silencing the alarm. Scot stopped in the middle of the living room.

Frank glared at Scot, as he approached. "What the hell are you doing here?"

"I need to see Marie."

"I don't give a fuck what you need." Frank grabbed Scot by the arm and pulled him toward the front door.

Scot resisted and shouted, "Marie! Marie!"

She appeared at the top of the spiral staircase, wearing sunglasses and a turtleneck. "Go home, Scot."

Scot wrenched his arm free and went to the staircase, with Frank right behind him. "Not until you take off those glasses."

"This is none of your business. You wouldn't understand."

Frank gripped Scot's shoulder. "Get the fuck out of my house."

Scot stepped away from Frank. "Don't fucking touch me. I'm calling the police."

"To tell them what? How you broke into my house?"

Scot ignored Frank, his gaze on Marie. "You don't have to be here. You can stay with me. You don't need his money." Scot held out his hand, beckoning Marie. "Come on. Let's go."

Marie removed her glasses revealing a faded black eye.

Scot pivoted and swung at Frank, his punch weak, but landing square on Frank's nose.

Frank bent over, holding his nose.

"Stop it, Scot," Marie said, hurrying down the stairs.

"God damn it." Frank stood upright, touched his nose, and looked at the blood on his fingers. Frank clenched his fists and stepped to Scot.

Scot backpedaled, showing his palms.

"Leave him alone, Frank," Marie said.

Frank shoved Scot, causing him to trip over his feet, but he didn't fall. Frank shoved him again, causing Scot to slam against the front door. Frank put his large hands around Scot's neck and squeezed.

Scot turned beet red. He tried to pry Frank's hands from his neck, but Scot was unsuccessful.

"Stop it, Frank," Marie pleaded in the background.

Frank let go, and Scot gasped for air. Frank opened the front door and gave Scot one final shove, sending him stumbling off the front stoop, and falling on the flagstone walkway. Frank stood in the open doorway, his hands on his hips.

Scot stood and fished his phone from his pocket. "I'm calling the police."

"Call Chief Waters. He's a close personal friend," Frank said, wiping blood from his nose. "He'll make sure you're arrested for assault and breaking and entering."

"I don't care if I get arrested. You're getting arrested for what you did to Marie."

Marie slipped past Frank. "Frank didn't hit me. I fell."

Scot twisted his face in confusion. "What are you talking about?"

She spoke without emotion, almost robotic. "If you call the police, I'll tell them that I fell."

"Why would you do that?"

Marie didn't look Scot in the eye as she said, "Because it's the truth."

CHAPTER 103

Family First

A red-spotted blackbird squawked in the nearby oak tree. Scot edged his client's front flower beds with one of Henry's old shovels. Then Scot dug out the weeds, putting the debris in his wheelbarrow.

Mrs. Redner exited her craftsman-style home, carrying a tray, with a pitcher of tea and empty glasses. The white-haired woman set the tray on the outdoor coffee table, shaded by the wraparound porch.

"Are you thirsty?" Mrs. Redner asked, looking down at Scot from the porch.

Scot stuck his shovel in the soil. "Yes. Thank you."

They sat across from each other on wicker patio furniture, drinking iced tea.

"It looks so much better already," Mrs. Redner said, gesturing to her front flower beds.

"Thank you. I should be done by the end of the day." Scot gulped his iced tea.

"I hope my little blackbird isn't bothering you."

"I think it's the other way around."

Mrs. Redner laughed. "She has a nest in that oak, so she gets a little territorial."

The bird squawked.

Scot glanced over his shoulder. "I think she heard you."

"Oh dear," Mrs. Redner said. "Your neck is very red."

"I burn easy."

"You need some sunblock." Mrs. Redner rose from her seat.

Scot stood too. "I'm fine."

"No. You'll be in bad shape tomorrow if we don't take action. I have some sunblock in the kitchen."

Scot finished his tea, while Mrs. Redner went inside to fetch the sunblock.

She returned with two tubes and handed one to Scot. "This is SPF 50. Put it on your neck and arms. It won't help the sunburn you've already gotten, but it'll stop it from getting worse."

"Thank you," Scot replied, rubbing the lotion on the back of his neck.

Mrs. Redner set the other tube on the table. It held a bright green lotion. "This is aloe. Put this on your sunburn before you go to bed. It'll give you some relief and help you heal."

Scot applied sunblock to his sun-kissed arms. "Thanks again. This is really nice of you."

She stared at Scot for a moment. "My late-husband was fair, like you. He loved to work outside, and I was always on him about wearing sunblock."

Scot wondered if he had died from skin cancer.

Mrs. Redner continued. "My Joseph always had his priorities in order. That's what I loved about him. Family first. That's what he always said. Family first."

★★★

At the end of the day, Scot packed his dirty tools in the trunk of his Mercury. With the wheelbarrow inside, the trunk wouldn't shut, so he tied a rope from the trunk lid to the frame, holding it mostly shut. Scot removed the envelope from his back pocket and climbed into the driver's seat. He stuffed the envelope in the center console. It was a check for three hundred dollars, more than he'd ever made in a day, apart from Bitcoin.

Scot smiled and drove a few miles down the road to Delia Russo's house. He moved the trash bags to the curb, under Mrs. Russo's watchful eye. When he was finished, she handed him forty dollars, the second half of his underbid garage clean-up job.

Scot shoved the bills into the front pocket of his jeans. "By the way, thank you for all the referrals. I have a flooring job tomorrow for Ralph Akers, and several jobs next week."

"As long as you do good work, I'm happy to refer you." Mrs. Russo narrowed her eyes. "But, if I get any bad reports from my friends, the referrals stop. Do you understand me?"

Scot nodded. "I do. I'll do my best."

"I know you will. Jane Redner told me she was thrilled with the gardening you did for her today."

Scot smiled. "She's really nice."

Mrs. Russo arched her eyebrows. "Unlike me, right?"

"Uh, no. That's not what I meant."

Mrs. Russo cackled, her wig off-kilter. "I know I'm a pain in the rear, but, if you can please me, you can please anyone."

"I'll remember that."

On the way home, Scot thought about what Mrs. Redner had said about family first. *Shit. My family's the opposite. It's every man, woman, and child for themselves.* He gripped the steering wheel, farmland on either side of the two-lane road. *Maybe that's the problem. Maybe that's why Marie's stuck in an abusive relationship and Heather thinks she has to do porn. I haven't heard from Heather since we confronted Mom and Johnny. How long ago was that?* Scot did the math in his head. *Thirteen days. That's not out of the ordinary. We've gone months without talking.* Scot pursed his chapped lips. He had an uneasy feeling deep in the pit of his stomach. *She seemed seriously depressed that night. I should text her.*

As he drove, he tapped her number, but it went to voice mail. Then he thumb-typed a quick text, his eyes flicking from the road to his phone and back again.

The Mercury drifted across the double yellow lines, as he focused on his phone. A horn jolted his gaze back to the road. He jerked the wheel right, barely missing the oncoming SUV. He pulled off the road and parked on the shoulder, his heart thumping in his chest.

"Holy shit," he said to himself. "That was close."

When he calmed, he finished his text to Heather.

> **Scot:** Hey. I haven't heard from you. I'm a little worried. I wanted to see how you're doing. Text me back.

Then he sent a text to Marie.

> **Scot:** My offer still stands. You can live with me anytime you want, for as long as you want.

CHAPTER 104

To Whoever Gives a Shit

At breakfast, Scot reread the text that Marie had sent last night.

Marie: I appreciate the offer, but Frank and I are good. Like all marriages, we argue, but he would never intentionally hurt me. I suggest you concentrate on finishing school.

Scot still wasn't sure how to respond. *He would never intentionally hurt me? That's bullshit.* Scot took a big bite from his Fruit Loops. He tapped a text to Heather. He still hadn't heard back from her.

Scot: Where are you? I'm worried. I'd like to stop by and see you today. I have a job this morning, but I should be done around five or six. Maybe we can have dinner. I can pick up takeout. Anything you want. Text me back, so I know you're alive.

Scot spent most of the day at Ralph Akers's house, installing the same hardwood flooring that was in his own house. After the job, Scot climbed into his Mercury, his back aching a little from working on his hands and knees all day, but not near as much as the first time he'd installed flooring. And he'd done a more professional job this time, especially on the corners. Mr. Akers had been complimentary.

Scot fished his phone from the front pocket of his jeans, checking his texts. Still nothing from Heather. So he drove across town to her mansion, situated on several acres of overgrown grass. Her neighborhood was the nicest in Lebanon, and her house was the biggest. Scot's nickname for the mansion—the House That Farts Built—didn't sound so funny anymore. He parked in her empty driveway.

He exited his Mercury and went to the garage door, peering into a window. Her red BMW was in the garage. The sun was still high in the cloudless sky, with a light breeze. Scot went to the front door and pressed the doorbell several times.

A minute passed. Nothing. Scot tried the door handle, and, to his surprise, it opened. He stepped into the foyer, shutting the door behind him. He winced at the faint smell of feces and rotten eggs in the air.

"Heather. Heather," he called out. "Are you here?"

He wondered if she'd gone away and had left out food, but the smell wasn't coming from the kitchen. He stepped beyond the foyer and through the living room, which was nearly all white—white walls, white furniture, white Oriental rug, and white curtains.

As he approached the stairs, the acrid smell intensified, and it gained in intensity with each step up the curved staircase. Scot thought that maybe some animal got in, couldn't get out, and then died in the house.

Scot lifted the collar of his T-shirt over his nose and opened Heather's bedroom door. The smell of rotting flesh, feces, rotten eggs, mothballs, and rotten cabbage flooded his nose and throat, causing him to choke.

A body was on Heather's lacy white canopy bed. Scot trembled, as he stepped closer to the bed. The bloated body vaguely resembled Heather. Foamy blood leaked from her mouth and nose. Her skin was puffy and yellowish-green. Scot gagged, hot bile running up his throat. He turned from the body, swallowing the bile, and noticing the envelope and open pill bottle on her dresser.

The empty pill bottle was Vicodin, prescribed to Laura Manning. The white envelope had a message in Heather's loopy handwriting. It read *To whoever gives a shit*. Scot grabbed the envelope, rushed from the room, and ran down the stairs. He ran through the living room, opened the front door, and raced outside.

On the overgrown lawn, on that beautiful spring day, Scot fell to his knees, and vomited several times, tears streaming down his face. When the vomiting subsided, he rose to his feet and staggered to the front stoop. He sat on the front step, held his head in his hands and sobbed.

When he finally calmed, he dialed 9-1-1 and said, "My sister killed herself." After giving Heather's address, he disconnected the call. While he waited for the police, he opened the envelope. The note was handwritten on printer paper.

> To whoever gives a shit,
>
> What's the fucking point? Why should I bother? My mother stole everything from me. My father disowned me. I don't have any friends. I don't have a boyfriend, and I never will. Men only want me for sex. After what I've done, I'll never be able to change that.
>
> There's nothing worse than a poor old whore. At least I'll only be two of those things.
>
> Fuck the world.
> Hot Heather

CHAPTER 105

The End of the World

After the police had asked their questions and Heather had been taken away in a body bag, Scot had made the appropriate calls. His parents and remaining sister. He'd left a voice mail and sent a text to Laura. Both messages were unrequited. Same for Marie. Scot had wondered if Frank had revoked her phone privileges. Eric had been stoic on the phone, saying all the right things, but Scot had wondered if he really gave a shit. Heather had talked about feeling abandoned by her father for his new family.

Scot parked his Mercury in the Target parking lot. Sunlight streamed into his windows. It was the same beautiful spring day a few hours after puking on Heather's front lawn. Scot exited his car and walked into Target. He wandered around the store, hoping to run into Anna, but he didn't. He left the store, returning to his car.

As he climbed into his Mercury, his cell phone chimed. He fished his phone from his pocket, checked the name, and swiped right.

"Hey," Scot said.

"I'm so sorry," Marie said.

Scot cleared his throat. "Don't be sorry for me. I'm not the one in a body bag."

A few seconds of silence passed between them.

"I can't believe this happened," Marie said.

Something snapped inside Scot. "Mom stole her money. Eric disowned her. What the *fuck* do you expect?"

"Don't yell at me. I didn't have anything to do with it."

"I know. I'm sorry. I just, … I was so fucking oblivious."

"No, you weren't."

Scot clenched his jaw. "I was. You tried to tell me about Mom. All I did was offer up excuses for her. She's … I don't know what she is. A psychopath? A con-woman? What kind of person steals from their children?"

Marie exhaled. "I don't know."

"What am I supposed to do now? Never talk to Mom again? Do I live my life like I don't have a mother?"

"That's what I do."

Scot rubbed his eyes with his free hand. "Heather told me that she felt abandoned by Eric. Obviously, I knew that Mom stole her money. She told me that she couldn't find a serious boyfriend. Guys didn't see her as girlfriend material. They saw her as a piece of meat. I knew all this, and I didn't do shit. I should've seen it coming."

"Don't do that. It's not fair, and it's not true. From what I know, you're the only one who tried to help her."

"It doesn't feel like that."

"It'll take time." Marie took a deep breath. "Do you know anything about the funeral?"

"Only that Eric's handling it."

Muffled shouts came from Marie's phone. Scot figured it was probably Frank.

"I have to go," Marie said.

"Yeah. Okay."

Marie disconnected the call.

Scot set his phone in the cupholder and watched people come and go from Target, still hoping to see Anna. Some wore masks; some didn't. Many had toilet paper in their carts and canned goods. Much more so than normal.

The end of the world.

On impulse, Scot grabbed his phone from the cupholder and

tapped Anna's phone number from his contacts. There was a quick busy signal, followed by his call being dropped.

Still blocked.

CHAPTER 106

What a Waste

Heather's funeral took place five days later, paid for by Eric. Scot sat in his Mercury in the funeral home parking lot. His window was down, letting in the warm breeze and the sounds of spring. He closed his bloodshot eyes and saw Heather's puffy face and yellowish-green skin. He opened his eyes again, not wanting to relive the moment. His head pounded from lack of sleep. Since her suicide, Scot had had a recurring nightmare.

The dream took place in their childhood home. Scot lay in his bed. Faint crying came from Heather's room next door. Scot padded to Heather's door and knocked. The crying ceased.

Scot knocked again. "Heather? Are you okay?"

Heather opened her bedroom door, her eyes puffy. "What do you want?"

"I want to help you."

She shook her head. "You can't help me."

Scot held out his hands. "Please. Let me help you."

"I need something for the pain."

A pill bottle appeared in his hand. He handed her the bottle, his arm not responding to the opposite impulse. Heather took the bottle, unscrewed the cap, and dumped hundreds of pills into her mouth. Then her face morphed from that of a beautiful young girl to a bloated corpse.

Then Scot always woke, thrashing in his bed, covered in sweat.

Scot glanced at the time on his phone—*3:59 p.m.* He had purpose-ly missed the viewing earlier that day, not wanting to see Heather's body or his parents. Over the phone, Marie had told him that it was an open casket, and, despite the mountain of makeup and embalming fluid, Heather appeared puffy.

Scot steeled himself, exited his car, and walked into the gothic funeral home. A man in a black suit and a surgical mask greeted Scot at the entrance. Scot had to give his name, as the funeral home only allowed those on the prearranged list. This was in response to Pennsylvania's new indoor-gathering limit of twenty-five people. The man directed Scot down a hall to the left.

Scot walked to the end of the hall, the carpet bloodred. A free-standing sign next to closed double doors read Heather Manning Funeral. Scot checked his phone. He was two minutes late.

Laura's voice came through the doors. "Thank you all for com-ing."

Scot slipped into the room, hoping not to be noticed, but the old door creaked as he opened it and creaked again as he shut it. Laura glared at him from the podium. Roughly fifteen people turned in their seats and gawked. Scot recognized a few aunts and uncles he hadn't seen in years. Eric and Janine, plus Marie and Frank, sat in the front row, but no Johnny. Scot dipped his head and sat in the back row, along the aisle.

"As I was *saying*, thank you all for coming," Laura said. "Heather would've been so grateful. She was my beautiful baby." Laura sniffed, her eyes glassy. "They say losing a child is the greatest pain a person can endure. When I heard that my baby died, my heart died with her."

Scot crossed his arms over his chest. *Her heart? What a bunch of bullshit.*

"I would give my own life for one more minute with my baby." Laura fanned herself to stop the tears from overflowing. "I don't know what I'll do without her."

Scot stood from his seat, like he had no control over his body, like he was in his recurring nightmare. "Bullshit."

The audience gasped. Everyone turned to Scot. Laura was slack-jawed.

"You don't know what you'll do without her *money*," Scot said.

Eric stood from his seat. "This isn't the time or the place."

Scot clenched his fists, glowering at his stepfather. "You're both hypocrites."

Marie stood from her seat too. "Stop it, Scot."

Tears slipped down Laura's cheeks. "I can't believe you'd do this to me."

"She'd still be alive if it wasn't for you two." Scot pointed at Eric. "You disowned her." Then he pointed at Laura. "And you stole all her money."

"That's not true," Laura shrieked.

Eric fast-walked down the aisle toward Scot.

"It is true. It was in her suicide note," Scot said.

Murmuring came from the audience.

"You need to leave. *Now*," Eric said, opening the door.

"What a fucking waste." Scot left the funeral.

CHAPTER 107

Sob Story

Scot left the funeral home and drove to Target. He wandered around the big-box store, wearing his black suit, hoping to see Anna, hoping she'd ask him about his suit, hoping for someone to give a shit. But she wasn't there, and Scot went back to his car.

Sitting in the driver's seat, he thought about Ray, his biological father. *Ray was telling the truth. He did send that check for Marie's college. Maybe he isn't the piece of shit that Mom made him out to be.*

Scot grabbed his phone from the cupholder and called Marie. After several rings, his call went to voice mail. He disconnected the call and scrolled through his contacts. Scot paused on Henry's contact, wondering what Henry might say, if he were still alive. *He'd probably quote some Stoic philosopher about death, something about death being a natural part of life.*

Scot shook his head and spoke aloud to himself. "There's nothing natural about this."

He continued to scroll through his contacts, stopping on Ray. He hadn't seen or talked to his biological father in over five years, not since he and Charlotte went there to ask for help with his college tuition. *That was a disaster.* Scot winced at the thought. Charlotte had told his stepmother, Brenda, to fuck off. Ray had kicked them out. *Maybe Ray was right not to help me. It's not like we have a relationship. Maybe that's my fault.*

Scot called Ray, his heart thumping in his chest, and his palms sweaty.

"Hello?" Ray said.

"It's Scot."

Ray hesitated. "Scot." He hesitated again, then spoke in a business-like tone. "What can I do for you?"

"Heather committed suicide."

"I know. Marie told me. I'm sorry, son."

Scot swallowed the lump in his throat. "I think, … I think I've been wrong about my mother. She filled my head with … things about you that …" Tears welled in Scot's eyes.

After a moment of silence, Ray said, "Are you still there?"

Scot's voice quivered. "I'm here."

"Where are you now?"

"In my car. In Lebanon."

"Not sure if you have plans, but, if you need to talk, you're welcome to come to dinner tonight. It's only 4:35. If you leave now, you can make it here by seven."

★★★

Scot had accepted the dinner invitation and made the two-and-a-half-hour trip to Altoona, Pennsylvania. When Scot had arrived, Brenda had grilled him about his potential Covid exposure.

"Have you been around anyone with Covid or anyone showing any symptoms?" Brenda had asked, guarding the doorway.

"Not that I know of," Scot had replied, standing on the stoop.

"Do you have a fever? Loss of taste or smell?"

"No."

Ray had finally saved him, inviting him inside.

Now he sat at the dinner table, with Ray and Brenda, eating lasagna. Their son, Ray Caldwell Jr., was home from school, as Penn State had canceled their in-person classes due to Covid, but he was at a friend's house. Ray appeared much the same as he did five years ago, fit and stern, with a hawkish nose and a white buzz cut. Brenda had aged, her Sandra Bullock face drooping and her body puffier than Scot remembered. He thought about what his misogynist ex-coworker Kyle used to say. *The wall comes for them all.*

Scot set down his fork, his plate empty. He wiped his face with his napkin and said, "Thank you for dinner. I haven't eaten all day."

Ray gestured to his wife. "It's all Brenda."

Brenda smiled, stabbing her salad with her fork. "You're welcome, Scot. It really is good to see you after all these years."

"I'm sorry it's been so long," Scot said, addressing Ray. "I've recently learned some things about my mother that I didn't know. I don't think she was always truthful about you."

Brenda huffed. "That's an understatement."

Ray frowned at his wife. "Let him talk." Ray turned his attention back to Scot.

"She said a lot of bad things about you over the years, and I think it clouded my judgment." Scot took a deep breath. "I'm sorry."

"I appreciate that. It takes a big man to admit that he's wrong."

"What happened with Heather, ... it really opened my eyes."

Ray and Brenda listened, as Scot told them the sordid tale of Heather's life and death, and Laura's theft, not just of Heather's money but also Scot's.

"Your sister filled us in on some of that. It's a terrible thing," Ray said.

"It's awful, but it's not surprising," Brenda said. "If the mother has loose morals, the child will have loose morals. The apple doesn't fall very far from the tree."

Scot stiffened. "Heather never hurt anyone. There was nothing wrong with her morals. She was just young and lost. And it wasn't just Laura who failed her."

Brenda set down her fork with a *clang.* "After everything, I can't believe you're still defending *that* woman."

Ray showed his palm to his wife. "*Brenda.*"

"That's what you think of me, isn't it?" Scot asked Brenda, raising his voice. "I'm one of those apples that doesn't fall very far."

Brenda pressed her lips together.

"You need to lower your tone," Ray said.

Scot turned to his father. "What about you? Is that what you think? That I'm like my mother?"

"I don't know," Ray replied, without emotion. "I haven't heard from you in five years. Last time you were here, you tried to shake me down for money, and now …"

Scot shook his head. "You think I'm here for money?"

"I don't know. You didn't mention anything about money on the phone, and now that you're here, you give us a sob story about your mother stealing your college money."

Scot drew back, his face twisted in disgust. "*Sob story*? Are you serious?"

"Last time you came here for money. And now you're talking about Laura stealing your college money."

"You don't think she stole my money?"

"I know she's capable of stealing, but I have no idea how much money you had, if any."

"Forty-six thousand. I told you."

"That's what you said, but—"

"But what? You don't believe me?"

"You're twenty-six years old, Scot. If you want to go to college, that's on you. It's time to take responsibility for your own actions."

Scot stood from the table. "This was a mistake."

Brenda said, "Just like last time. He doesn't get what he wants—"

"Shut the fuck up, Brenda."

Ray sprang from his seat, his face beet red. "Get out of my house and don't come back. We're *done*."

Scot nodded, talking to Brenda, but staring at his father. "You're right, Brenda. It's just like last time." As he walked past his father to leave, he said, "You're wrong about me."

CHAPTER 108

Closing

On the way home, Scot stopped at the Target in Lebanon. He drove through the parking lot, searching for Anna's Honda Civic. He saw several Civics of varying model years and colors, but not Anna's, although Scot had no idea if she still drove that car.

He wandered around the store. It was mostly empty that Monday night. As he passed the children's clothing section, he saw a brown-headed associate with a red mask, hanging clothing. Scot stared, sure it was a mirage.

The woman did a double take, then stared back, her eyes wide.

Scot smiled and walked over to Anna, his hands in his pockets.

She stiffened as he approached. "What are you doing here?"

Scot shrugged. "Shopping."

Anna arched her eyebrows. "Without a cart or a basket?"

"I just need a couple things."

Anna nodded. "What's with the suit?"

Scot nearly told her about Heather, but he didn't want to emotionally blackmail her. "I was at a formal … get together. So how are you doing?"

"I'm doing okay." Anna reached into the boxes at her feet, grabbing a hanger in one hand and a onesie in the other. When she rose, she put the onesie on the hanger.

"How long have you been working here?"

"A few months." Anna hung the onesie on the rack.

Scot peered into her eyes, desperately wanting to see her face. "Are you still saving for vet school?"

She grabbed another hanger and onesie. "I don't think that's going to happen. It's tough enough to keep the lights on, pay for food, rent, my car. Not much left over, you know?"

"Yeah, I do."

She hung the onesie on the rack. "What about you? Are you working?"

"I'm working for myself. Handyman stuff. I'm saving up for a van."

"Good for you," she said, her inflection telling Scot that she meant it.

Scot smiled. "Thanks. That means a lot coming from you."

"Are you still investing in crypto?" She reached into the boxes and grabbed another hanger and onesie.

"No. I have a few dollars still in the market, but it's not much at all. I don't even look at it anymore. Too busy working."

"Maybe that's for the best." She hung another onesie.

"Probably."

A voice came over the loudspeaker. "Target will be closing in five minutes. Target will be closing in five minutes. Thank you."

Scot glanced up at the ceiling. "I guess I should … get going."

Anna nodded. "Yeah …"

Scot turned to leave, but then pivoted back to Anna and said, "I'm really sorry about what I did to you."

Anna was stunned for a beat. "It's ancient history."

"No, it's not. I wish I could go back in time and fix it all."

"It's over. Really—"

"You wanna go out sometime?" Scot blurted out the invitation, speaking rapidly, as if he might not have the courage to finish the sentence.

Anna blushed. "I'm sorry. I can't, um …"

Scot dipped his head. "I understand. I wouldn't go out with me either."

"It's not that. I have a boyfriend. It's new, but I really like him."

CHAPTER 109

One Year and Two Weeks Later ...

Scot parked his van in his client's driveway. The sun warmed his face, as he walked to the rear doors. Scot Caldwell Handyman was lettered on the van, along with his phone number and web address. He opened the rear doors and grabbed a small stack of vinyl siding.

A horn startled him. He turned around to see a yellow Lamborghini near the driveway apron. The driver honked again and held out his hands. Scot left the siding in his van and walked toward the car.

The driver powered down his window. He appeared younger than Scot. Maybe in his late teens or early twenties. "You're in my space."

Scot turned and looked back at his van.

"Are you deaf? Move that piece of shit."

Without a word, Scot went to his van, shut the rear doors, and backed out of the driveway. It wasn't a piece of shit. In fact, Scot had paid $40,000 for the lightly used van. The young man and his Lamborghini parked in the driveway, revving the V-12 engine for no apparent reason. Scot parked along the street and carried the siding across the lawn.

As he walked to the house and work area, he noticed the vanity plate on the Lamborghini—*Coiner1*. The young man went inside. Scot set the siding on the lawn and gazed at the exposed house wrap on the second floor of the Cape Cod–style home. A bad wind storm had come through a few days ago, and his client had lost a few pieces of siding.

Scot went back to his van and hefted his ladder from the roof-mounted rack. His arm muscles bulged from the effort. Scot carried the ladder across the lawn and leaned it against the house. This was no small feat. Despite being made from lightweight aluminum, the forty-foot extension ladder was quite heavy.

Over the past year Scot had embraced his new business, applying his work ethic to the underserved handyman market. He took any job, no matter how small. If he wasn't sure how to do something, he learned how to do it. When he made mistakes, he made sure that he paid for them—never his clients. His client list had grown, along with his skills and reputation. Sixty hours was a typical workweek.

His client exited the front door.

Scot smiled at the middle-aged man as he approached. "Good afternoon, Mr. Higgins."

Mr. Higgins smiled back. "Afternoon, Scot. Thanks for fitting me into your schedule on such short notice."

"It's no problem. I should be done in about an hour."

"That's great." Mr. Higgins hesitated. "I, uh, wanted to apologize for my son." He gestured to the Lamborghini. "He made a fortune in crypto. Now he thinks he's an F-ing genius. He's become very entitled."

Scot nodded. "I understand. It's okay."

"It's not okay, but I appreciate that. This crypto's been on a tear lately. I've been saying it's a bubble for the longest time." Mr. Higgins frowned. "My son's happy to point out how wrong I've been."

That night, as Scot ate dinner at his kitchen table, he thought about what his client had said about crypto being on a tear lately. Out of curiosity, Scot checked his Coinbase account. It had been over thirteen months since he'd last looked at his account. Back then he had $1,200 split between three cryptos that he'd chosen with dart throws.

Scot gaped at the screen on his phone. "Holy shit. *Holy shit!*"

Your Portfolio
LiteCoin 11 LTC $3,810.07
Ethereum 3 ETH $7,997.61
DogeCoin 235,294 DOGE $63,529.38
Total Balance = $75,337.06

CHAPTER 110

To the Moon

Over the next ten days, Scot watched his account continue to grow. He resisted the urge to call Marie and to tell her the good news, not wanting to jinx it. *I doubt she'll pick up anyway.* Marie rarely called Scot anymore. Since Scot had broken into their house, he was *persona non grata.* Scot had invited Marie to live with him several times since the big blow-up, but each time seemed to push her further away, so, when they did talk, they stuck with superficial topics.

On Friday night, he ate dinner at his kitchen table and checked his Coinbase account. He grinned, his eyes bulging at the digits on his phone screen.

> Your Portfolio
> LiteCoin 11 LTC $2,856.15
> Ethereum 3 ETH $10,454.19
> DogeCoin 235,294 DOGE $159,999.92
> Total Balance = $173,310.26

"This is crazy," he said aloud to himself. "If it keeps going up like this, I'll be a millionaire by the end of the year."

He thought about having millions of dollars. *I won't blow it this time. I could live anywhere. Do anything. I wouldn't have to work anymore. What would I do?* He thought about his work, how the hours passed in the blink of an eye. Working at Big-Mart had been the reverse, with time moving at a glacierlike pace. He thought about his clients. Hundreds of them who depended on him for everything from minor plumbing and electrical to flooring, painting, and gardening.

He thought about the elderly widows on fixed incomes who raved about his reasonable pricing.

Scot gaped at the screen, specifically at his total balance. *One hundred and seventy-three thousand. Where have I seen that number before?* Scot stroked the stubble on his chin for a long moment. Then he leaned back in his chair and said aloud, "It's not where I've seen it. It's where I've heard it." He paused, still thinking. *Maybe Larry Boyd could help me with that.*

Then Scot went back to his phone and sold everything.

CHAPTER 111

Marie and The Abyss

Marie padded into Frank's home office, carrying his old fashioned. Frank slumped in his leather chair, staring at multiple screens, featuring stock charts and ticker symbols. Marie sidled up to him, taking his empty glass, replacing it with the fresh whiskey drink.

"This fucking market keeps going up," Frank said, his breath and his pores emitting alcohol.

"Going up is good, right?" Marie asked.

Frank glared at her. "If you're long. I'm *fucking* short. It's a bubble, and all these idiots are bidding this motherfucker into the stratosphere. It's all Fed funny money and stock buybacks. It's all a fucking sham."

"You're a great investor, honey. You'll figure it out."

Frank chugged his old fashioned and threw the glass against the wall, shattering it.

Marie ducked and covered her head.

"What the hell do you know?"

Marie smiled, trying to keep him from falling into the abyss. "What would you like for dinner? I was thinking about making crab cakes."

"Get me another drink." He gestured to the glass on the floor. "And clean that shit up."

Marie left his office, went to the supply closet, and grabbed a broom and a dustpan. She tiptoed into his office, not wanting to divert his attention from the screens. Marie swept the glass into the dustpan.

"Where's my drink?" Frank said.

"In a minute," Marie replied, with annoyance in her voice.

Frank sprang from his seat and slammed Marie against the wall. She dropped the dustpan, glass shards spilling across the hardwood. Marie slapped him across the face. Frank threw a right cross, connecting with Marie's left cheek. The impact knocked Marie to the ground. Everything went black.

When she came to, Frank yanked her to her feet like a rag doll and slammed her against the wall again. The room spun around her. Her bare legs burned, with several glass shards penetrating her flesh. Frank gripped Marie's neck with his large hands and squeezed. Marie clawed at his face, raking his flesh, creating three bloodred lines across his cheek.

The urge to breathe was stronger than anything Marie had ever felt. Frank continued to squeeze, glaring at Marie with bloodshot eyes. Her vision blurred. Her body went limp, and everything went black again.

CHAPTER 112

Marie and The Breaking Point

Marie lay on her back, her eyes closed, listening to the rhythmic breathing of her husband. Her aching cheek throbbed like a pulse. She'd been hit before. Not just a slap. She'd been punched on many occasions. That wasn't new. She'd been choked before too, but never to the point of a blackout. Since their wedding, Frank had slowly increased the abuse, starting with light verbal abuse. It had happened so gradually that Marie had endured the abuse, as if it were the natural order of things. But even the meekest have a breaking point. The near-death experience had been Marie's.

Marie turned her head, checking the clock, her neck barking in pain. It was midnight. Frank had been sound asleep for about an hour. She slipped out of bed. Frank groaned and rolled toward Marie. She stood frozen, like a deer in headlights. He went still again, his breathing rhythmic.

Marie padded to their bedroom door, leaving her cell phone on the bedside table. She rarely used it anyway. Frank tracked her movements with her cell phone and demanded full access to her phone at all times. She touched the door handle and turned back to Frank. He was sprawled in the middle of the bed, still asleep.

She turned the knob slowly, then opened the door just wide enough to slip through. As she crossed the threshold, she turned back again, expecting Frank to wake and to finish what he had started earlier. But he was in the same position. Marie tiptoed across the landing, then down the stairs to the kitchen. Moonlight filtered into the windows, giving her just enough light to navigate.

Around the corner from the kitchen, she entered the laundry room. Here, she turned on the light in the confined room, knowing that the light wouldn't filter upstairs. She opened the dryer and removed a backpack. It was stuffed with clothes, her wallet, and toiletries. Just the bare necessities.

Marie changed into her sweatpants, running shoes, and a turtle-neck to conceal the bruising on her neck. She stuffed her pajamas into the backpack and zipped it up. She put on the backpack and cinched the straps tight. Marie cut the light and crept through the kitchen, living room, and foyer, to the front door.

Her heart pounded. Sweat collected under her arms. She turned the dead bolt slowly, trying to avoid the audible *click*, and failing. When the lock clicked, she looked at the spiral staircase, expecting Frank to burst from their room and barrel down the stairs after her, but the house was still quiet.

She stared at the alarm on the wall next to the front door. The red light was on, signifying that it was armed. This was the moment she dreaded. She'd have to enter the four-digit code, then the Off button. Five buttons, each of them creating an audible *beep*. No way around it.

Marie took a deep breath, covered the speaker with her hand to muffle the sound, and punched in the code 3-4-6-7-Off. She looked upstairs again, listening and expecting Frank to stop her, but nothing happened. She opened the door, stepped onto the front stoop, and carefully shut the door behind her.

Then she ran. She ran on the macadam, through her neighbor-hood of fancy mansions. As she ran through the deserted streets, she smiled, sucking in the sweet air of freedom. She ran five miles, a distance she already knew she could run from her long runs on the treadmill. Frank insisted that she stay fit. On multiple occasions he'd said some version of "I won't be caught dead with a fat-ass wife."

She slowed to a jog, once she reached the parking lot of the twenty-four-hour Wegmans grocery store. Marie went inside, the automatic doors opening for her, and went to the customer service desk.

A sleepy young woman sat at the counter, her head propped up with her arm. The young woman straightened, as Marie approached. "May I help you?" the young woman asked.

"Could I use your phone?" Marie replied.

"Of course." The young woman selected an open line, turned the phone to Marie, and handed her the handset.

Marie put the handset to her ear and dialed the number. The phone rang on the other end. *Come on. Pick up. Pick up.* The call went to his voice mail. *Shit.* Marie dialed the number again. As the phone rang again, Marie scanned the grocery store, imagining a red-faced Frank marching toward her, his rage concealed just enough so nobody would intervene.

"Hello?" the sleepy voice answered.

Marie said, "Scot. I need you to pick me up."

CHAPTER 113

Marie's Out of the Frying Pan

Marie loitered by the shopping carts, watching the parking lot from just inside the Wegmans grocery store. A white van parked along the curb. Big vinyl lettering proclaimed Scot Caldwell Handyman. She exited the store, looking both ways, as she hurried to the van. Scot met her next to the passenger door, giving her a tight hug, the van idling.

When they separated, Scot inspected the bruising on her cheek. "Are you okay?"

Marie nodded. "I'm fine. It's nothing." Luckily her neck was covered by the turtleneck.

"It's *not* nothing. We need to go to the cops."

Marie shook her head. "It's over. I'm fine."

Scot raised his eyebrows. "*Marie.*"

"Going to the police will only make it worse." Marie looked around, still paranoid. "Can we get out of here?"

Scot opened the passenger door.

Marie tossed her backpack in the footwell and climbed inside.

Scot shut her safely inside and hurried to the driver's side. He drove them away from the Wegmans in Villanova, headed for his house in Lebanon.

Marie stared at the dark forest passing by at seventy miles per hour.

"You want to talk about what happened?" Scot asked.

Still peering out the passenger window, Marie replied, "No."

"What's the plan?"

"I don't know." Marie turned to Scot. "I just need a place to stay for a while, so I can figure things out."

Scot glanced from the road to Marie several times, as he said, "You can stay with me as long as you want. I have an extra bedroom and bathroom for you. I just renovated the bathroom. I mean, it's probably not as nice as what you're used to …"

"Sounds great. Thank you."

"Of course."

A moment of silence passed between them.

Scot glanced at Marie. "You think he'll come to my house for you?"

"I don't know," Marie replied. "He doesn't know where you live."

"I'm sure he can find out. I still think we should call the police."

Marie shook her head. "Absolutely not. The police won't be able to hold him. He has plenty of money to make bail, and he's friends with the chief of police. He'll be furious when he gets out, and he'll take it out on me. Trust me. I know him."

"If he shows up at my house, we should call the police immediately. I doubt he knows anyone in Lebanon."

"Okay." Marie turned away from Scot, leaning on the window. After the adrenaline rush of her escape, and the late hour, she drifted off to sleep.

Marie peered into Frank's bloodshot eyes, as he squeezed her neck. She scratched at his face, but it had no effect. Her vision blurred, dimmed, then went black.

Marie sat upright, rigid, gasping for air.

Scot leaned toward her, shaking her by her forearm. "Wake up, Marie. You're having a bad dream."

Marie looked around, her breath modulating, as she scanned the interior of the van.

"We're home," Scot said.

"Sorry."

Scot placed his hand on top of hers and squeezed. "You're safe."

Scot led Marie along the brick-and-stone walkway, landscape lighting illuminating the path. Manicured hedges and flowers framed the front of the brick rambler. Marie inhaled the woodsy fresh mulch smell.

Inside, the living room was sparsely furnished with a plaid couch and an open armoire, housing a television. The walls were painted a pale yellow, which matched the furniture and shiny wood floors.

"Your house is really nice," Marie said.

"I still need some more furniture, but, yeah, I think it's coming along."

Scot led her down the hallway. He flipped on the light and gestured to the bathroom. "This is your bathroom. I just put in new tile and a new sink."

The small bathroom had a shower tub, sky-blue walls, dark-blue tile in the shower, and a quartz countertop.

"You did all this yourself?" Marie asked.

Scot smiled. "I learned a lot of stuff by fixing up this house."

"I'm impressed." Marie dipped her head. "I'm sorry I never came over."

Scot had invited Marie to see his house on multiple occasions, but Frank wouldn't allow it, not after Scot had taken a swing at him.

"You're here now." Scot led Marie to the bedroom across the hall from the bathroom. He flipped on the light. "Sorry, it's a little empty. We can go out and look for furniture this weekend, if you want."

A single bed sat along the wall, along with a wooden dresser.

Marie hugged her brother and said, "It's perfect."

Before falling asleep, Marie snatched the large knife from the kitchen set and stashed it under her bed.

CHAPTER 114

Marie and Meaning

The next morning Marie sat at the kitchen table, pushing eggs around her plate. She wore a pair of jeans and a clean turtleneck. Scot had stared at her covered neck, when he'd seen her that morning, but he hadn't said anything. Marie worried that, if Scot saw the bruising, he'd renew his plea to go to the police.

Scot sat across from Marie at the table, most of his food already gone. Between bites he said, "I have a clogged sink to fix, but, after that, I was thinking we could go shopping for whatever you need."

"You have to work today?" Marie asked, distress in her voice.

It was Saturday.

"It won't take long," Scot replied. "You can come with me, if you want."

She exhaled. "I'll come with you. if that's okay."

"Yeah, sure. You can see me in action." He pointed at her plate. "Are the eggs all right? I have cereal, if you want something else."

Marie set down her fork. "Sorry, I'm not very hungry."

Scot nodded. "Do you know what happened to my kitchen knife?"

Marie blushed, embarrassed by her fear. "I'm sorry. I … I slept with it under my mattress."

"*Jesus*, Marie. If you're this scared, we need to go to the police."

"I'm fine."

Scot blew out a breath. "You're fine, *huh*? What's under that turtleneck?"

Marie looked down. "It's not important."

"Show me."

Marie hesitated, then pulled down her collar enough to show some of the bruising.

Scot winced. "Does it hurt?"

Marie raised her gaze and her voice. "I'm fine, and I'm *not* going to the police. If you do, I'll deny everything."

Scot showed his palms. "*Okay.* That's your decision. You know what I think."

"I do."

"If that piece of shit comes here, we're calling the police."

"I know."

They ate in silence, Marie picking at her food, while Scot cleaned his plate.

Scot wiped his face with his napkin and said, "I hate seeing you like this. I wish I knew what to do."

"There's nothing to do. I've ruined my life. It's already done."

"Please don't talk like that. You're scaring me. Heather was saying things like this."

Marie frowned. "Don't worry. I'm not brave enough to kill myself."

"That's bullshit. You got away from him. You left everything behind. That took guts."

Marie swallowed the lump in her throat. "I'm worthless."

"*He* made you feel worthless. It's a lie. You're priceless."

Tears welled in her eyes. "I have no skills, no friends, no family. I'm nothing."

"That's not true. You have me, and I *need* you." His eyes were glassy. "You hear me? I *need* you. Don't you ever think about leaving me."

Marie wiped the corners of her eyes, before the tears could fall. "My life has no meaning. That's the truth."

"No, it's not. Do you remember when I was a mess after my divorce?"

PHIL M. WILLIAMS

Marie nodded.

Scot leaned toward Marie, putting his elbows on the table. "You're the one who got me off my ass. Who knows where I'd be if it wasn't for you?"

Marie nodded again. "What about you?"

"What about me?"

"What's your meaning, your purpose?"

"I don't know." He thought for a few seconds. "Maybe I'm supposed to help you, like you helped me, like Henry helped me. Maybe I'm supposed to fix stuff for people. Maybe we're all supposed to try to be the best versions of ourselves, knowing we'll never actually reach that goal because we're imperfect. But that doesn't matter. It's the trying that matters."

CHAPTER 115

Marie and The Devil

Later that Saturday night, Marie and Scot sat on his couch, sharing a bowl of popcorn, watching *Seinfeld*. Neither of them had been alive when the pilot had aired in 1989, but the nineties' sitcom had seen a resurgence among young people due to streaming services, such as Netflix. They laughed when David Putty emerged from his bathroom, with his face painted like a devil.

A hard knock came at the front door. Marie and Scot looked at each other with wide eyes. Scot stood from the couch. Another hard knock caused Marie to flinch. Scot crept to the front door. Another hard knock nearly took the door off the hinges.

Frank shouted, "I know you're in there, Marie. Get your ass out here."

Marie sprang from her seat and grabbed Scot by the wrist.

Scot turned to his sister.

Marie shook her head and mouthed, *Call the police.*

Scot nodded, pointed toward the bedrooms, and whispered, "Hide."

Marie tiptoed to the hallway. Before she ventured out of sight, she glanced back at her brother. He punched three digits into his phone. Marie went to her bedroom, searching for a good hiding place. She opened her closet, but it was small and mostly empty. So, she hid under the bed, tight to the wall.

She lay under the bed, listening, her heart thumping in her chest.

"Marie," Frank shouted, his voice coming from the front corner of the house, right outside Scot's bedroom window. "Marie. Marie."

It sounded like Frank was walking around the house, his volume rising as he moved along the back of the house, nearing Marie's bedroom window.

"*Marie.*"

She startled, Frank's voice just outside her window.

"Marie," Frank said again, his voice now moving away from her bedroom.

She exhaled, not realizing that she'd been holding her breath.

Frank knocked again, this time at the back door by the kitchen. "Marie. Get your fucking ass out here!"

Scot shouted back from the kitchen. "Go home, Frank. The cops are coming."

"Let me in!"

"Get off my property."

A crash came from the flimsy back door.

"What the fuck are you doing?" Scot asked.

"I want my wife," Frank replied, his voice no longer muffled by the back door.

"She's not here. Get the fuck out of my house."

Another crash came from the kitchen, followed by glass shattering. Then a heavy *thud*, followed by grunts, many more *thuds*, and Frank's voice. "You little piece of shit. I'll fucking kill you."

Marie scrambled out from under the bed, grabbed the kitchen knife from under the mattress, and ran down the hall to the kitchen. Frank straddled Scot, his back to Marie, pummeling Scot's face with both fists. Scot lay motionless, his face an unrecognizable mash of blood and tissue.

She rushed to them, the knife raised with both hands. She screamed—her own war cry—before she plunged the knife into Frank's back. The scream caused Frank to straighten his upper body at the same time Marie plunged the knife into his back. But his movement caused Marie to miss the mark. She'd been going for the center of his upper back, but, when he straightened, Marie plunged the knife into the back of his neck, the blade stopping at the hilt.

Marie let go of the blade and stepped back, in shock. Sirens whirred in the distance. Frank felt the blade vaguely with his bloody hands. He staggered to his feet and slowly pivoted to Marie. His face and shirt were bloodred. The tip of the blade pierced his throat, just to the left of his Adam's apple. Marie backpedaled into the living room. Frank stumbled toward her, his hands held out front, as if ready to choke her.

Except this time, he fell face-first on the hardwood. Blood pooled on the floor from his neck. His fingers pulsed, as if still trying to grab her. Marie rushed past him to the kitchen. The sirens were close now, right outside. She kneeled next to her brother. Tears streamed down her face as she put two fingers to his neck, confirming what she already knew to be true.

CHAPTER 116

Marie and The Best Version of Ourselves

Marie stood behind the podium, dressed in black, a ball of tissues in hand. A table was beside her, featuring flowers and a blown-up picture of Scot. The crowd was jam-packed with people she'd never met, mostly elderly clients from Scot's handyman business.

Laura and Ray weren't in attendance. Laura had wanted to give the eulogy, but, when Marie forbade her from speaking—which she could enforce, since she was paying for the funeral—Laura had bowed out of the funeral entirely. Marie thought that was addition by subtraction. Ray apparently still held a grudge against Scot, since their last argument. Also addition by subtraction. Their stepfather, Eric Manning, did attend alone. So did Scot's ex-girlfriend Anna.

Marie took a deep breath and spoke into the mike. "Thank you all for being here. I'm Marie, Scot's sister. I apologize in advance if I can't get through this."

From the front row, an elderly woman wearing a black-haired wig said, "It's okay, honey. You take your time."

Marie forced a smile, then said, "What do you say about someone who gave their life for you?" Marie's throat tightened. "On the day he died, I was questioning my own worth as a person. I told Scot that I was worthless, that I was nothing." Marie dabbed the corners of her eyes with her ball of tissues. "He told me how much he needed me. How much I had helped him in the past." A tear slipped down her cheek, followed by two more. "That's not entirely true. I disappeared from his life for a time, leaving him to figure it out alone, but you know what? He did figure it out."

Marie blotted her face with her tissue ball. "I asked him about his purpose in life. You know what he said?" She paused for a beat. "I remember it word for word because it struck me like a bolt of lightning. He said, *Maybe I'm supposed to help you, like you helped me, like Henry helped me. Maybe I'm supposed to fix stuff for people.*"

Many people in the audience cried quietly, their faces buried in handkerchiefs and tissues.

Marie's voice cracked. "*Maybe we're all supposed to try to be the best versions of ourselves, knowing we'll never actually reach that goal because we're imperfect.*" Marie wiped her face again and continued. "*But that doesn't matter. It's the trying that matters.*"

★★★

After the eulogy, Marie met many of Scot's former clients. They regaled her with stories of Scot's hard work and generosity, often charging less than he should.

Delia, the woman with the black-haired wig said, "He was patient and kind, even to a cranky old bat like me."

Their stepfather, Eric Manning, hugged Marie and said, "It was a beautiful funeral." Then he was gone, back to his family.

One woman waited patiently, until everyone was gone to approach Marie.

Anna offered a small smile and said, "I'm so sorry for your loss."

Marie hugged her. When they separated, Marie said, "Thank you for coming, Anna."

"This is going to sound really strange, but something happened two weeks ago, and I think Scot had something to do with it."

Marie furrowed her brow. "What happened?"

Anna wrung her hands, standing in her long black dress. "I got a phone call from Larry Boyd—"

"The attorney?"

Marie had also been recently contacted by Larry Boyd, as she was the sole beneficiary of Scot's estate. She had been surprised that someone as young as Scot had a will. Larry had said that Scot had come to him on other business, and Larry had suggested the will, telling his clients what he always does. "You never know."

Anna said, "Yes, he was Henry's probate attorney. Henry was our mutual friend who died last year."

"I remember."

"He told me that I was the beneficiary of some trust, but he wasn't allowed to tell me where it came from."

"You think it came from Scot?"

Anna nodded. "I do."

Marie tilted her head. "Did you ask Scot about it?"

"I called him several times, but he never returned my messages. He eventually sent me a text."

"What did it say?"

"He congratulated me and said it must've been Henry, but Henry's been dead for over a year."

"Henry could've set it up before his death. Maybe he wanted it to be anonymous for some reason."

Anna shook her head. "It had to be Scot. It's a very specific amount of money. One hundred and seventy-three thousand, which is exactly the amount I told Scot that I needed to finish my bachelor's degree and veterinarian school." Tears welled in Anna's eyes. "I've wanted to be a vet ever since I was a little girl. I gave up on my dream a long time ago."

"And now?"

She stood a little straighter. "I'll try to be the best version of myself."

If you enjoyed this novel, … you'll love *Cesspool.*

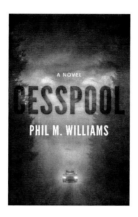

Would you become a criminal to do the right thing?

Disgraced teacher, James Fisher, moved to a backwoods town, content to live his life in solitude. He was awakened from his apathy by a small girl with a big problem. James suspected Brittany was being abused and exploited by his neighbor. He called the police but soon realized his mistake, as the neighbor was related to the chief of police.

Most would've looked the other way. Getting involved placed James squarely in the crosshairs of the local police. James lacked the brawn or the connections to save himself, much less Brittany. The police held all the power, and they knew it. But that was also their weakness. They underestimated what the mild-mannered teacher and the young runaway would do for justice.

Buy *Cesspool* today if you enjoy vigilante justice page-turners with a side of underdog.

Adult language and content.

<u>What Readers Are Saying</u>

"Wow. Just wow. This book was amazing. Every chapter, every page had me thinking about ideas, philosophies, current events, history in a different way."

– Elaine ★★★★★

"The writing is excellent, the pace quick, the characters and dialog believable. An excellent read."

– Dusty Sharp, Author of the Austin Conrad Series ★★★★★

"I have enjoyed this author before, but this is his best yet. If you want a story that will keep you reading, this is it. The story, the characters, and the cunning displayed by the hero is some of the best fiction I've had the pleasure to read. Do yourself a favor and pick up this book. You won't lay it down until the end."

– Patrick R. ★★★★★

"Wow! This was one of the best books I've read in a while. Twists, turns, and unexpected events in every chapter. What a movie this would make."

– Kindle Customer ★★★★★

"This book was incredible! I read it in three days—the entire story is a whirlwind of fantastic characters, a perfect constancy of ups and downs throughout."

– Rae L. ★★★★★

For the Reader

Dear Reader,

I'm thrilled that you took precious time out of your life to read my novel. Thank you! I hope you found it entertaining, engaging, and thought-provoking. If so, please consider writing a positive review on your favorite retail site. Five-star reviews have a huge impact on future sales. The review doesn't need to be long and detailed, if you're more of a reader than a writer. As an author and a small businessman, competing against the big publishers, I greatly appreciate every reader, every review, and every referral.

If you're interested in receiving two of my novels for free and/or reading my other titles for free or discounted, go to the following link: www.PhilWBooks.com. You're probably thinking, *What's the catch?* There is no catch.

If you want to contact me, don't be bashful. I can be found at Phil@PhilWBooks.com. I do my best to respond to all emails.

Sincerely,
Phil M. Williams

Gratitude

I'd like to thank my wife for being my first reader, sounding board, and cheerleader. Without her support and unwavering belief in my skill as an author, I'm not sure I would have embarked on this career. I love you, Denise.

I'd also like to thank my editors. My developmental editor, Caroline Smailes, did a fantastic job finding the holes in my plot and suggesting remedies. As always, my line editor, Denise Barker (not to be confused with my wife, Denise Williams), did a fantastic job making sure the manuscript was error-free. I love her comments and feedback.

Thank you to my mother-in-law, Joy, one of the best nurses on this planet. She is always gracious with her time and extremely knowledgeable about all things medical.

Thank you to my beta readers, Ray, Saundra, and Ann. They're my last defense against the dreaded typo. And thank you to you, the reader. Without you I wouldn't have a career. As long as you keep reading, I'll keep writing.